SAVAGE THEORIES

SAVAGE THEORIES

Pola Oloixarac

Translated by Roy Kesey

SOHO

First English translation published in 2017 by
Soho Press
853 Broadway
New York, NY 10003

Library of Congress Cataloging-in-Publication Data

Oloixarac, Pola, author. | Kesey, Roy, translator.
Savage theories / Pola Oloixarac; translated by Roy Kesey.
Teorías salvajes. English

ISBN 978-1-61695-735-3
eISBN 978-1-61695-736-0

1. College students—Argentina—Buenos Aires—Fiction.
2. Couples—Argentina—Buenos Aires—Fiction. I. Title
PQ7798.425.L65 T4613 2016 863'.7—dc23 2016017075

Interior design by Janine Agro, Soho Press, Inc.

Printed in the United States of America

10 9 8 7 6 5 4 3 2 1

For Maxie and EK

All collaboration, all the human worth of social mixing and participation, merely masks a tacit acceptance of inhumanity.

—*Minima Moralia*, 5 (trans. E. F. N. Jephcott)

This thing of darkness I acknowledge mine.

—*The Tempest* (V, i, 275)

SAVAGE THEORIES

Part One

1

In the rite of passage practiced by the Orokaiva communities of New Guinea, the young boys and girls are first tormented by adults who crouch hidden in the foliage. Pretending to be spirits, the adults pursue the children, shouting, "You are mine, mine, mine!" They drive the initiates onto a platform similar to those used for the slaughter of swine; there, hoods are drawn over the heads of the terrified children, leaving them blind. They are led to an isolated hut deep in the forest, where they are made witness to the torturous rituals and ordeals in which the history of the tribe is encoded. Anthropologists have confirmed that it is not uncommon for children to die in the course of these ceremonies. In the end, the surviving children return to the village wearing the same masks and feathers as those who'd first threatened them, and join in a wild boar hunt. They are now not prey but predators, and they too shout, "You are mine, mine, mine!" Similarly, among the Nootka, Kwakiutl, and Quillayute tribes of the Pacific Northwest, it is wolves—that is, men in wolf masks—who torment the children, driving them at spearpoint into the dark heart of the rites of fear. When the ritualized torture is complete, the children are taught the secrets of the Cult of the Wolf.

The life of little Kamtchowsky began in the city of Buenos Aires amid the violence of the Years of Lead, in the late 1970s; her earliest memories dated to the return of Argentine democracy known as the Alfonsinist Spring. Her father, Rodolfo Kamtchowsky, came from a Polish family that had immigrated to the city of Rosario in the 1930s. Rodolfo's mother died quite young, and he was sent to live with his aunts—the only man in the house. As early as primary school, he demonstrated an exceptional gift for abstract thought, and his fourth-grade mathematics teacher, who'd been to university, spoke glowingly of his capacity for formal innovation. When little Rodolfo brought this news home to his aunts it frightened them a bit, but they nonetheless decided that when he turned thirteen they would send him off to the capital to continue his studies.

Rodolfo was a happy child, but very shy. He spoke little, and at times appeared not to hear what was said to him. When the time came to move to Buenos Aires, he was taken in by yet another aunt, who lived across the street from Lezama Park. He enrolled at the Otto Krause Technical Institute, and later earned his engineering degree in record time.

Neither his timidity nor his chosen field had done him any favors in terms of meeting girls. In his engineering courses there had only been two female students, and he hadn't really considered them *girls* as such—they were rather dumpy, almost misshapen, much as his own daughter would one day be. It soon become clear that fate and inclination had obliged him to be heterosexual, monogamous, and faithful. It was thus only natural that as soon as Providence brought him a woman (one belonging to the set known as "Girls"), Rodolfo would cleave to her, much as a certain type of mollusk swims freely through the ocean before driving its muscular appendage down into the sediment like an axe, its shell or mantle equipped with the ability to line the mucus-coated appendage with layers of calcium, though of course the lining will at some point disintegrate, and the mollusk will once again be adrift between death and the ocean's depths.

When he first spotted her, she was walking along Corrientes Avenue: a short, dark-haired young woman in a tight turtleneck sweater, her black eyes lined in black, mask-like. Though Rodolfo had known of similar sets of empirical data, impressive only because of how perfectly generalizable and thus ordinary they could become, there was *something* in the moment's avalanche of concrete detail—perhaps the way the pleats shifted beneath her buttocks, perhaps the bus ticket protruding from her back pocket—that he perceived as supernatural. *Something* beyond what he'd come to expect of this world. This passageway between a set of environmental data and his individual, untransferable status as eyewitness to it, as synthesized into the phenomenon of "her," led him to experience a sense of decisiveness. He followed her down the street as if keeping watch over her. Then he noticed that others were watching her too, that an awareness of her was spreading, and as he came to understand the *worth*, in some sense, of his target, he likewise understood that she couldn't possibly be oblivious to the fact that he'd been following her for at least ten blocks. Of course, this latter thought was of no importance whatsoever to the present stage of the process—he had already intuited its programmatic nature—and he resolved to stop thinking altogether.

Then a miracle occurred: it started to rain, and Rodolfo was carrying an umbrella. The young engineer quickened his pace. His heart filled as the young woman laughed a bit distractedly and accepted the protection he offered. They stepped into a bar called La Giralda to warm up and dry off; as Rodolfo had hardly gotten wet at all, he concerned himself exclusively with warmth, and blushed a bit, but she didn't seem to notice. She peeled off her wet sweater, giving Rodolfo a glimpse of her flesh-colored bra, and he hid his erection by sitting down as quickly as he could. They ordered hot chocolate, and she wolfed down a few croissants.

Later that same afternoon, caught up in the flood of chatter and delighted with his newfound and apparently innate ability to talk to the girl and imagine her naked simultaneously, Rodolfo told her that the aunt with whom he lived in Buenos Aires had said that his other aunts, the ones who lived in Rosario, had had to work as prostitutes to provide for him. The girl was a sophomore psychology major; she responded languidly that in fact Rodolfo believed that his own mother had been in that line of work. The girl gazed at her reflection in the window, practicing her Evenly Suspended Attention, then glanced at Rodolfo to gauge his reaction. His mother had died of cancer, and in her final years she'd been unable to rise from her bed; stunned, he took a bite of the chocolate-covered churro in his hand, and let his thoughts drift.

The following day he went to the university to look for her. The Psychology Department was divided into two areas of study—"psychosocial" and "humanistic"—both housed in Philosophy and Letters. Like Rodolfo, the future mother of little Kamtchowsky belonged to the first generation of middle-class youth to throw itself more or less en masse into the market for higher education. In 1968 the Psychology Department produced twice as many graduates as it had the year before; its explosive growth continued, peaking in the early 1970s at more than four hundred graduates per year. When the Peronist party returned to power, the university gutted and rebuilt all of its departmental programs, the course offerings now influenced by the entire spectrum of Marxist doctrine. Many once-mandatory courses became optional, and in 1973 the department's plan of study was reoriented to emphasize the field's social aspects, in particular its communitarianism and fieldwork. The new approach downplayed the importance of professional training through coursework and curricular obligations. Marxist epistemology determined that the main priority should be support for popular struggles; the specific obsessions of fields less reliant on partisan imperatives were given second-tier status at best. Enrollment rates had grown precipitously, and forty-five percent of the new female students chose the psychology department, where women outnumbered men by a ratio of eight to one.

For a university graduate, the statistical probability of interaction with either a professional psychologist or one in training was thus extremely high; nonetheless, this was Rodolfo's first time. Never before had he received the look of scientific condescension native to a mind that is forever tracing deep connections between unscientific postulates and the world itself. Psychoanalytic jargon allowed both respectable professionals and those en route to respectability to pepper their vocabulary with genital references that would have been out of bounds even in openly lowbrow entertainment contexts such as cabaret shows. Government censors could close striptease joints and ban certain films, but psychoanalysis was perceived as a sort of linguistic vanguard, a close cousin of "freedom of thought," and the members of its lexical entourage had managed to insert themselves into the moist cavities of the middle class.

The key to the enthusiasm with which society had embraced the field was undoubtedly its medical origins—its very existence was justified by its alleged ability to alleviate pain. To Rodolfo, the constellation of words that calmly orbited the anal and vaginal orifices seemed indescribably mature and daring, unlike anything he'd ever known (and in this sense much like love); the implications left him all but priapismic. The young woman often let her eyes fall closed as she spoke, interlacing her speech with significant pauses. She seemed intelligent, but it was impossible to know for sure. When she spoke earnestly of the Oedipal myth, of Little Hans and the *vagina dentata*, of autoerotic mothering in Melanie Klein, Rodolfo hid his surprise as best he could and scrutinized her face, trying to determine whether or not there was, beneath all the eyeliner and mascara, a member of the lettered elite who actually took all this nonsense seriously. It seemed reasonable to him that between the demands of romance and those of political militancy, she wouldn't have time to get a real degree. Each time she spoke of the passion of the people's struggle, of mobilizing the masses from below, of shattering the shell of the individual once and for all, Rodolfo got such a hard-on that he could have filled the mouths of all those rebel Marxist woodcutters in Chaco with proteins and fatty filaments, each last one *Made in Kamtchowsky*. And somewhere in the course of one of these interludes, little K was conceived.

2

As the sexual tussle that would result in the birth of little Kamtchowsky was getting underway, another Argentine—a psychiatry student and philosophy TA—was awarded an *ad honorem* post caring for teenage microcephalics at the Montes de Oca Colony. Slovenly and socially awkward in person, pretentious on the page, Augusto García Roxler's natural habitat was the shadows of academia. His future as one of the foremost theorists in his field was so much in doubt as to be quite literally unforeseeable; he prowled through the scabrous libraries of the Department of Medicine, blind to everything but his own ideas (and what he took to be prodigious signs proving their validity), living as if walled off from the rest of the world, and in particular from the majestic, blood-drenched corridor in which the great events of his time were taking place.

He was too shy to be openly pedantic and too nondescript to inspire any sense of mystery. His genius would remain hidden for decades; more importantly, when it finally filtered through—its rays thin and tentative, the bony extremities of a blind man groping about in the darkness—it would only ever reach a single consciousness. Only one (the chosen one, the perfect one) would decide its fate. Only one would gather and sustain its battered photons, rebuild them, send them flitting spirit-like across the monstrous face of the facts. But before that, long before that, back when young Augusto was still spending his days measuring microcephalic crania and undressing oligophrenics and catatonics for his experiments, there was a book, and then a night, a single terrifying night, in which his theory caught its first whiff of the earth's crust. He was thirty years old, or perhaps a bit older, when he finished the first draft of what would eventually become his Theory of Egoic Transmissions.

The Theory's earliest progenitor had sent its first tentative shoots into the air back in 1917, when the Dutch anthropologist Johan van Vliet published an article in *Nature* describing a series of experiments on human subjects. An inveterate traveler and confessed admirer of Jean-Jacques Rousseau, Professor van Vliet saw no reason why his field of study should focus exclusively on wealthy Westerners, or on the proletariat of the remotest corners of Europe. He believed that in order to formulate an authentic theory of human psychology, a theory that would speak to the deepest modes of human action, it was necessary to work with elements taken from outside the process of choreographic adaptation known as Culture.

For his *Ad intra res cogitans* experiment—its title was taken from that of his diary—Johan van Vliet organized a small expedition to Dahomey, now part of Benin, in West Africa. At the time, Dahomey was relatively accessible for European travelers, thanks to its two-hundred-year history as a producer and exporter of palm oil and slaves for the White Man. France had recently overthrown the country's last native dynasty; the consul general (who happened to bear an extraordinary resemblance to Voltaire) gave Van Vliet directions to a Fon encampment that lay en route to the northern jungle. Two of Van Vliet's disciples—Dr. Fodder and Dr. Fischer—had recently arrived from England. As they stood in line for quinine pills at the consular infirmary, Van Vliet, eager to get into the jungle as soon as possible, forced himself to thumb slowly through an old copy of *Le Figaro*.

The Fon people treated them kindly, gave them campsites with good views into the bush, and provided them with smoking materials. The Fon believe not in a single, all-powerful God, but in a spirit-world that is complex and unstable, and shortly after arriving at the encampment, Van Vliet—a genuine pioneer in psychological experimentation—began skulking about wearing nothing but a loincloth. He smeared mud all over his flabby academic flesh so as to move about "unseen" at night. He walked barefoot at all times, and spent hours staring at the moon (which seemed much bigger and brighter than it had during his expeditions to the North Sea, where he'd been researching conflict theory in sea spiders). At times he fell asleep seated there on the porous soil, his notebook still in hand. He took notes using ink made of resin, palm char, and bone ash, and one day while mixing up a batch he befriended a small monkey with almond-shaped eyes. As he anxiously studied the language of the Fon, he quickly learned that of the birds, and set up a provisional academic office complete with all his notebooks high in the branches of a topped tree that had once been home to a family of bushbabies.

At this point in history, psychological theory was having itself quite *un moment*. In 1917, Alfred Adler had concluded his fifty-two page work on homosexuality, showing the phenomenon to be the result of an inferiority complex toward one's own sex. In 1920, Sigmund Freud published his *Jenseits des Lustprinzips* (*Beyond the Pleasure Principle*). Three years earlier Jung had arranged for a private printing of the seven sermons to the dead he'd written and ascribed to Basilides of Alexandria (*Septem Sermones ad Mortuos*), and in 1926, Burrhus Frederic Skinner, having recently decided that he possessed neither the talent nor the experience a literary career required, abandoned his dream of becoming a fiction writer and applied to do a PhD in psychology. Inspired by Bertrand Russell's commentaries on Watson's behaviorist theories, Skinner's earliest experiments on pigeons ("'Superstition' in the pigeon," 1947) were followed by others of subtle mechanistic design applied first to individual human beings, and then (albeit only in theory) to massive groups (a territory previously considered the exclusive domain of utopian literature); these mega-groups lived in communes where the children were raised according to a strict creed of operant conditioning and various other protocols of social engineering.

Given this context of psychology on high boil, and the

fact that Johan van Vliet didn't belong to any of his field's prominent schools of thought, it will come as no surprise that his radically original projects were dismembered by the jaws of time without ever putting up a struggle. In fact, amidst the murky circumstances of Van Vliet's disappearance into the jungle, Time's appetite left the new theory headless. One of his disciples, Manfred Fodder, who'd managed to get the results of the African sojourn published in *Nature*, was eventually absorbed into the Skinnerian hordes; the other, Marvin Fischer, continued to impart the master's theory at occasional conferences until finally giving up and joining the legions of Otto Rank—who, in 1926, was excommunicated by none other than the Father of Psychoanalysis himself for the sin of "anti-Oedipal heresy."

In spite of their firsthand experience of Van Vliet's genius, neither Fodder nor Fischer was capable of serving as medium for the Dutchman's voice when seated at the wide oak tables of academia. Neither had his gift for the sort of edge-of-your-seat conceptual theater that might impress their fellow intellectuals, most of whom had given the man up for dead. Neither knew how to summon the murmur of Van Vliet's singular theory up through the sublunar language of workaday academics. A man with a theory is someone who has something to shout, but a dead man with a theory requires a séance, and even then his spirit is a wad of half-chewed bread lolling about in the medium's mouth, occasionally pushing back against the teeth but certain to disintegrate and destined to be spit out. The academic presentations given by Fodder and Fischer came out sounding like the bleating of two goats lost and alone in the far hills. Translated into English and German to accommodate the ears of their colleagues, the content resembled the strange unintelligible wailing of a newborn, at best indistinguishable from other theories. The year after Rank's exile began, Fischer published *Cerebral Response and Egoic Transmissions: An Introduction.* He and Rank met regularly to discuss their respective hypotheses, but it wasn't long before Fischer passed away, leaving no philosophical descendants.

The Montes de Oca Colony (founded in 1915 as the Coeducational Asylum-Colony for the Retarded) is located in the district of Luján approximately eighty kilometers from Buenos Aires, and its grounds cover two hundred thirty-four hectares. The patients live in a group of buildings surrounded by vast green spaces—woodlands of elm and acacia, of cypress, of river oak and eucalyptus—interspersed with immense open meadows that stretch to the horizon, on the edges of which are a series of bogs and pits into which the patients sometimes fall to their deaths. Days and even weeks can pass before the scavenger birds begin to circle above the site; at other times it is the asylum's guard dogs who suddenly appear chewing on shreds of clothing and human bones. In either case the proper form is promptly filled out to document the disappearance.

It was in the course of a stormy night here at the Colony that young Augusto, while reading in his pajamas on the cot in his small bedroom in the infirmary, first understood the implications of Van Vliet's theory. The realization coursed through his body like an electric current. Far too excited to sit still, Augusto threw on a shawl his mother had knitted and walked out onto the porch, which lay half in ruins. Rain filtered through the slats of the overhang; a sludge of water and splintered wood dripped down his face. He thought of Van Vliet's visage, of the pointy tip of the man's nose, of the flaring nostrils, a face more similar to that famous portrait of Hobbes than Augusto's own genetic *corpus* could ever have mustered, and now the Dutchman's shade watched him from the core of the night, both maw and wolf. The theory was practically unprecedented, and long misunderstood; more importantly, it had the sound of a precursor to Augusto's own fantasies. The raindrops kept falling, and he opened his mouth to drink them in. He had in his hands the fetal tissue of intuition. Now he had only to flatten it against the throat of his beliefs, to beat down all other voices, to submerge, to expunge the outside world from his mind until his mission was complete. A flash of lightning set the sky aflame; the rain curtained his vision in all directions. Augusto dried his face, then let out a shout. A spectral figure was coming toward him up the gravel path.

The infirmary was set somewhat apart from the rest of the asylum's buildings (labeled Incontinent, Oligophrenic, Violent, Catatonic, Gerontological, Crippled, and Women, respectively); the evening curfew applied equally to patients and doctors, forbidding them from leaving their buildings unaccompanied at night. Lightning seared Augusto's vision, and his imagination's soliloquies bore him into space. The specter was now within meters of the porch on which the horrified Augusto stood: scrawny legs and pointed skull, some random John

Doe drenched to the bone and white against the dark, still drifting toward him. The man's brain couldn't have weighed a whit more than 104 grams, the weight of Prévost's brain as described by Paul Broca in his study of murderers executed by guillotine ("Le cerveau de l'assassin Prévost," 1880, *Bulletin de la Société d'Anthropologie de Paris*, pp. 233–244). Augusto opened his mouth, but no words came out. The shawl slipped from his right shoulder; he stretched out his hand as if to control the man telekinetically. It was only Titín, one of the microcephalics. The rain washed down through the rags in which he was clothed; his filth-matted hair hung stiffly along the sides of his face. His eyes shot wide open, and a flash of horror lit Augusto's face; Titín screamed as his Pavlovian conditioning kicked in and he began to remove his clothes. Augusto slipped quickly back in through his door, locked it, and double-checked all of the shutters to make sure they were properly latched. Outside, the storm raged ever stronger, lashed at the fields and graves, sent bolt after bolt down into the trembling trees.

The ideas that sprang into being as a result of this meeting of the three agents required of all theories (viz. the Precursor, the Theoretician, and the Victim) remained comatose for most of the twentieth century. Then, though no clear connection had yet been made between them, the hypothetical possibilities that had been created by their proximity to one another found, like the spirit gods of the Fon, the perfect body in which to make themselves manifest.

3

Beginning around age eleven, Kamtchowsky suddenly found herself in a series of classroom discussions wherein the teachers wished to know if the boys were masturbating yet, and whether anything milky came out when they did. The classes were co-ed, and everyone enjoyed them. The teachers, all women in their thirties, were careful to keep their expressions serious.

Thanks to some cosmic scheduling wisdom, sex ed and civics were part of a single course that most often came right after biology. The classroom slogan "Ask anything you want to know!" attempted to clarify the relationship between happiness and knowledge by tying the concept of "body" to that of "communication," an associative bundling that led in turn to the concept of "sexuality." The abstract notion of pleasure presented itself as the subset of thought contiguous to the action of estrogen and testosterone upon the students' bodies, as evidenced by the accumulation of fat in the girls' buttocks and busts, and the swelling growth of the boys' scrotal sacs.

Sooner or later (and everyone knew it was coming) nervous laughter would be followed by a furtive glance at a classmate, who would nod in turn, and from that point on it was simply a matter of "letting oneself go," especially for the girls, though there were no instructions given for the procedure in question.

It was only natural that anxiety would permeate the classroom. Given this diagnostic, instead of cutting the students' vulgarities short, the teachers hardly even registered them; for the most part they merely furrowed their brows a bit, discouraging such comments while also dispensing a dose of sympathy, and even complicity. Punishment was left programmatically vague, as if it were some evil gas that prevented oxygenation from occurring within the pulmonary alveoli, and its absence thus allowed everyone in the room to breathe freely. The occasional loss of control or outbreak of violence could be foreseen, but not completely avoided. When necessary, the problem child would be asked to step to the front of the class; ever so sweetly, the teacher would make the student look like an idiot, thereby taking the royal scepter back in hand without feeling dictatorial. One teacher did however make the mistake of pushing a student too far. "All right," she said, "if you're really so fond of talking about your wiener, why don't you pull it out and show it to us?" The boy obliged, then peed in the face of a female classmate, whose giggling became a horrified gasp. (At the next PTA meeting, several parents were visibly upset; they spoke of a similar case that had resulted in post-traumatic stress disorder, the victim now incapable of drinking apple juice.) During recess that same day, Kamtchowsky went to the restroom and found her panties stained with blood. It was viscous, and dark, and difficult to rinse out. Back home, she put off telling her mother for several hours.

Night came, and with it her mother's reaction, wherein she mentioned that they hadn't named her Carolina because they were afraid that her classmates would call her Caca. Little Kamtchowsky's skin was indeed relatively dark, but it *wasn't because of that*, her mother hastened to add. The ominously empty hallways of the girl's mind began to fill with thoughts harboring the somber intuition that there was something repulsive, something really repulsive going on with her, and she had to hide it any way that she could. She suddenly understood that she'd known this since she was very young, because there was simply no way not to be aware of it, even if she couldn't quite explain what *it* was, not even to herself.

That same year, Kamtchowsky's mother decided that she was at last old enough to begin typing up the handwritten notebooks of her Aunt Vivi, which she—little K's mother—was hoping to get published. She believed that aside from their indisputable historical value, the journals were possessed of a fundamental authenticity evident in their use of the present tense, the untidiness of the hurried handwriting, and a certain lack of structural coherence. She asked her daughter to correct nothing but spelling errors. Kamtchowsky's suggestion that the project be accompanied by a raise in her allowance bore no fruit whatsoever.

Not long after Kamtchowsky's mother had gotten married,

Vivi, her younger sister, had been kidnapped while handing out pamphlets in an Avellaneda factory. Rodolfo Kamtchowsky had accompanied his new bride as she made all relevant inquiries, but in truth there was little to be done. Vivi never reappeared, though there were rumors that she'd been seen in the Seré Mansion, a secret detention center in Morón. She left behind a few flowery dresses, a broken Winco record player, and this multi-volume diary written in first and second person, wherein she described the events of her life right up to the week she was kidnapped. From the age of seventeen or so, most of the entries in her diary consisted of letters to Mao Zedong, heroic leader of the Red Army; she hid his identity by changing a single letter of his name.

The hardback, folio-size notebooks had been hidden in a leaky basement; they smelled pretty bad.

Dear Moo:

There's some weird kind of tremor in the streets, a sense of disturbance, of madness and the future. Life, it must be. They're not going to silence us, those sons of b------! These are some fucked-up days, Moo, black days. Both personally and politically. Things aren't going well with L.; it's hard not to feel like we're growing apart. I also think he's seeing another girl. I know that we've got an open relationship, and I feel like a hypocrite because it's not like I ever told him I wanted us to be one of those little bourgeois couples—if anything, I wanted the opposite. I always supported his militant opposition to the putrid values of society. We both reject bourgeois repression, and together we've chosen a new path, unswerving and brightly lit but full of thorns. I know that if at some point I can't stand it anymore, then all I have to do is get out of his way, and it will be over. But I can't, Moo. The truth is that I love him, and it hurts me, the way things are right now. I realize that there isn't much I can do to change things, and that if I really want us to stay together, what has to change is my way of seeing the situation.

For example, the other day he came over, and we were getting along great, drinking mate *and talking, mostly about him. He told me that in his Local Party HQs he'd been reunited with a bunch of comrades from the Tendency, and everyone was very excited. I noticed that he was acting kind of weird, as if there was something he wanted to tell me, but didn't dare. I told him that he could trust me, that I would always be here to support him—I know, maybe it sounds a little cheesy, but that's how it came out. He took a wrinkled piece of paper out of his pocket, and read it to me:*

But what kind of Argentina is this?
The people came out to defend the government they'd wanted
and the police swore at them, sent them running with tear gas, flew
after them on motorcycles and in squad cars.
Not even Lannuse ever dreamed of this.
The magnificent youth poured into the streets

to show that spilled blood was non-negotiable,
that the most loyal Peronists could never be prisoners,
that the people, victorious on March 11th
and September 23rd, could not be
forced to put up with all this, the officers
who'd repressed the people for eighteen long years
promoted for treating the people as if they were the enemy.
The people regrouped and advanced once again.
The facts speak for themselves.

When L. stopped reading, he seemed overwhelmed with emotion. I spoke gently, said that we shared the same feelings of powerlessness. (It wasn't long ago that the crowds were chased out of Plaza Once—I hadn't gone because I was having my period, but L. went.) He interrupted me, saying, "No, baby, it's a poem, a poem that Silvina wrote. Boy, I shouldn't show you things like this—they're too intimate." I felt myself growing red with rage, Moo, I swear. I wanted to kick him right in the you-know-what. Why in the world would he show the poem to me if it was so intimate? Then he said, "I found out her real name by accident. But nobody else knows that I know, so don't tell anybody I told you anything." I could feel my face burning, as if I'd just eaten a whole bag of hot peppers. He calmly put the piece of paper back in his pocket. I was furious, but hid it by speaking as fast as I could:

"So, but why, why shouldn't you know her real name?"

"Because of our roles in the cause, Vivi, why else?"

He was dead serious this whole time. Then he got impatient with me, and a little while later he left. Forgive me, Moo, but what he read me was no poem. That the girl wrote the thing herself, fine and dandy, with any luck it doesn't even have any spelling mistakes (here's hoping, anyway—I swear to god, most of these Peronists, it wouldn't surprise me to see them carrying signs urging us on to "Bictory") but where is the poetry in it? Okay, I get it, you're going to say that I'm judgmental, that I've got no feel for artistic freedom, the formless form, whatever, that I'm afflicted with that typical bourgeois blindness. (I'm happy to admit that the poem's lack of actual poetry could in fact be a good thing, like with the music of Stockhausen, which isn't, shall we say, all that musical.) But all of a sudden my mind was full of doubts. I bet if L. had stayed, I would have stared at him with absolutely no expression on my face.

I was in such a bad mood by then that I couldn't sleep, couldn't think, couldn't do anything at all. I was so depressed that I actually started paging through a copy of Siete Días *that we had there at the house. What a terrible magazine! But if that other thing was a poem, then this jeans ad in* Siete Días *is also a poem. (In the photo there are two guys and a girl, all wearing jeans with huge bell-bottoms, their makeup like something out of* Nosferatu.)

The ghosts
were seen appearing, luminous spirits
in the penumbra of nightfall.
They were young, and they laughed at the
cold.
Because they felt the caress of their Levi's.
Soft as the light of the stars.
Warm as the glow of a campfire.
The ghosts were possessed
by the magical joy of life.
They had Levi's.
And they sang.
But the gray ones—those who believe that joy
has no place in this
world—they did not understand.
"Phantoms," they murmured.
And locked their doors tight.
The ghosts hadn't seen them,
had already disappeared,
singing, into the night.
Kept warm by the spell of their Levi's.

I'm not one of the gray ones—never was, never will be. I'll risk everything for the things that matter. I believe in my own inner world, and in my fight against the closed-off hearts of the bourgeoisie. I'm not about the individual as a solution. I'm all about the causes that affect the Third World, the poor and the working class, those who fight back day after day. I will not stand motionless beside the path, as Benedetti puts it, and no I will not calm down. Oh, Moo, I swear I'm trying to get my head around it, trying to accept the idea that L. and I are in an open relationship, but it's just so hard. Fine, we're all as free as you please, but it pisses me off, nothing I can do about it. The other day I went by the unit—mine, not L.'s, because if I'd gone by his we'd have ended up in a fight. So, they told me to sit down and wait, and a little while later a guy came in, dark-skinned, super cute, long curly hair, big mustache. I was glad I was sitting down so he couldn't see that my backside's a little flat (I told you that already). He told me his name was Fernando—I wonder if that's his nom de guerre *or his real name. "Hi, Fernando," I said, "I'm Vivi." Well, in ten minutes it felt like we'd known each other all our lives. I felt so strange, Moo, as if the logic of my footsteps and the cipher of my days (the signs in my dreams) had carried me there, to that little desk, once and for all. Or maybe I'm being too dramatic about it—I was reading Borges at the time and his way of thinking about how events unfold is really contagious. Later I told L. about it over the phone, and he hung up on me—he didn't even believe me.*

All the same, I don't hold grudges—I went to see him, and gave him a copy of Libro de Manuel, *because we'd both always loved Cortázar, who's like some kind of talisman for us. I remember one time we went out for dinner at Pippo, and L. started calling me "Maguita," as in La Maga from* Rayuela, *then we went back to his apartment and made love and it felt like I was floating up in the clouds, loved for the way I am, cherished by the one I loved. Moo, just so you see the difference: this time L. tore open the gift paper, looked at the book, and said that it was garbage. That in this exact book Cortázar had lost his way politically, and even more so artistically. Or vice versa, depending on which matters more to you. But how can you know that if you haven't even read it, I said. L. is very intuitive but it's not like he's clairvoyant. "Well, you know, I was hanging out with Pelado Flores, and he showed me a couple of passages—totally pathetic," was the best lie that imbecile could come up with. I realized that he must have read that article on Cortázar in* Crisis, *because he was just repeating the author's taunts—he spent the whole afternoon making fun of Cortázar and calling him a bullshit firebrand, acting like such a bully, as if he were lord and master of revolutionary truth.*

L. says that the hippy motto is total nonsense—why make love not war, if you can do both? "War is an aphrodisiac," he says. "It heats up your blood just like love. Plus it's summertime!" If he had kissed me right after saying that, I swear to god I would have led the people's insurrection myself—the Fifth International, pro-China and pro-Viet Cong, and you know what else? After that I would have nationalized everything, thrown all that Peronist nonsense straight out the window, a

> *workers' insurrection pure and simple, government of the people. Oh, Moo! What I wouldn't give to have him between my legs again, and we'd do it slow, everything he wanted, and then we'd do it again!*

At about this same time in Kamtchowsky's life, the Brazilian wave of Gal Costa and Maria Bethânia, of "Eu preciso te falar," of "Amanhã talvez" and Rita Lee's hit "Lança perfume," came to an end. An extensive marketing study determined that the wave's commercial success had been due mainly to a certain timbre in the treble equalization; apparently the sound engineers had set out to light up the same cerebral pleasure circuits that respond to cocaine. Against all reasonable expectations, the wave's popularity was immediately usurped by César "Banana" Pueyrredón's pop ballad "Conociéndote," followed by a final twitch from the death throes of his career, "No quiero ser más tu amigo." Then Kamtchowsky's father left for Chile to manage the construction of a new factory, and she never saw him again.

The fifteen years that passed between her initiatory bloodshed and the beginning of this story proper were difficult ones for Kamtchowsky. It was all too clear that other people found her frankly unattractive, and her mother seemed to wish her dead. She suspected that she had no idea how to "let herself go," and soon proved this with Mati, a classmate who was quite ugly himself. Kamtchowsky tried to adapt herself to his rhythm; she parted her lips lasciviously, threw her head back. Some of the "sensual" moments were frankly uncomfortable, but she did her best to please.

Mati and Kamtchowsky spent most of their time rubbing

their stubby little bodies together, then staring meekly at one another, waiting for *emotions* to occur, mirroring each other's expressions as best they could. The activation of their reproductive apparati was compulsively enriched by Mati's onanistic research. While most of what went on could clearly be termed *exploring* (an adventurous euphemism for all activities related to physical development), the bulk of their efforts went into the process of working through the script that begins with Curiosity and proceeds into the singular experience of Romance. In fact these were two separate stages—one instinctive and animalistic, the other human and rational—and the natural thing was to progress from one to the other. Loving and being in love were also important, of course, almost as important as homework. Mati and Kamtchowsky generally got bored fairly quickly of all the thrusting and staring, put their clothes back on, and hooked up the Atari. Mati was rather chubby, with thick lips and bulging eyes that gave him the look of a stunned beetle; a few years later, during his growth spurt, his eyes would migrate toward the sides of his head, making him more of a tadpole, as if to indicate the potential that croaked softly within. That was also the period during which he discovered that he was ambidextrous in terms of jerking off and of drawing pictures with his pee in the urinals.

Kamtchowsky was strangely conscious of the fact that this relationship was no more than a test run for the future, and in general she let Mati have his way. She suspected that he acted as he did in order to seem cool, though he obviously couldn't pull it off; she wanted to caress his little gel-stiffened quiff, to say that he could calm down, that they would learn soon enough. Then, much as her father had discovered how to calculate Fourier series functions at the tender age of ten, Kamtchowsky made her own unoriginal and thus trivial discovery: that fucking consisted of a set of procedures which *could* be serialized. Given the constant acceleration of repeated motion aligned vertically inside her (glans [G] = force vector), the mathematical operation in question would result in Kamtchowsky lying beaten to a pulp against the wall with her skull pierced along its horizontal axis (the abscissa) as follows:

$$\mathrm{d} = \frac{W}{pGu^2 f\left(\frac{u\sqrt{G}}{v}\right)} \quad \frac{1}{\cos(\pi)}$$

When the sense of decency inherent in his self-awareness gave out, Mati dedicated himself to the art of hurting Kamtchowsky precisely where she was most vulnerable. He told her he'd figured out that she faked all of her orgasms, that she was cold as a fucking fish, that if she wanted to turn him on, she should come over here and suck him off, and if she was lucky, just maybe he'd stick a finger up her ass and cum on her tits. The two of them moaned their way through an emotional duty-free zone where erratic and relatively aggressive behaviors soon to include eating disorders, suicidal tendencies, substance abuse and stress were celebrated as rites of passage demonstrating a particular sensibility given a relatively orderly freedom to develop. Both Kamtchowsky and Mati had grown up in nurturing environments that encouraged displays of sensitivity, creativity, and originality, particularly on the raised stage that is sex, sphere *par excellence* of liberty and play. Kamtchowsky became furious. Something—feminine intuition?—told her that she was smarter than him, that she always had been, that she shouldn't just let him win. She shot a glance at his crotch, let drop a particularly acidic bit of commentary, and walked out the door.

Generally speaking, successful theoretical models of standard adolescent behavior show a pattern of superficial benevolence; the empirical soil in which these models are grown, however, is swampy, demoralizing, and vulgar. Kamtchowsky's classmates spent their post-pubescent years working through a catalog of *personality vectors*, each of which could be accessed by exaggerating personal details that they had come to understand, suddenly and at quite a young age, as *belonging* to them as individuals—which is to say, as authentic, as *real*. Identifying these details enabled them to draw up strategies they could use to call attention to themselves, thus giving them additional mechanisms for regulating their minimum caloric intake of personal self-esteem, in accordance with the formula whereby the *audience/empathy* binomial becomes an existential modality. In *Bambi* (1942), the fawn's emergence in the forest initiates the hero's apprenticeship in full view of the multitude. The creatures of the forest gather to watch him rise to his feet for the first time; his mother nudges him with her muzzle, and Bambi staggers, lurches back and forth, strains to stay upright, then tumbles to the ground. He's charming. He's also very young, and thus clumsy and weak, in need of attention, of care: it is by falling flat on his face that he gains the love of his woodland audience.

In order for initiational observations to be transformed into personal belief systems, the little subjects must be convinced to dive deep into their own pasts, believing wholeheartedly that within the timeline of their life there lies a key. The process of searching for ways to atone for one's behavior naturally favors those with a predilection for dwelling on the most sordid, violent facts of one's past—those moments when the little ones' humanity is delineated with great quickness and clarity. Likewise, the process trains the little ones to accept as naturally as possible the camaraderie of older men and women who refuse to conform to proper models of adult behavior.

One day, however, Kamtchowsky grew up and said:

–Given the absence of any binding objective morality, we have no option but to entrust ourselves to the privacy of an *ethics of mental processes*. This is where a form of personal responsibility branches off. Such a system, of course, has nothing to do with any sort of Kantian obsession. At no point have I assumed the existence of any true "us" whatsoever.

Shortly after jotting down this affirmation, Kamtchowsky managed to land herself a boyfriend. His name was Pablo. He wore glasses, and paired every bodily movement with an expression of pained discomfort. They'd run into each other several times at the MALBA cinema, had watched each other from afar, but both of them thought themselves too horrible looking to be desirable even to someone who was equally repulsive. Moreover, each detected the repellent top note given off by the biographical elements they had in common. Both had quickly abandoned the simplistic comics of *Anteojito* for the ineffable *Humi*, the magazine for progressive primary schoolers; both had parents who'd never put much effort into hiding their copies of *Sex Humor*, giving the hormonal development of their children a completely unfounded air of natural ease; growing up, their loyal companions had been video cassette recorders, microwaves, and yogurt makers rather than some guilty-looking dog snuffling at the air and hoping for permission to defecate.

At about this time, Kamtchowsky decided to start wearing skirts: she was afraid that her backside would burst out and hurt someone if she kept trying to encage it. The eyeshadow she used was a particularly repellent shade of green, and she hid her double chin under scarves. She wore platform shoes, and socks with patterns involving microchips and circuitry. She sat near the front of the cinema to avoid the promiscuous laughter of others; there, she sprawled across her seat, sucking on chewable mints and pretending no one could see her.

Pablo had similar moviegoing habits, having cribbed them from her. Now he waited for the lights to dim, and sat down two seats away. She moved her backpack into the empty seat between them. He matched her peevishness by lowering his rucksack ever so slowly to the ground and staring at her for the rest of the film. Kamtchowsky sees everything, saw everything, but left her legs splayed wide open on the back of the seat in front of her.

The movie was Pabst's *Don Quixote* (1933). Kamtchowsky ignored Pablo programmatically throughout the film. At the end he leaned over surreptitiously and whispered in her ear: "Smart-ass lil' bitch." Then he stood and walked away.

When Kamtchowsky came out after the credits had rolled,

Pablo was waiting for her, holding a small bouquet of grass ripped out by the roots. "I'm sorry for insulting you," he said, "but I didn't want to come right out and say that I find you very attractive." She made it clear that she understood perfectly, and taught him how to make her cum with a packet of Sweet Mints. And thus, though she hadn't moved a muscle while Pablo (hereinafter known as Pabst) drilled a hole in her silhouette with his laser-like vector of ugliness, she had been *reading* in the most fundamental sense, had been sharing in the pertinent signs.

4

Pabst added Kamtchowsky's blog to his blog roll, and she added his to hers. His had a black-and-green background, with multicolored text in Helvetica. It manifested a serene sense of nostalgia for the 1990s, the decade that had seen him develop from a fat little dwarf into a person of normal proportions, albeit completely devoid of beauty and vitality. The blog was thick with references to the singers and songs that had once sent him running from the quinceañeras of all those girls who were out of his league. Milli Vanilli, Jazzy Mel, Ace of Bass, Technotronic—the entire soundtrack that played in the background whenever the innocent face of Flora G. or Caro T. or Maru Z. appeared. Nowadays, Pabst listened to these same songs as he worked himself into a froth of humiliation—an appetizer he'd only recently discovered—*very* exciting.

In the fantasy world of his wanking, the plot was structured as follows: the birthday girl made her way from table to table, posing for a picture with each group of invitees, and Pabst came up to her from behind, spun her around, grabbed her by the shoulders and locked his lips onto hers, pressing himself up against her breasts as best he could. She pushed him away in disgust, wiping his saliva off her chin; his feet got tangled in the hem of her dress, and he tripped and fell to the ground in full view of everyone. Bringing this mental residue to life, Pabst stroked himself harder and harder until it started to hurt; he wanted to put an end to the whole mess once and for all. The abrasions grew more and more painful; ejaculation tended to take a while, which gave time for the other guests at the imaginary party to make all sorts of unpleasant comments, competing amongst themselves to see who could insult him with the greatest degree of precision and ingenuity. The culmination was a mixture of tears and semen, and it *felt* extremely therapeutic.

His blog was peppered with encoded references to this habit in the form of short poems:

Lore—no law, no lei
has stained—the Dress—with salsa
the Salsero shakes and—won't dance to Vilma Palma.

He had lost all contact with his classmates from those days of mediocre betrayals, of wiping boogers and zit-pus on the bottom of the classroom desks, so there was no one left to offend. And nobody read Dickinson any more.

On his blog he maintained an updated list of online resources for sharing pirated software, as well as an interesting selection of macabre pornography. It wasn't that contemplating the systematic abuse of pregnant women gave him as much pleasure as cyber warfare, but that his mind, already polluted with obsessions particular to unassailable self-esteem, had concluded that the access protocol for modern empathy involves the intelligent, glamorous use of cruelty.

Pabst had established deeper and more interesting relationships while sprawled back in his desk chair caressing a plastic bowl and masturbating than ever before in his life; he had gotten to know nicer people, who enriched his life with funnier, defter, haughtier comments, and he had an arsenal of mp3s and jpegs to share. Out there—that is, inside the heads of others—the same epic play of the pollywog scrivener who assists at the call to Being was being staged. Pabst had glimpsed the underlying structure of this logorrheic art of the *I* in love with its own vulnerability, and thoroughly enjoyed terrorizing the weak.

To Pabst's own solitary surprise, verbal sadism and high-speed typing weren't the only skills that could be combined to produce highly tolerable tête-à-têtes and contacts leading to personal satisfaction. New psychopathic plains emerged spontaneously, and Pabst was proud to see that a certain subterranean connection between evil and voluptuousness had (at long last) begun to play in his favor. Much as "lactescent," "milky," and "spurt" can be satisfactorily combined to evoke the mental image of semen, Pabst's discursive brutality and his superciliary control over discussions—demonstrations, both, of his superiority—were together apt to attract (much as certain orchids use the smell of the insects decomposing within them to attract still more insects, who are apparently convinced that they are somehow different from the others, that they can feed there safely) those who sought some strange, tortured, doomed beauty; some majestic castle to which only the few are admitted, and allowed the short-lived pleasure of sliding unprotected yet unharmed through the cacti. Through his daily regimen of hating all and sundry, Pabst gained access to a new self-image, one richer in the flair of lucid Adonis than Pabst could ever have managed on the strength of his physical attributes. All of which is to say that Pabst told lots and lots of people to fuck off, and was told to fuck off by lots and lots of people.

At long last he was able to make good use of the personal liberty for which his education had prepared him—a sharp contrast with the crap uses his garbage life had thus far been able to make of it. Exercising his anonymous right to violent aggression, Pabst fought bloody battles against invaders and enemies (all of them potential admirers). Trolling about in his native element, he seemed preternaturally gifted at creating irritation and discomfort in others, as if born with foreknowledge of the winding paths of electronically manifested disdain.

Pabstian cruelty was most often decoded as "critical" in some sense, as part of some larger program of self-improvement, thanks to one very simple principle: striking a passive-aggressive or openly destructive attitude obliged one to articulate the weaknesses of that which was being read/disdained, texts whose *I*, unweaned of its need for attention and thirsty for distinguishing traits, was always fodder for discussion. His regular visitors, their absurd nicknames favoring "alternate spellings" using k's instead of c's or q's, insulted his posts with varying degrees of candor, precision, and lucidity, turning his blog into a theater of war. Pabst's taunts consisted of categorical judgments sprinkled with references to films, TV series, people with facial burns, pop miscellanea from the '80s and '90s, nudists, zombies, Sideshow Bob, giant squid, and all kinds of other irrelevancies. His observations were concise, categorical, and invariably right. The Internet provided a context wherein the protocols of association permitted one to *control* both one's own spontaneity and that of others, thus providing a social context that was far more sophisticated than the mere bad weather of raw behavior. Violent as they may have been, Pabst's relationships with others came to seem like a twisted form of affection: in the long term, paying attention to something and disdaining it became one and the same project. Dealing with a certain amount of contempt was not only possible, it may even have been healthy. Each act walked the fine line between spontaneous conduct and *performance*; and even in the worst of cases, one always had the consolation of thinking oneself "misunderstood," which linked the writer to his or her favorite forbears, namely other misunderstood individuals, tortured souls, film characters, accursed poets, et cetera. Even masochism itself grants its victims a certain distinction. In such a swamp, the path toward existence postulates that any given child can find access to an audience in exchange for making him or herself visible, and thus vulnerable. Of course there was hatred embedded in the judgments of others, but—and this was the most surprising discovery of all—there was love, too. The search for like-minded beings gave all the pollywogs the opportunity to praise themselves over and over, yielding sensations in turn multiplied by thousands upon thousands of hyperlinks, producing a style of communication that was both intimate and open all at once.

As Pabst himself explained it, in the playful style of early Wittgenstein:

> *Regarding Solitude as Inalienable Resource for the Administration of Nourishment to the Ego*
>
> *1. Embarrassment on behalf of others causes an infection in one's own eye: momentary euphoria.*
>
> *1.1 It is an interactive process: the individual actively participates in making the infection worse.*
>
> *2.1 The (psycho)logical portrait of bare (human) facts is thought (of embarrassment on behalf of others) itself.*
>
> *2.1.1 René Descartes seated by the fire in his meditation room: immovable pieces of furniture are immovable persons. Little René has a wig on, caresses his curls. He is at the center of the world: without leaving his armchair he commences the activities, his* je *and his* pe . . .
>
> *2.1.2 In these moments of pleasure, little René seems to forget that his curls are clearly inferior to those of Leibniz.*
>
> *2.2 The act of partitioning the set of all desirable things logically requires the ability to make oneself despicable.*

At the end of the post there was an image of the folk singer Soledad, twirling her poncho. As for the victims of Pabst's ire, some were accustomed to it; they soon stopped attempting to defend themselves, and always came back for more. (As Pabst was the first to admit, the medium made it hard to actually *see* them bowing down like servants before their master, acknowledging the Reign of Pabst once and for all, but each typo, each spineless rebuttal, each grammar or spelling mistake in their responses served as a distant column of smoke—proof positive that their home village had been torched.)

Kamtchowsky liked Pabst's blog; also, he was thin, and towered over her by almost a foot. It wasn't the 1990s but their very childhoods that were back in style. Now that Kamtchowsky and Pabst had the criteria necessary to appreciate their youth aesthetically, they no longer skittered about like tiny fawns terrified of the rest of the herd.

Strictly speaking, there is nothing exactly ugly about any of Pablo's facial features. Considered as an ensemble, however, they give the sensation that a mistake has been made, that he is some stumpy species of mammal that should never have made it past the starting gate in the race against extinction. The revulsion he inspired can perhaps be explained by its subordinacy to the syntactic consensus regarding what it means to belong to a given species.

Splayed out on his bed, with Kamtchowsky's dark foot in his hand, Pabst reflected on all this:

–In the 1970s, on the other hand, it was impossible to sound cheesy. You could announce that your object in life was to be a tormented poet, and no one would laugh at you. Now it's different. Our age group is more highly evolved, aesthetically speaking, by which I mean that our mental posture is *spontaneously* critical of the events that occur, not merely *dragged along* by preordained actions. I have no idea how many neurons must be called into play to configure that sort of perceptual arc, but surely it is a substantially more complex operation than simply "believing oneself to be a constituent force" of something. Furthermore, one must take into account the fact that the conditions that make someone "interesting" at any given moment correspond to a specific, *legible* modality. Your environment can *always* be used to justify being a jackass, but not all justifications are valid. That is to say, adherence to an ethical structure that makes it harder to descend into imbecility can immobilize you—the *effects* of said adherence produce a kind of paralysis—but at least the inherent dignity of reflection and self-awareness are kept intact. Of course here I'm referring to the middle class, specifically to the middle class youths most likely to engage in healthy introspection.

Kamtchowsky mentioned that the generational difference was perhaps a function of the distance between suffixes and prefixes. As seen morphologically in things like "consciousness-*in-itself*" and "consciousness-*for-itself*," the Suffix Generation focuses on that which *results*, that which extends *a posteriori* (syntax never lies) from consciousness; the following generation, on the other hand, discusses the issue of consciousness in terms of the biases inherent in its gaze, and thus opts for the prefix, for the *preceding* and therefore intrinsic characteristics of this selfsame ability to reason (e.g. *self*-consciousness). Pabst agreed enthusiastically; the significance and preponderance of huge posteriors amongst the Suffix Generation was beyond question. Classics like *Los caballeros de la cama redonda* (1973), *Expertos en pinchazos* (1979), *El rey de los exhortos* (1979), *A los cirujanos se les va la mano* (1980), *Te rompo el rating* (1981),[i] and certain blameworthy camera angles in the films of Enrique Carreras showed all too clearly the growing prevalence of carnal suffixes on Argentine soil. Likewise, the advertisements for Hitachi televisions—specifically those with the slogan "Hitachi, How Good You Look" superimposed on Adriana Brodsky's derriere—express concisely the protean quality of information tucked into privileged areas so as to convey certainties.

This gluteal liberation, undergirded by the rebirth of Argentine democracy, found an ideal habitat in a particular *kind* of sex comedy: those with military settings. Examples of this include *Los colimbas se divierten* (1986), *Rambito y Rambón, primera misión* (1986), and *Los colimbas al ataque* (1987).[ii] The adult nature of these films contrasted sharply with the anodyne clothing and de-eroticized vocabulary of the gang of adolescents in the television series *Pelito* (1982–1986). The series' innocent family-based plot lines involving divorce, daddies who smoke, and what to do with the poor little black classmate (most notably the character of Cirilo Tamayo in *Señorita Maestra*, 1983) portrayed a love between boys and girls that was as stereotypical as the anal fetishism of the military comedies, though at least the girls of *Pelito* were safe from lordosis—as were those of *Cantaniño cuenta un cuento* (1979). Nonetheless, neither the prominence of anti-slut moralism nor the phenological custom of crossing oneself at each sighting of a noteworthy ass can successfully explicate what Pabst and Kamtchowsky took to be a more widespread sociological phenomenon.

Moving smoothly to block Kamtchowsky's first objection before she'd even made it, Pabst admitted that for his digression to be sustainable, he would have to establish a correlation between the Prefix Generation and the current-day obsession with tits—as things stood, it was still far too early to tell. All the same, the theory didn't need to be all-encompassing in order to be accepted (here in this bed full of crumbs, books thick with underlined passages, computer cables, and packets of Sweet Mints) as an irreducibly wise hermeneutic manifesto.

Pabst and Kamtchowsky were profoundly politically incorrect in their praise of McDonald's. They loved that it regularly hired senior citizens—the only local business to do so—especially old women who had nothing to do with their lives. Its absurd molesto-clown mascot notwithstanding, McDonald's was the only truly democratic space they knew of. Everyone stood in line as equals, and no one got more than they'd hoped for; the thirty-year-old employees with Down syndrome smiled widely even though they weren't allowed to work the cash register. At times the place was a Limbo full of slum-dwellers, but most often they did their begging outside, leaving the middle and lower classes to cohabit in peace.

Pabst and Kamtchowsky went out fairly often. In those days Buenos Aires was a cultural amusement park bursting with protoentertainment options. Kamtchowsky's relative celebrity—a documentary she'd made about herself had caused quite a stir in certain circles—brought constant invitations to the city's rash of exhibitions, multimedia happenings, screenings of youth-oriented films, and performance art pieces of varying degrees of topicality, forcefulness, interest, and mediocrity. As neither Pabst nor Kamtchowsky was at all attractive, they could wade into conversations about the relative sex appeal of other entelechies with precisely the amount of earned resentment necessary to make their opinions colorful and fun. Their disdain for themselves and their families was an inalienable good whose elasticity in the field of autobiographical analysis gave cover to their commentaries on everyone else; for example, as Jews, they smelled particularly Jewish precisely because of their anti-Semitism.

The social balance at these events was less delicate than at the private parties they often attended, where, according to the revisionist vice then in fashion, the menu was precisely that of the childhood parties their parents had thrown for them: Cheetos, popsicles, hot dogs. Every party had the equivalent of a clown, usually some geezerly egotist making a fool of himself. Those who'd emerged victorious from the womb during the Years of Lead meandered around like little animals hypnotized by their own hypersensitivity.

The financial well-being of the attendees' psychoanalysts depended on their ability to convince the youths of a modest truth: that once armed with the sinister petulance that comes from "assuming the burden" of belonging to a dysfunctional family, they could kindly forgive themselves for their phobias, mistakes, body odor, and lack of general culture; these were pseudo-illnesses to be exhibited as bizarre curiosities, or, more precisely, as clear proof of one's *distinction* amongst equals. Anything placed under the redemptory halo of words like "sickness" or "problem" tended to awaken kindness in others, creating the protocols necessary for communication between flawed egos particularly susceptible to contagious infections such as empathy. The innate idea of a "personality" was easily substituted out for a Science Corner interminably packed full of neurasthenic pets. Treating egoic diseases (the what-how-when, the instructions and antidotes) was as simple as treating a disease that attacked iguanas: the iguana should eat one of these bugs every so often, and make sure it stays out of the cold; the person can't stand these bugs, and likewise can't stand the cold. Thus it was that little by little, everything once seen as a moral defect was converted into visible proof of one's individuality.

The more nervous Pabst and Kamtchowsky felt at festive occasions, the more carefree they pretended to be as they sipped from the cup of dissipation. Neither Pabst not Little K were sufficiently trained to survive a running Cooper Test throughout possible worlds, lying sportingly so as to avoid the judgment of others, which was of course inadmissible. Their youthful *politesse* led them to take for granted that following each new interlocutor's opening comments (usually only half-understood, as the music was invariably loud, and only half-agreed to, as early reviews are generally bad, even when deep down they're good), one or the other would smile a certain smile, having just been granted the title of "deep thinker" for the duo, a mistake that would inevitably lead to additional future misunderstandings.

Kamtchowsky preferred not to admit it, but she was obsessed with sodomites. Standing there at the edge of the wall of humanity that lined the dance floor, it was hard for her not to stare at them idiotically as they moved to the music. She didn't exactly envy their happiness, their fleeting success as a race, their tight little tees; she wondered how it was possible to achieve sufficient dilation for one's sex life to be centered on anal rending. While it was obvious that as a muscle the anus had its place down there in the shadows, she wasn't clear how often one could, so to speak, jog eight laps around Palermo.[iii]

Pabst kindly offered to ream her in the ass so she could stop obsessing about it once and for all.

–I don't want to. I get too much pleasure just thinking about it. I'd rather leave it as my body's one pristine, unreachable destination.

Thus, having located a new Neverland within the borders of her backside, they hugged, and slept until dawn.

5

Amongst the Gahuka-Gana and Gururumba tribes in Papua New Guinea, young boys dressed as tigers are brought to the river, the air around them thick with the chanting and howling of the warriors. There they are confronted by a group of men standing knee-deep in the water; the men are masturbating, and pushing sharp leaf shards farther and farther up their nostrils until they begin to bleed profusely. The initiates imitate the men's actions until they have induced their own hemorrhaging; they are then taken deep into the woods, where they spend a year living in the warriors' huts. During this period they have almost no contact with women, and dedicate themselves to learning the arts of nosebleeds, vomiting, and playing the flute.

Augusto García Roxler's first steps in the company of men were likewise systematic and shadowed. Certain university legends (pejorative rumors that perished during the voyage from the Department of Medicine to his current kingdom in Philosophy and Letters over on Puan Street) have him fondling his pudenda during written exams: not exactly a hero-on-horseback effigy of Argentine letters. I was able to discover (through covert operations I will not discuss until the time is ripe) that his contact with the fair sex had been held to a minimum. On the other hand, the impression he gave—timid, vulnerable—led several unattractive female members of the administrative staff to trust him enough to take part in his experiments. Emilia "Piggy" Sosa was the first subject to complete his strange set of questionnaires, and to bear stoically the horror that such original, mysterious versions of the Theory produced. Apparently, the flaws in his nude physique made the research easier to conduct; when combined with other factors, the effect was such that his subjects *voluntarily, instinctively* recognized him as a predator. He was also careful to take precise cranial measurements. By the time I entered the department, however, he had lost his way, and abandoned all of these practices.

Personally, I didn't think much of his theories at the beginning. I smirked each time I heard or read his name, and if I happened to come across a text of his while rummaging through boxes of used books, I pushed it aside without a second thought, much as you'd separate out the uncoordinated children, or those who can't write a proper sentence. Closing my eyes now, I can see him making his way down the Main Hall, his expression serious yet absentminded, a gray overcoat, papers and books falling out of his pockets, and I see myself languidly chewing bubble gum, or raising one condescending eyebrow, or doing both at once; the wild years of

Augustus's theories were history, and not the kind that leaves disciples, prefaces, and fear scattered in its wake.

The fact that he was still around was less an honor for us than proof of a doddering ecosystem wherein doddering academics were allowed to coexist peacefully amidst the institutional deterioration, much as they had all their lives; the only thing expected of them was the *possibility* of (doddering) emeritus-type appearances. Thanks to these individuals, the university had quite a collection of pictures of Dorian Gray—automaton portraits for an antiquated university that never quite managed to be proud of itself. Even before I entered the department, Augustus's intellectual life had come to an end. The weakening of his higher faculties had given him a certain charm . . . but as for reading his books? No one but me, with my omnivorous appetite and devotion to the task of learning, would ever have bothered with those spurious texts.

As is well-known, it is difficult to separate sense from sensibilities as regards one's contemporaries—and even more difficult if the contemporary in question looks like the cousin of some minor sub-species of Tyrannosaurus rex. The one thing I can state with certainty is that when I finally heard his voice for the first time, his phrasing had the cadence of absolute fact. And at that moment, the impossible occurred: the star pupil, the rampaging tigress of the classroom (*moi*) took an interest in the aged beast, the out-to-pasture professor, Augustus. And *ensuite*, everything changed: our inverted romance took a decisive turn as the brio of my youth combined with a gift for action that can only be acquired though training in the humanities, and I threw myself into an investigation of the possibilities that inhered in his theory.

García Roxler himself agreed to send me a copy of his seminal article from *Rivista di Filosofia Continentale*, which I later returned to its author accompanied by a brief tribute and a lengthy appendix. I then went straight to work, putting off research that was perhaps more urgent. I wrote in tiny, seraphic handwriting, filling loose pages that I carried around with me everywhere; I later translated those outbursts of thought into the docile calligraphy of the computer—so much more legible. I soon became an adherent of the illustrious theory that disdains linear representations of time, leaving past, present, and future all as yet unwritten. I tracked down seemingly untrackable articles published long ago in New Haven, Río Cuarto, Aix-en-Provence, Leipzig; I even managed to locate a handwritten copy of "Do Cave Paintings Dream of Syntactic Structures?" I also bought a fish, (Yorick, a red *Betta splendens)* because sooner or later I was going to need the company. I simply couldn't stop.

The peaks of intensity, the moments in which my intuitions became more or less perceptible to the human eye, generally took place either early in the morning or after dinner; only from the hours of rose to the hours of violet (i.e. 4 to 7 P.M.) did my mind permit itself to rest. Outside of that interval, my constant clacking at the keyboard kept my fingernails worn to the nub. I used wrist braces to avoid carpal tunnel cramps. I read, argued aloud, scrawled premises, undid conclusions; I read Augustus's books and class notes, returned to my own notes, crossed things out, corrected errors in the margins, and went back to writing again. Augustus had taken the first step in a tactically forbidden direction: his approach to Van Vliet's Theory of Egoic Transmissions combined metaphysical intuition, anthropological depth, the real-world potential of political philosophy, and language that was seductive, daring, rationalist. I don't believe I'd come across such a swarm of theoretical activity since my tumultuous affair with Clausewitz's theories of war and Van Vliet's own *Maanloos Geschriften (Written on Moonless Nights)*. I simply couldn't stop.

5.1

Anyone who reads these pages before meeting me in person[1] should picture a woman in her twenties with a jet-black mane, wearing a beige overcoat. Emotion has given a rosy tint to her cheeks. She pushes her hair back from her face, and tiptoes through a glass door leading to a vestibule whose marble floors are lined with red carpet. Like a *débutante* from imperial Russia, the young woman blinks delicately at the rabble of which the world before her is composed—a world her glaucous feet do not yet dare enter. She has come to another doorway, this one thick with people pushing their way in; knocked off balance by the moderately brutal elbows of those alongside her, she stumbles into the ballroom.

The event in question is an embassy reception in honor of a young writer from the Yucatan who has come to visit Buenos Aires; the promise of free drinks in a decorous environment

1 Other than Augustus, who knows perfectly well who I am.

attracted the cream of the local intelligentsia. Mariachis musicalized the environment. Small gatherings of ladies and gentlemen stood in animated conversation around certain luminaries; there were groups of bohemians, philobohemians, academics, and bald guys with canine silhouettes. A somber army of waiters handed out glasses of champagne; the atmosphere was relaxed, the public well-disposed toward the mariachis in their sparkling vests, who now struck up the bolero "Sabor a mí."

Our young *débutante* slides furtively along, wading through the undulating light that streams in through the art nouveau windows, looking discretely in all directions. She stops for a moment, thinking of nothing in particular; when the mariachi trio reaches the lines, "*No pretendo ser tu dueña / no soy nada, yo no tengo vanidad*,"[iv] she recovers her motor/cranial skills. There is no sign of Augustus anywhere.

She gulps down the champagne she is offered and bolts a bacon canape, her lips atremble. The song mutates surreptitiously into "Piel canela" (also known as "Me importas tú"). One of Augustus's teaching assistants, a stable boy from his nepotistical duchy, now crosses the room bouncing off of other guests. It's chubby little E.G., and he's coming toward her. Horrified, the young woman tries to blend in with those around her. The waves of humanity continue to knock E.G. around; in the end they toss him up beneath the windows, and she slips out along the shore break, hopefully in the direction of the restrooms.

Drawn by her unescapable gravitational force, men gaze at her, speak to her, attempt to stop her from leaving. But she can't afford to be distracted by the idle chat of those who aren't part of her plan. She finds a place where she will be safe from the jackals; sadly, it is not long before a waiter stoops politely to ask what she's doing under the table, and whether she's feeling all right. Though still separated from her prey by dozens of meters and guests, she can already smell him. He cannot hide from her. She stands and accepts the champagne the waiter offers. Her acid lips gleam.

And suddenly the noun García Roxler is made flesh, here he is, blue gabardine, gray trousers, I can see him clearly. Towering, magnetic, graying hair, inexpressive smile—perhaps he feels a slight disdain for the *quidam* before him, who used to be the Municipal Secretary of Culture. Oh, I could certainly have drifted between the ex-Secretary and his incredulous captive audience like a mermaid carved on the prow of a ship, but that was not my plan! I wasted no time in extending my hand exquisitely.

–Dr. García Roxler, good evening. I have an impossible project to offer you.

It wasn't the first time that the vigor of my candor left someone perplexed. He recoiled a bit, a modest *avis*, and in the act of distancing himself he displayed (*Majestitas Domine!*) the slightly absentminded, obscurely romantic aplomb—the reticent, innately seductive aura—of a genuine South American academic. The ex-Secretary inclined his bald head toward me, affecting an air of Parisian refinement; I took my lip between my teeth, voracious.

Habitually a man of few words, Augustus thought it sufficient to respond (to me) as follows:

AUGUSTUS: I trust your instincts. How about if you don't offer me the project, and I don't accept.

ME: Don't think that wouldn't be a mistake on your part. Of course, the conditions are such that you feel obliged to turn me down. But those conditions aren't, shall we say, entirely objective.

AUGUSTUS (*a bit impatient*): To what do you refer?

I explained with all due deference that certain of his essays suffered from a series of errors, rather *serious* errors let us say, serious and contagious enough to infect his other texts, which otherwise might be considered rather powerful, or at least of certain interest. Moreover, I happened to find myself in a position to correct those errors, and I very much preferred to say so here at this party rather than destroy him publicly at some future congress. The ex-Secretary seemed very amused, and asked for my name. Augustus held him back with a gesture (perhaps one born of jealousy) and, prey to unwarranted certainty or inborn spite, he leaned toward me ever so slowly, *parsimoniously*, and said:

–I doubt, Miss, that your characterization of my work, however energetic it might be, would interest me much.

The moment of silence grew thick: at once open and furtive. Often, in his classes, I've felt him monitoring me closely. I was aways surprised by the firmness of the pact of submission that he maintained vis-a-vis one particular region of my anatomy. Simply put, his position never softened. I let my eyelids fall half closed in reverence, sensing that these dark arts only work when one is still. A prodigious yearning rose up through my knees, surged across my amatory triangle. I can see it, can see it all: Augustus rising to write something on the chalkboard; and Augustus suddenly stopping, struck by the bolt of some fabulous, ungodly idea, eraser in hand. Augustus tolerating interruptions, slowly clenching his fist of fury. Augustus caught up in a spirited circumlocution, and no one is listening; he paces up and back, stops skeptically, stares at the ceiling panels. I see him changing his mind (returning to the fork, the two paths leading to different worlds, choosing the right one this time) and carefully snapping a stick of chalk in half. His face turns back and forth between the empty chalkboard and the empty faces of the students in the first few rows; then he slumps down into his chair, draws a few yellow candies from the inside pocket of his blazer, and continues his lecture, speaking as if completely alone, the rest of us participants in some strange, repetitive act of homage, the eminence García Roxler made manifest, and now he stands in the center of the classroom, dedicates his somber hendecasyllables to me—sublime messages that no one but I could decipher.

I answered slowly, as if drawing near to a little woodland creature, letting my words fall like candies amongst all the little woodland creatures. He said nothing in return, eschewing his linguistic dexterity, overconfident in the power of his facial rhetoric. (Actually, he did say a thing or two, but, *noblesse oblige*, I prefer to swathe that fetid outburst of saliva and post-structuralism in an equally brusque silence.) I stood unscathed, my empty champagne glass trembling in my hand. Ideas pertain to a fortress built of syntactic densities; they can only communicate their own purity through a *deliberately precise execution* of the facts. I was able to read the back side of his plot's tapestry, and could have told him what I knew, could have retreated with the hygienically clean conscience of one who, before striking the death-blow, explains to the fallen that after the dagger will come the fire, the siege, the strategic concealment of the pyres. Could he see, with those atrophied optical nerves of his, how the terrible shadow of this ever-so-young Athena, *si sage et si combative*, was rising up to blot out the ancient stars? I insisted once more that he take into account my corrections to the Theory of Egoic Transmissions—and here I slowed my speech—*at this*, *the dawn of its radicalization.* The echoes of my decisive coda had only begun to fade gracefully into the tulle of silence when the left corner of Augustus's mouth started to twitch; just then, plump E.G. materialized beside his fair lord, held out a glass, blanketed me with jealous looks.

The most prudent of my readers will say that this was the moment to disappear, quietly humming *So long, farewell . . .* And while I was able to detect this signal emanating from the labyrinth of fabrics, foul air, disjointed sentences, and sweat known as the world, I did not budge. *No, sirree!* To the contrary: this fatidic male trio had unwittingly solved the combination, setting loose a rebellious army within me. I was taken by a sudden voluptuous fit of desire to recite a few verses in the manner of Von Clausewitz:

But the annihilation of the other (the adversary)
cannot consist merely of a simple logical negation;

to the contrary,
it must be a dialectical negation engendered by the conflict itself.
To the extent that the conflict is developed—that is,
to the extent that its potentiality is developed—
it manifests not as a strength in itself
but as a product
of a reality created
by antagonists who are
likewise
real.

I stayed silent, however, choking back my desire. Something similar, perhaps, to what cats feel as hair balls advance and retreat along their laryngeal passage. (And do I play with the hair ball, or does the Hair Ball play with me? So might wonder Montaigne, my kitten. Soon I'll tell you more about Yorick, my fish.) This, this is the silent dilemma of Time and Space teetering at the edge of existence; in my personal Synesthesia-Foundational-Synesthesia dictionary, pure apnea, sliding under pressure through my deepest passages. It is as if the surface were getting farther and farther away, becoming vague and porous, much like the three men who now appear ever more distant, ever darker, submerging themselves in other wells of meaning, distancing themselves along other rocky peninsulas.

I know that he pivoted slightly, taking care not to let the others see—his personal way of saying, "See you later." But I don't want to get ahead of myself, don't want to, as the

Americans say, "push the envelope" in examining any given intuition, any cold explosion of empathy long held in check, in assessing the relative severity of a sneer, or of the distant, collegial glow that grave souls emit in the presence of an equal. The excuses of your pride shall not blind me.

I want you to see, Augustus, to make note of the crystalline piety with which I shall have to act for now. I know that in principle you may have convinced yourself that disentangling the key to your theory is a task that is yours and yours alone. (For the moment I allow myself to speak to you as an equal, but in a moment I will cease doing so, carried along by the local intonation—as sober, as somber and neutral, as flat as our Río de la Plata.) I understand that it is often difficult to transfer the power of a determination—one that is seemingly autonomous—to the allure (and probably the fear) of seeing it hunted down, dangling from bloody fangs amidst a chorus of voices, a sight I will soon show to you as I advance upon your comrades-in-arms, your Is that are almost you, those yous that are almost me, chosen by your true you within you.

Because your theory is incomplete without me.

6

Pabst and Kamtchowsky agreed that in terms of aesthetic obsessions, the return of pure sensibility ran parallel to heresy. The truly sad things of this world had become so exacerbated that the tale of the Ugly Duckling was now a minimalist iteration, a myth of origin that gave structure to the tragedy lived by the many millions who had eyes to see and thus knowingly *stood observed and demoted (by themselves and the rest of the world) on the basis of homeliness.* Modern songbooks were full of delicate hymns to the certainty of intrinsic patheticness, to self-consciousness regained as mirrors. This is precisely the story of Pablo's childhood. The disquieting mirrors in his desperate soul weren't tucked away at the end of some psychic hallway—they covered the walls of the very living room. And the evidence they provided made intercourse—the *possibility* of intercourse—unthinkable. The Spanish word for mirror, *espejo,* shares a root with the word *species;* the mirror shows each species for what it is, and lays bare the shoddy reasoning that has led each to think itself unique. Pablo recently wrote a blog post confessing all this, and a number of other things as well. He promised that he would soon post a few homemade snuff films starring individuals ("see charts below") who had systematically denied him attention and affection, then headed off to bed.

Elton John's "Sacrifice" was ranked first on Pabst's list of best possible background songs for the humiliation of the chronically adolescent individual. His distrust of anyone younger than himself was positively canonical. Little Kamtchowsky quickly became suspicious of them as well—she hewed instinctively to the latest sociological trends. The two often shared the vertiginous impression that all conversation was but a prelude to some new prejudice—and to the extent that one was conversing with the right people, this prejudice would be ever riskier, ever more outrageous, ever more decadent.

Kamtchowsky often picked her nose in public, and the habit had given her a special ability to sense furtive glances in her direction. This evening, she and Pablo were headed to a goth party in Suipacha y Viamonte, where they hoped to test a number of their pet theories. She was wearing a black flared skirt, socks with polka dots, and Mary Janes. He was wearing Puan-gray trousers, three T-shirts one on top of another, and had his ever-present, notebook-stuffed rucksack hanging from his shoulder. In sum, then: two researchers doing fieldwork in the city.

Pabst had often observed that the sexual conduct of standard adolescents gave evidence of a strikingly peculiar numerical discontinuity. In their first relationship they had intercourse once or twice with a given partner; their second relationship was much the same; but from there they jumped straight to six-person orgies. What sort of exponential function did this imply? Could one derive from such behavior a logarithmic calculus of generational disdain for the nobler sentiments? His own sexual history had been devoid of courtly love the same way weapons of mass destruction have been cut short of deploying their powers in full; both had only been able to exist as threats. And yet, Pabst never fully abandoned the project of emotional reciprocity, the fest of blowing and catching kisses on air. With astonishing speed, the current sociological hypothesis had dissociated itself from that which only comes after years of heartbreak, and its similarity to Rousseau (his work as portrait) encourages one to demonstrate that sexual conduct pertains specifically to *the precise facet* of the individual that allies itself *only* with the will of the majority. Pabst had addressed the topic on his blog as follows:

> "In effect, the concrete development of the common self on one hand and of the general will on the other both presupposes and implies—as a logically necessary postulate rather than as a historically real act—the existence of the social contract."

Their hypothesis duly established, they were still a good ways from the entrance, the crowds had already grown thick, and it seemed fairly unlikely that the bouncer would let them in. Every five minutes Pabst had to push his eyeglasses back up the bridge of his nose; the oily film covering his skin had them perpetually sliding down. He was nervous, and thought it unreasonable that someone as good at taking tests as he was should have to put up with being grilled by the ignorant galliform at the door. To console himself, he chewed through a series of syllogistic mantras:

–So, the human brain is designed to establish relationships only within small groups, and seeks constantly to reproduce the feeling of being "just amongst us." All attempts at socialization are intended to recreate within us a series of previously successful patterns of empathy, because . . . Aha! Because the only *real* human instinct is to flee into the forest depths. If this weren't the case, why would the State expend so much effort teaching us to love that which is social, and why such frantic insistence on the amorous-gregarious nature of the glorious Fatherland? Social training is an operating system composed of customs designed to minimize the panic one feels at finding oneself *completely surrounded*. Social aristocracies are brought into existence as a form of technology that enables the elite to tolerate the proximity of others, as another way to address the need for human contact felt by the *I* while simultaneously protecting it from the unwashed hordes via membership cards and club protocols. The presence of the bouncer ensures that the favored group will stay small. The charm exuded by the elite is the *Ersatz* of an evolutionary defect related to our genetic inability *to be alone*, which is to say, *to rid ourselves* of our fear of the forest—and to do so with sufficient speed.

The later it got, the more intense grew the couple's desire not to be turned away at the door. But they knew how imprudent it would be to push forward with so little evidence of worthiness at their disposal; average adolescents would only reveal the hidden diamond of their conduct to those who dare to share the same dream of sweaty skin, black light, and crystal meth. Kamtchowsky heard Pabst sigh, noticed his trembling hands, and decided to buck him up.

–The whole concept of the urban tribe is both fallacious and stupid, she said. All of these people want exactly the same thing: a simple straightforward fuck. Or else a lucid fuck, one they won't feel the need to try to forget tomorrow morning. And it's easier to fuck someone who dresses the same way you do, albeit not so much because of some alleged empathy based on textile preferences—the fact is, you'd fuck *anyone* willing to fuck you. The key, then, is to maintain a strict policy of defrauding your own conscience, which has no way of knowing that you'd be perfectly happy fucking anyone at all. Deciding with whom to associate on the basis of fabric color and texture allows your conscience to verify empirically that in fact you are *not* fucking absolutely *everyone*, but only a *select few*. That is, it's not so much that the modern self has broken down and now finds itself at the mercy of much stronger unconscious forces, but that it perpetually designs ever more sophisticated strategies for maintaining control. And in this case, the chosen means of control requires that one mimic a tactical strategy of unknowing.

Kamtchowsky had one lip curled, as if a pane of glass were pressing against her face. From that point on she would take recourse to this same expression whenever she needed to express surprise, disdain, or anal dilation.

–Hey, said Pabst, the *select few* are checking you out.

–You're the one they're checking out.

–Does it matter?

The girl waving to them was a redhead with a cute little turned-up nose, big eyes, bright blue eyeshadow. Beside her was a boy with a friendly smile and short curly blond hair swept up in a half-crest. Both had that indefinable glow that all beautiful people exude so effortlessly whenever they smile.

Pabst and Kamtchowsky fell silent and tried to breathe normally as they watched the couple approach. The girl was wearing a short vintage dress, the cloth patterned with little pine trees in lilac and green. From closer up, they saw that her dress was almost translucent, and that her nipples were almost as attentive as her smile.

–Hi! she said to Kamtchowsky. Aren't you the girl from the documentary?

–Well . . .

It was a simple question, but Kamtchowsky couldn't think of the answer, and decided at last just to close her mouth.

–How's it going? Don't you remember me? Rotstein introduced us one day maybe halfway through the film festival—the day they were showing that new Fassbinder film, the one named after a woman . . . *Monika*, maybe?

Kamtchowsky took a symbolic step backward so that Pabst could join in, which he did, as laconic and solemn as ever:

–*Summer with Monika* is a Bergman film. *Martha* is the Fassbinder.

–Oh, that's right! Of course!

The girl shot a glance at her watch, a cute little number decorated with the Swiss flag.

–Anyway, we've got some time before the party gets going. Would you guys let us buy you a drink?

The Research Commission agreed to allow a quick break at the downtown apartment that Mara and Andy shared—Kamtchowsky and Pabst didn't learn their names until a nervous silence in the elevator, one that gave Mara the opportunity to seem carefree and solvent while Andy smiled ironically in the background. The apartment had high ceilings, and living room walls with curves instead of corners. A coquettish window gave onto an intersection that was silent at this time of night. A mirror ball hung in the center, its red and blue lights flashing across the black-and-white photographs that covered the walls—a series of extraordinary images of Buenos Aires.

The room's centerpiece was a gigantic photomontage. In it, the rocket-shaped Kavanagh Building had been turned on its head and embedded in the roof of the Álzaga-Unzué mansion. Next to it slumped a hotel (the Hyatt, or maybe the Four Seasons) that had been digitally retouched to make it look as if an enormous fire had destroyed the side that gave onto Cerrito y Alvear Avenue. A low-angle shot showed the landmark Rulero Building collapsing onto the 9 de Julio Expressway; another showed the Alas rotated forty-five degrees, looming like a massive gargoyle about to slam into the Hotel Catalinas Suites. The National Congress building had been reduced to charred ruins, its dome riddled with holes. There were also two photographs of automobile accidents. One had taken place on the infamous Curve of Death where Figueroa Alcorta swoops beneath the train tracks, a dotted line overlaid to show the path of someone who had run wounded into the trees, then collapsed and died. The other had occurred out toward the boardwalk near La Mosca Blanca, along a shortcut that runs from the wrecking yard to Retiro.

As the guests contemplated her work, Mara put a hand on her waist and launched into an appropriately languid commentary:

–I wanted to push the accident theme a little harder, but at this point it's already kind of a cliché, right? Because of *Crash*, I mean. It's all . . . you know. Anyway.

–*Crush* is a dead soft drink and nothing more, said Pablo, drawing closer to study a series of blurred images of the Río de la Plata. In places the surface of the river had been sliced into geometric shapes, as if whole buildings were drifting crosswise in the current, architectural skeletons of rebar and concrete. Then his gaze was drawn to a blurry mass covered with blood and loose grass beneath a bridge.

Andy returned from the kitchen bearing drinks. He was wearing a batik shirt, and thanks perhaps to the magic exuding from the rest of his persona, which had apparently been carved exquisitely by hand, the shirt managed to look almost good on him. He sat down on a beanbag chair and folded his legs into the lotus position, gave them all a tranquil gaze, and cracked his neck joints. Pabst turned his eyes skyward like a scandalized priest, but Kamtchowsky couldn't look away from this trim modern Buddha on his ground-bound throne, not even when she realized that he was staring right back at her.

–Excellent, isn't it, he said.

He moved his head in slow circles, a sort of auto-massage.

–What?

–The drink, I mean. Isn't it great?

Kamtchowsky managed a *hm!* of agreement.

–It's called an "Andy Wants . . ."

–A what?

–An "Andy Wants Dot-Dot-Dot . . ."

–And what exactly does Andy want? asked Pablo, more than a bit irritated.

Andy spoke as if from some tawny beach in Thailand:

–You're supposed to complete the sentence in your head, with thoughts of your own. Like a fill-in-the-blank, you know, those exercises they gave us in English class.

–I know what fill-in-the-blanks are.

–Okay. And you also know what thoughts are, right?

Pablo propped himself up against the wall by slapping his sweaty hand flat against the gigantic photograph of the blackened remains of the Hyatt. All of the morbid admiration that kept his relationship with Kamtchowsky erect was based on that old chestnut of natural selection, according to which ugly people are inevitably more intelligent than beautiful people, because they've had to develop more sophisticated means of obtaining things. This pull-string Ken doll was not only destroying the theory as far as Pabst himself was concerned; he was also torching the cherished prejudices that Pabst and Kamtchowsky had shared up on that quiet, serene hilltop where, their cheeks caressed with greasy pizza crumbs, they were occasionally able to dream of superiority.

–Actually, no, said Pabst. I haven't the faintest fucking idea what thoughts are, nor–

–*The stuff dreams are made of*, said Andy, smiling, his sudden English almost Etonian, *and yet, what is this quintessence of dust?*

Pabst noticed an emphasis on the word "dreams" as Andy had looked him up and down.

–. . . Nor what's in this drink, nor who *the fuck* you are . . .

He almost added, *Nor what planet people like you come from*, but caught himself in time. At least he'd nailed the British accent on "fuck."

–Hold on! said Andy, rising to his feet. Nobody shouts at anybody in here. Nobody gets to be Toshiro Mifune—not me, not you, nobody. Mara's apartment is . . . well, it's Mara's apartment. Nothing but good vibes allowed.

Pabst sighed in relief. From that point on, the mockability of "good vibes" became something of a talisman for him. He was happy to see that Kamtchowsky had found an interesting object on the floor to stare at, even if it happened to be invisible to him, and made her bow her head somewhat ashamedly (and perhaps this was how she went about disapproving of Andy's vibes? One could hope!). Then Mara stepped out of the shadows, and gently corrected her boyfriend:

–Andy, the vibes here aren't just good. They are *excellent.* Absolutely and extremely excellent.

She laughed, turned and put her hand on Kamtchowsky's shoulder.

–I think you guys are the best.

Kamtchowsky was by now fairly drunk, and felt like she was going to throw up.

–Really? she said. What's so great about us?

She lifted her head and opened wide her caca-colored eyes. Mara smiled as if about to caress a child's hair. She went to speak, laughed instead, looked at Andy as if hoping he'd step in. Then she scratched her head charmingly.

–I'm not very good at explaining things. Let's see . . .

Andy seemed to be cheering for her silently.

–Look, Andy's my boyfriend and I also think he's a really special person. That seems obvious, right? Well, it is and it isn't. Hold on.

In two quick hops Mara reached the corner of the room, and pressed a pair of buttons on the wall; the maelstrom of disco lights quieted, the reds and blues fading to a glow of rose and orange. The entire space was now lit warmly, deliciously. It felt like being inside an apricot.

–Close your eyes! said Mara.

Pabst and Kamtchowsky squinted, then obeyed, leaning into one another like tipsy soldiers. Mara wrapped herself in a vaporous shawl dotted with tiny silver stars, twirled like a fairy godmother, and planted a kiss on Kamtchowsky's open mouth. The moist lips, the smell of grape-and-strawberry lip gloss, Kamtchowsky shivered, and now the bewitching, the meandering, the soft, slow, fleshy tongue. For several long moments Kamtchowsky kept her eyes closed, and concentrated on mimicking these luscious movements, but now she could hear Pabst bleating from where he lay struggling beneath Andy atop a floor cushion.

–What are you doing? shrieked Pablo, now clutching the cushion to his chest. Get off of me! What are you doing?

Kamtchowsky unwound her scarf and straightened her skirt, embarrassed by Pabst's shrill outburst. She glanced at Mara, hoping to find her way back to that extraordinary mouth, but the moment was gone. Pabst was still howling hysterically, his incredulity now incontrovertible. "They brought us to their apartment to pin us down and fuck us because we're ugly—they think that because we're ugly we can't say no!" he shouted, giving voice to his refusal to allow this lack of equal opportunity to result in his intentions begin taken for granted. Pabst defended his independence from the social dictates of what one should do or seek; sleeping with any given gorgeous human being was something he could luxuriously indulge in rejecting.

Even so, Kamtchowsky was baffled by Pabst's analysis of the situation. She dried the saliva at the corners of her mouth, wondering if there was any easy way to re-interpret the situation that didn't make her feel so unabashedly stupid.

–Yes! continued Pabst. They think we're desperate because we've never fucked anyone who isn't as ugly as we are! Because no one else will fuck us! They think we're dying to touch them but we . . .

He seemed to be on the verge of tears, but in fact he just had a runny nose. Andy stood nearby, his shirt half-open, his hair artfully mussed. When he shook his head to deny what Pabst had said, it was a most beautiful, taciturn gesture.

Kamtchowsky took a deep breath. She was, after all, an

important young woman: only a few weeks before she'd been offered a job running the Young Jewish Cinema segment of the Independent Film Festival.

–So, I guess there's just the one question, she said. Why do you want to sleep with us?

Mara and Andy looked at each other for an instant; they were ready to confess.

6.1

For a brief moment, the silence that followed Mara's answer glued them all in place. Pablo wasn't in any condition to ask for specifics; he had a feeling that if he'd been in a different mood, he would have found the answer frankly insulting, and couldn't overcome his desire to flee. Kamtchowsky followed him out of the apartment and pulled the door closed with a bang.

What Mara had said was, "Well, who knows, maybe because you two are just like us?"

Pabst and Kamtchowsky walked down the hall, and the *us* from only seconds ago was now a distant *them*. Then, waiting silently for the elevator, they heard laughter coming from inside Mara's apartment. Pablo stabbed at the elevator button. Kamtchowsky tugged at his sleeve. He turned to see Andy hanging from the door frame by his fingertips, gazing sleepily at the two of them.

–Guys, we're sorry. We didn't know that . . . Well, but you also didn't have to take it like that, right?

The small bulb overhead covered him in a crystalline, pious light, and Kamtchowsky caught her breath.

–Do you want us to call you a cab? asked Mara.

She'd poked her head out through the space under Andy's arm. Together they formed a bicephalous monster with exquisitely beautiful young features.

–Okay, well, bye then, and again, sorry if we offended you. Oh, and you, Documentary Girl, you never told me your name.

–It's Kamtchowsky.

–No, I mean, your real name.

Squat dark K stared intently into Mara's eyes for a moment, her own eyes wet with sadness. Then she stepped into the elevator, and Pabst slammed the grill shut.

Down on the ground floor, they heard the panauricular screech of a passing garbage truck.

–As researchers go, observed Dr. Kamtchowsky, we're awfully prudish.

–No we aren't, said Pablo, his voice trembling slightly. This isn't the 1970s.

Dr. K observed the nervous expression on Pabst's face as he shouldered his rucksack and checked the ground obsessively to make sure he hadn't left anything behind. His erroneous diagnosis of the Argentine zeitgeist made her suspicious. She was willing to admit that the whole armed rebellion thing had pumped the '70s full of sexual energy, but actual sexual follow-through—which is what he was referring to—hadn't exactly been its strong point, regardless of its many feverous desires, its profound sense of imminence, its well established *petite mortes*, or *petites mortes en masse*.

Of course this wasn't the '70s; the only thing that had anything to do with the '70s was acting like promiscuity was a thing from the '70s. Which meant that Pabst was just jealous. Which meant that he loved her. She put her arms around him and gave him a kiss.

–You're an idiot, she said.

–I know.

–We could have fucked them, could have seen what they looked like naked.

–Yeah.

–And afterwards we could have gone right back to fucking each other.

–You think? But you'd have seen his dick . . .

K lit a cigarette.

–Oh please. And now who knows when we'll get another chance. What happened to you? Did it freak you out because he's a guy?

She expelled the smoke sharply.

–I don't think he's just a guy, whispered Pabst. He's built like Achilles.

–Do you want to go back?

–Do you love me?

–Yes. Do you love me?

–Obviously.

–Damn it, there goes the elevator.

–There's got to be a service elevator somewhere.

The second time I saw Kamtchowsky, it was in footage shot that night in Mara's apartment.

7

He can't have failed to notice how frequently we've been running into each other—he must have sensed the appearance of a new celestial body whose orbit intersects his own, destroying its symmetry. But he has no idea which law determines such movements. I have closed in on him slowly, inexorably; I know that he is feeling the temptation to glance up at what is going on around him, but he hasn't yet been able to pinpoint the new source of gravitational attraction, can't yet explain the sense of urgency brewing deliciously behind the curtain of his thoughts. As far as he is concerned, I am still just a specter circling a bastion of contingencies. I'm sure that a fondness for me will soon overlay his initial paranoia.

Augusto García Roxler arrived half an hour late to our most recent class. He was wearing his little gray pinstriped suit, with a white dress shirt under a v-neck sweater; all his clothes were old and worn, but the overall effect was charming. As a national holiday was drawing near, he had a flag pin stuck in his lapel, which gave his lecture an infinitely more tender feeling than usual.

I suppose it would be trivial of me to point out the prevalence of misunderstandings in this world, or to note that errors are simply a function of the subject's distance—be it moral, physical, what have you—from the object. As I said at the start, my early experiences of Professor García Roxler's theories involved a fair amount of rejection and denial on my part. To my kindly but not inexpert eyes, Professor García Roxler was the embodiment of a herd leader locked in a repertorial morgue: stooped over a shapeless mass of decomposing ideas, scalpel at the ready, mask to block the stench. My views must have started to change when I first began attending his classes, wandering in like some sleepwalker at midnight, irresistibly attracted to the sound of his voice. Or, strictly speaking, to the *hypnotic system of language secreted by his mouth*—the labial art of Augustus.

There was something inevitably precise about his way of speaking—something that came to life as naturally as voices spreading out through one's brain. There was nothing accidental about the musical cadence of his speech; he knew the exact progression of each sentence's interior drama, knew the clever workings of each velvet-smooth hinge. To gloss the secret shape of the world, a very special set of paraphernalia is required, along with, in Augustus's case, a series of intricate proofs—their hordes of subordinate clauses lined up in columns behind their enlightened Subject—whose complexity occasionally bordered on confusion. (My kingdom for a footnote supporting—*organizing*—these scattered crystals!)

But like one calming a spirited steed named Panegyric, or Redundancy, I shall prevent myself from going on about this at length, perhaps because as History (and her Aegean scribe, Melpomene) are wont to teach, this drama's true protagonists are not to be found in the stimulus itself, but in the extraordinary repercussions said stimulus provoked *in me*, the glowing pitcher of their echoing voices.

I was sitting in the center of the classroom, my hands resting chastely on my knees, and this is what occurred: little by little, the blackish mass of other listeners disappeared, and as if in slow motion, the raised hand of Augustus drew near me, the lips of Augustus drew near, the center of the classroom trembled, the light turned to ardor pure. I took a deep breath. What I was seeing had the tenor, the force of reality itself—it had truth seeping from its very pores. I let my eyes fall half-shut, much as theater curtains are pleated to intensify the *mise-en-scène*; your voice advanced toward me, flaring hot against my eyelids, and again he nears, his mouth-speech thrown like a rope around my neck, my own voice inside my head. His raised hands passed through solid objects. I was alone, chosen from among the rest.

I had accepted the challenge.

Somber, dominant, Augustus paced the hardwood floor. His eyes, orbiting planets, traced a revolution around me. He threw a question into the air—something viscously answerable by any mole who'd ever had a look down the shallow Hegelian tunnels of the assigned readings. His gaze swept past the raised hands of those few willing to attempt an answer, as if he were looking for "someone."

I took advantage of the lowered tension that followed an interruption—a couple of bearded guys asking for donations to help fund the daycare center for children with Down syndrome that had recently opened on the ground floor—and slipped my hand in through the buttons of my blouse, *à la* Napoleon. Then I stared at Augustus, nodding in silence.

Without noting my demeanor, or even my presence, *Herr Professor* took a few more slow-motion steps, which carried him far to the right, the darkest side of the room. Then he spun abruptly around and gave a pat on the back to E.G., *Éminence Grise*, his chubby TA with the little goatee and the pink toad-like face. E.G. commenced sending little packets of saliva to everyone in the nearest rows as he held forth on a series of obvious and trivial points from the reading.

I've always defended myself candidly from all hostility. I crossed my arms and legs, gazed distantly (and, yes, disapprovingly) at Augusto, and waited for the class to end. Then I walked casually up to the dais on which his desk rested. Oh, he had no way of foreseeing the ferocity of my plan, the selfless devotion of my search. (Nor could he intuit it transcendentally, no matter how pure a Kantian he was.) He placed a book in his briefcase—fluorescent green spine, *Die Diktatur*, Carl Schmitt, the same translation that I have. He slid the '79 edition of the *Cartas privadas de Nicolás Maquiavelo* in on top; still on the desktop was a volume of *Leben des Generals von Clausewitz*, and a copy of Lenin's commentaries on the Prussian's strategic doctrine. That Clausewitz book contains a magnificent sentence:

> Regardless of whatever pleasure I may take in telling the story of my life to the world, my path leads me always across a vast battlefield; unless I enter it, no lasting happiness shall be mine.[2]

I wobbled a bit, overcome by the thought. Just then, Augustus hurled an ice dart my way: "You already passed this course—why are you taking it again?" He continued to fiddle with his books, not daring to lift his gaze to the human height where my own gaze awaited. I confess, I didn't know what to say. I had no proof that he'd received my latest missives regarding his lectures, which I had diligently placed in the humble dusk of his fourth-floor office so that he could absorb my elucidations without the pressure of having to reason coherently *in praesentia mihi*. It is not often that one has the pleasure of seeing for oneself in real time that one has won an argument, simply because people don't like to change their opinions in public. Likewise, as there were witnesses present, it was hardly the right moment to point out that this semester's study program included a number of changes that clearly reflected *observations* ("suggestions") I had made. The Old Man, as some students call him, is also an older man. He should share my position not because I've forced him to, but as the result of a careful examination of evidence consisting of brute facts and the manner in which they developed and in which they will continue to develop, whether he likes it or not.

2 Schwartz, Karl. Leben des Generals von Clausewitz, Friburg: 1887, p. 45.

And *still* the man couldn't imagine—was not yet able to read—the ferocity of my hidden plans.

Whenever I am obliged to penetrate the depths of the Main Hall, I tend to walk quickly—I have a number of admirers with whom I prefer not to cross paths. The same goes for a group of students (batik clothing, dreadlocks) who dared to "confront" me[3] in response to my pseudonymous cybernetic Lugonian crooning—I think it all began with me posting on the web forum the verse "Liberty, Liberty, that Venus of the Commoners." At any rate, my elevated tone and structural daring were sufficient to light the ardent wicks of those Gulag punks. My "crime" was of course perfectly lawful (I avoided even mentioning that the fateful lines were drawn from the period of *La Montaña*, the anarchist newspaper where the definitive Voice of Río Seco—Lugones himself—shared top billing with that charlatan Giuseppe Ingenieros). The key element of my experiment was that I knew who they were, but they never found out my real

3 It didn't take long for the news of my intellectual intimacy with Augustus to spread. As part of a smear campaign intended to slander both Augustus and me, certain cowardly and not unsarcastic elements let fly with criticisms such as, "Oh, sure, a treatise on political erotomania—at best it'll be the kind of esoteric mumbo-jumbo you'd find in some realist novel." This public statement was issued on the 2nd floor of the department, spoken through a cud-like mouthful of bread—perhaps a key experiment intended to determine whether carbohydrates can be used to strengthen one's scrawny opinions, with no results to speak of. I had the good sense to put forward my answer in writing, from the comfortable solitude of my pied-à-terre: "Ah but no. As distinct from realist novels, the theory of AGR takes into account the manner in which decisive processes depend upon maniacal evolutionary developments based on the System of Personal Pronouns intrinsic to the Grammar of Romance Languages." In this book, Cf. Section 2.1 et seq.

name. All of which proves conclusively that my rate of speed in the Main Hall at that moment was a justifiable acquired response, not a sub-product of the contingent fact that Augustus was walking ahead of me, and there I was still trying to think up a clever form of revenge. How wise of him to jump into a taxi at his earliest opportunity.

For all I know, lots of things happened that week, but I never found out about any of them: so little seems relevant except for what comes from books, or one's deciphering of them. (Of course, some perhaps overly dainty individuals hold that there is no difference.) Regardless, I can confirm that this was roughly the point when a number of faunal modifications were made to my ecosystem.

In my *pied-à-terre*, I have cultivated an expansive sense of austerity. Heaps of books and papers live in close cohabitation with my computer and other electricity-dependent species. On this somber stage, my omnivorous library has pride of place, ruling majestically over the rest of the incubi. At any rate, I was feeding good Yorick (my little red fish) when my kitten Montaigne began mewing archly from the foot of the bookcase. In keeping with her confrontational nature, Montaigne had been entertaining herself by gnawing on the little signs I put up to denote the various sections of my library—"Hobbesian Frenzy," "A Social Engineering Night's Dream," "Police Academy 9: The Positivists Return." To this day I don't know how many sections it actually has.

Those were the facts. I chose a book at random (an old edition of Skinner's *Walden*) and smacked Montaigne across the snout—a common technique for introducing conduct-altering data into small animals. (In fact I have certain doubts as to its efficacy. Once, when Montaigne tried to eat Yorick, I used the same method, rapping a book against the side of the fish bowl. This seemed only to excite the kitten even more—I always carry a little log book called *Small Animals Journal* for animal-related thoughts that occur at untimely moments. The proximity of the fish had powerfully awakened the predatory interest of the kitten, whose threatening behavior intensified: hackles raised, ichthycentric orbit, Yorick's movements monitored through the crystalline penumbra.) I then left off observing my pets, abandoning myself to labors more properly celebratory of the divine within the human, or vice versa. Montaigne Michelle mewed plaintively and snuggled up against the warm computer; I continued typing through the hours of night and into the dawn.

I draw your attention to these delightful domestic vignettes, the intimate nucleus of my abstract bestial affections, in order to make more tangible the drastic transformation that the following pages hold. As preface to the horror, suffice it to say that the waters of this tranquil pond rose up in fraught crests as if driven by Sirocco winds; that the most profound spirituality was transformed into a hurricane. Kind reader: this is not a tale of obsession. My private tragedy, which shouldn't be of particular interest to anyone else—anyone except you, Augustus, you who look at me now—is that I was forced to abandon my natural habitat, the velvet-lined home of my solitary, lettered existence, and plunge deep into the brutal swamplands of a monster.

8

The four-hands idyll that Mara and Andy played with Pabst and Kamtchowsky included visits to the zoo and a couple of different cinemas. As the latter two didn't consider themselves sufficiently perverse or attractive to make it worth the trouble of hiding their true personalities in an area as fraught as sex, there too Pabst and Kamtchowsky played their customary roles of lucid, intellectual pessimists. For them, sex was a commodity much like oats or rice; it was expected that someone else would take charge of adding value. Despite the morbid fantasies to which Pabst clung, Andy did not in fact suffer from some strange syndrome that let morons quote Shakespeare with the accent of a British scholar. His golden curls, fabulous shirts (or so they seemed to Pabst—in fact they were rather ridiculous), and carefree aplomb notwithstanding, Andy was a reasonably articulate guy who carefully hated all the things one is meant to hate. He was self-sufficient and far-seeing enough to have taken an otherwise colossal bourgeois failure (he'd dropped out of college) and turned it into a point in his favor: he now worked in the film world and made far more money than any mediocre academic, as he explained one day to Pabst, who sat there gritting his teeth while Andy nibbled on a brightly colored tab of paper.

In general, Pabst preferred to stay off to one side and masturbate. He considered himself to be something of a monk, albeit one with well-whetted appetites: the simple satisfaction of curiosity wasn't a big enough bribe to convince him to give up the pleasures of misanthropy. He jerked off while walking around the apartment, or let himself drop gracefully into a beanbag chair; here at Mara's he treated his penis with a long-lost affection, as opposed to back at his own desk, where solitude led him to twist it brutally back and forth in a spasm of emotional helplessness, sadism, and sadness.

Like some retired Nero too lazy to bother lighting the torch of any given desire, at times he laid back under the shifting lights of the mirror ball and let his eyes fall half-closed, his gaze drifting over the photographs of the destruction of Buenos Aires, the long avenues and ornate buildings in ruins, while Poppaea Kamtchowsky, backgrounded by a Puerto Madero laid waste (the *A Grosso Modo* series), took it from both ends at once. At other times he played the roll of DJ: with his pants down around his ankles and his cock safely in hand, he connected his mp3 player to Andy's PC. (He'd once managed to awe Andy just by removing the CPU case, leaving all the colored cables and skeletal components of the drives and connectors in plain sight—a science nerd aesthetic that was just starting to catch on amongst hipsters.) Pabst took the role seriously, adjuncting the sessions for all he was worth—the fucking of others, his own jerking off—he and his fabulous alter-ego DJ Milk Blow, brought to you by a.a. cumming, inc.

Once, rubbing himself up with a bath towel, a pair of panties tucked into each nostril—Milk Blow was in charge of the outfits—Pabst saw a massive column of flame shoot up from the gothic fog of Buenos Aires. His mouth twisted, spasmed, he masturbated harder and harder, he murmured *Kristeva and Chomsky, hold on tight!* and his eyes rolled back. What followed was a disgorgement of theory, a spew of staggering dimensions; he could imagine his classmates from college, who'd always hated him, fighting each other barb and nail to see who would blog it first. The narrative was a recurring fantasy of his, a sort of "Jesus raises a ruckus in the temple"—he could visualize the shocked looks of the students with all their hippy accessories as he stalked the department halls like some justice-dealing tiger, shredding the banners and kicking down all the little stands with the Che Guevara merchandise and the garish Paco Urondo flags, the "We Shall Triumph" signs. In the end everything was in ruins and Pabst couldn't stop talking, couldn't stop laughing diabolically and pointing at the spelling mistakes on their posters.

Pabst agreed with Milk Blow that the notion of a masturbating DJ was in fact a redundancy, or an analytic truth, or a tautology—lately, Pabst himself preferred enumeration to synthesis. The songs they chose ran the gamut from "Personal Jesus" (either Marilyn Manson's cover or Johnny Cash's) to *excerpta* from the Guns N' Roses album *Appetite for Destruction*, via Alien Sex Fiend, Butthole Surfers, Rage

Against the Machine, Pixies, Rammstein and Sepultura. According to Pabst's theory, the true tip of the sexual peak was the '80s, when for the first time vanity knew no limits. That said, whenever it came time to choose a musical background for the day's hump session, he never dismissed the furious, threatening rhythms most appropriate to the unfurling of the historical materialism of vanity: evil just makes you want to fuck.

The other force guiding his musical selections was his loyalty to Kamtchowsky. If he chose more playful songs ("Don't Talk Just Kiss," mid-'80s Madonna, Britney) or any of the more specifically seductive offerings, most of them by black singers, ("Doctor's Orders," "Love to Love You Baby") he would be obligating her to demonstrate aptitudes which, all condescension aside, not even the most doting grandparent would be willing to testify she possessed. He took for granted that deep inside one or another of her organs, Kamtchowsky, currently down on all fours and mooing with pleasure, much appreciated this thoughtfulness on his part. The songs that, statistically speaking, were most likely to make adolescent girls spread their legs up on the speakers presented a perverse sort of challenge within Kamtchowsky's graceless universe. For other girls, each specific motor activity correlated to a series of musical instructions that functioned like a private language hidden deep within a given community; for Kamtchowsky, however, hearing those instructions was like finding herself in the middle of a massive chessboard, and realizing that she isn't a chess piece at all. It was as if those songs were in a language that Kamtchowsky could understand, but was incapable of speaking.

As for "Mars, the Bringer of War" (Holst's *The Planets*, track 4), Pabst decided to hold off until they were all at least thirty years old. Otherwise these idiots would squeal with pleasure thinking that they were listening to the *Star Wars* soundtrack; they would pump each other furiously, with Pabst left bobbing his head in managerial silence.

After each orgy, they gathered to compare notes. Mara praised the beauty of Kamtchowsky's feet, politely passing over the rest of her; when it was Andy's turn to talk, he crossed his legs and pretended to take great huge bites out of the air. Pablo played a fundamental role, and not merely that of the birds that keep the ruins of Tlön from disappearing; his masturbation fulfilled the group's expectations as regarded yet another metaphor for love. He also brought a number of deeply penetrating sociological insights to the table.

–Nowadays when we talk about the sexual revolution, we're finally back to using "revolution" the way Copernicus originally meant it. In *De Revolutionibus Orbium Coelestium*, his treatise on revolutions, it refers to the immovable, reiterated, *fixed* manner in which the planets trace their routes around the sun. A perfect term for that which is stable and permanent, "revolution" had from the beginning the scientific and etymological meaning of a cosmic status quo. This powerfully conservative meaning held sway until the Jacobin brouhaha started in France. The alleged sexual revolution of the 1970s was a fallacy that has only now acquired its true meaning: *conservation* as the ideal modality for capitalism. Sex is a stable system of egotistical forms revolving around the sun of vanity. Promiscuity's spirit of exchange proposes a new version of the foundational myth of democracy: namely, that participating in the exercise of assuming that all are equal should, by definition, enable us to transcend the obstacles of private activity, of mere intimate contingencies. Only now, depoliticized and thus cold and pure and free of all teleological nonsense, does the sexual revolution regain its *true* Copernican meaning—the conservative instinct of vanity as the moral and aesthetic triumph of democracy.

Mara and Andy had been listening carefully; Pabst and Kamtchowsky were sharing a beanbag chair.

–Yeah, said Mara, that whole '70s thing was bullshit. You see how fucked up those guys are now, and you realize it was all bullshit. The other day I had a job shooting this extremely cool electro-hardcore group (Andy, remember? We saw them in that little underground club over on Constitución?) called Tradition, Family, and Private Property.

–Ha! Nice name. Go on, you were saying?

–Good, right? Anyway, the singer's name is Dantón, and he plays with these two other guys—it's a power trio, guitar and computer and voice. Somebody was profiling them for some crap newspaper supplement, and the singer was driving them crazy, saying that here in this country the only difference between the right and the left is which side their dick hangs down.

Pabst felt almost beautiful in these moments of laid-back sophistication.

–Well, she continued, doesn't his position seem like an ethical/political option worth highlighting?

Mara stiffened, then joined the others in their laughter.

The scarcity of resources in the neighborhood (two girls, their non-infinite number of orifices) often caused a sort of emergency amongst the males: they kept brushing up against each other. Even in a context of peaceful cooperation, the inclination to compete was unavoidable, albeit generally limited to simply verifying the other's whereabouts. Accustomed as he was to an existence in which resentment was a form of lucidity, and thus of vigilance, Pabst was extremely conscious of these iterations. Tranquility, on the other hand, was Andy's domain. If asked about said competitions, he would have laughed at the questioner and dismissed the hypothesis out of hand. His carefree attitude belied the irrevocable superiority that only extreme physical beauty can confer. Andy set his glass down on the floor and ensconced himself in his beanbag chair.

–I'm going to attempt to establish a relationship, he said, surely more modest than that last one, between the tools of sex and the implicit truths of the masses. In the 1960s, a man named Michael Condon undertook a research project whose consequences have been, to this day, insufficiently explored and poorly understood. His objective was to decode a film clip that was four seconds long. In it, a woman says to a man and a child, "I hope you enjoyed the chicken. I prefer it without bacon." He divided the clip into second-long segments of forty-five frames, and set himself to watching them. It was a year and a half before he made his discovery: *the woman moved her head at precisely the moment the man raised his hands*. He began to reconstruct other micro-movements that were repeated time and again; in a given frame, a character's shoulder might move just as someone else lifted an eyebrow or changed direction, and another series would begin. Condon surmised that all group behavior functioned on the basis of communicable, synchronous empathy. According to his theory, people's actions are driven less by allegedly intellectual motivations than by *systems of contagion* that have no need of language whatsoever.

Pabst was about to say something (he'd just realized where these ideas were coming from) but Andy, alert to that danger, kept talking:

–What I'm saying is that it's plausible that the irresistible instinct to act *en masse*, to replicate the irresistible circuit of empathy, constitutes a sort of private language for our species, one that is older than any spoken language, its source residing deep below the conscious mind. The phenomena of synchrony and contagion may yield only a single visible detail in a vast and complex field of study. Perhaps the implicit languages that modulate our conduct depend on some quality that we've been dragging along with us since Pleistocene times. Perhaps those languages . . . perhaps they're associated with the superimposition of multiple supposedly meaningful messages at a particular time and place!

Pabst scratched his chin, careful not to let his fingertips brush against a pimple that was crowned with a minuscule carbuncle of pus. If he added examples, complementing Andy's thoughts with a series of Pabstian über-cool opinions—that is, if he assented to the proposed format of literary dialogue—the situation could well develop into something resembling masculine *bonheur* or camaraderie. Pabst wavered; it was an awfully complex scenario. He had to act carefully, as he didn't want his narcissistic interest in unfurling his own opinions to lead to some fraternal handshake as regarded the mysteries of the human species—not by any means. His hand settled alongside his balls as he began.

–There's an extremely common type of amoeba (*Dictyostelium discoideum*) that, whenever the colony is spread out in the grass or across the trunk of a fallen tree, which is where it's most often found, looks very much like dog vomit. These amoebas have a simple unicellular structure, and spend most of their time moving around individually, completely independent of one another. But under the proper circumstances, millions of them will unite and coordinate their actions, creating what amounts to a single organism that slides across people's yards, eating rotten leaves as it goes. The changes that affect the colony can be tiny ones. If the temperature drops two degrees, the great amoeba becomes disorganized, disintegrates back into the myriad unicellular organisms it was before; if the temperature then rises a little, the process of dissolution reverses itself: each one becomes part of a single "them" whose behavior indicates that they are all blindly obeying the unified decision-making *I* of the Prime Amoeba. Now, what exactly is organizing this myriad of tiny dots that is suddenly acting as if it were a single body, and beyond that, how do they know which direction to go? (I forgot to mention that in August of 2000, Toshiyuki Nakagaki managed to train one of these amoebic organisms to find the shortest route through a maze.) The earliest hypotheses simply correlated to the researchers' own political notions: they posited that there was a group of elite amoebas who gave orders to the rest, a sort of vanguard that sent back instructions so that the others might follow. This "vanguard hypothesis" was extremely difficult to prove, and for twenty years scientists believed that their inability to find any elite amoebas showed only that they, the scientists, lacked sufficient data, or that their experiments were poorly designed; the commandos had to be somewhere, and if they weren't, well, that only meant that the means of searching for them was flawed. Later, Keller and Segal proved that the transformation from "one" to "us," from individuality to coordinated action, is based on a purely chemical process. When the local amount of cyclic adenosine monophosphate (cAMP) was altered, the amoebas were carried along on pheromones generated by their comrades—the signal created a positive feedback loop, with each amoeba increasing its own production of cAMP, inciting all the others to do the same. This loop actually combines two types of behavioral rules: syntactic and chemical. The combination of the two results in the phenomenon known as imitation. Same thing with Dante in *The Divine Comedy*. Take the case of Paolo and Francesca. One day, the two of them innocently start reading the story of Lancelot. When they come to the part where the knight falls in love with Queen Guinevere, both of them blush; when they read that the two characters kiss, Paolo and Francesca have their first kiss as well. They fall deeper and deeper in love as they read deeper and deeper into the book. Their fascination with the written word, with imagining the text's binary game of "her and him" coming to life through their own bodies, convinces them that they are a chapter in the general history of absolute passion. (Not for nothing does Spanish allow certain verbs to use the same conjugation in both first and third person: decisive detail!) Neither Paolo nor Francesca realizes that they are erasing the mediator—Dante's book—and the amoebas likewise pass information along without ever realizing that they are obeying a law of general association. The moral of the story appears to be this: the most interesting part of the narrative curve is that which has the greatest number of possibilities for emitting and absorbing warmth; Nature and Dante agree that in heat, contagion is perfectly non-trivial.

Pabst let himself fall sweetly, softly back; he closed his eyes and popped the zit on his chin. He had subtly compared the two theories, leaving Andy with the weaker one; he had connected two authors with absolutely nothing in common; he hadn't displayed any symptoms of Due Deference Syndrome, or shown any desire to put an end to the discussion once and for all. As for the honeyed glob of pus on his fingertip, at some point he'd find something to wipe it on—at some point Andy would take his shirt off once again, the women's eyes would lift, feverish; no one would notice anything.

Andy had first heard about the holocaust of the 1970s at the age of five, in Pinamar. Apparently he was pulling at his mother's skirt because he wanted an ice cream. Susana, his mom, leaned down to him—jangling Balinese earrings, Farrah Fawcett hair. She hooked her fingers through his belt loops and looked lovingly into his eyes. "Do you see that sign up there? All right, now, your grandfather already taught you to read. What does the sign say?" Andy maintains that this was the first time he was ever aware of actually shrugging his shoulders. Looking through the pines he could see a Bavarian-style cottage, where there was a huge cone topped with a pink ball, the image completed by a slender maternal finger, nail gleaming with polish: Massera Ice Cream. "Well, Massera is an evil man who threw a bunch of people out of an airplane, okay? Why don't we buy an alfajor instead? Look, there's a Havanna right over there." Susana ruffled his bowl-cut hair, and reassumed her adult posture. From then on, the boy looked suspiciously at every airplane, but Massera's dulce de leche remained his favorite flavor until Volta finally opened its doors.

At Mara's high school, on the other hand, the students were encouraged to contemplate the sort of disturbing issues that would lead them to compose essays about the Disappeared and poems about the dictatorship during their Speech and Drama class. After crying a little and drinking her first few cups of strong coffee, Mara had written a piece called "Song of the Grandmother Who Speaks from the Depths of the Wolf":

> *DAUGHTER: There is an auburn-tinted dream in which I can't see anything, my head is covered with a hood, and I hear the voice of someone who hates me and yet wishes to paw at me.*
>
> *GRANDMOTHER: These things that seem made for stabbing, they are men, my little girl. They stab themselves into you. They fear nothing. Your voice nestles*

inside my ear, without you ever making a sound. Their tongues stab deeply into you as well. I too am wearing a hood, like Little Red Riding Hood. The teardrops of sweat fall from the walls that enclose you, drip onto the back of my neck. My neck bends down, my body a circle, a circle closed in vain.

DAUGHTER: Knock, knock. Who's there? The stick wants to know if there's anyone inside my body. There's nothing inside his because he's solid wood. Carved from a single piece of painstaking certainty, a macho comic opera: in short, a man. In the evil glow of his presence, I sense that he won't want the flavorless parts of me. I whisper: that he won't want. His breath hangs lasciviously around my neck. I have been pressing my thighs so tightly together that they seem to have become one. The dust, motes of imprisoned skin, a cascade of sparkling golden flecks floating down to the pool of water on the floor.

THE END

The heat and the filth—push rivers across, inside my skin—nothing separates blood from other blood. I am nothing but a sense of hearing, porous, awaiting the sharp ring of ironclad footsteps—those who have come to choose me. The blue smoke betrays my presence like a light shining down on the dead. I step forward into his outstretched arms and cannot breath. In this basement, lying beneath this guy, it's impossible to breath. It's too dark for anyone to see me shaking my head, but it can be felt. I'm so afraid he'll kill me that I can't even scream.

* * *

It was published in the school paper (her classmates suggested changing the title to "Hit Me and Call Me Esma") and when Mara brought a copy home, her mother hugged her and wept wildly out of sheer pride. She sat down at the kitchen table of their apartment in Palermo Sensible, snug up against Villa Freud, and offered her daughter another cup of coffee. Mara accepted tearfully; an intense chat was clearly in the offing. Her mother opened wide her enormous green eyes and caressed Mara's smooth, elegant forehead. Mara, she said, when your father and I first met, he had a girlfriend and I had a boyfriend. I was a Trotskyite and he was a Montonero. My best friend and I were always arguing with the Montos. I don't know why, but they had all the cutest guys—big mustaches and long hair, all committed intellectuals. On the night our department held its elections at the university, we went out to stir up some trouble in the streets. We were already pretty drunk, and Liliana had hooked up with one of the FAR guys. Well, long story short, what a bunch of assholes the PST guys turned out to be. (Remember when I told you, Uncle Robert was with them for a while but then he left?) The thing is, I really liked the one Liliana was with, but there was a blackout, and I ended up fucking the guy's friend, Martín. They killed Martín two days later, and Juan Carlos (the cute one) got his teeth drilled for the cyanide pill the day after that. He came to the house to see me (I was living with Liliana back then but it was obvious that he'd come to see me instead, because when I went to the corner window he gave me a little signal, and I snuck down and met him a block away. It was a bit cold out and we did it up against a wall, it doesn't bother you that I tell you all this stuff, right?) and he said that he was headed for Formosa, that a big operation was about to get underway. I told him, I said Juan Carlos, I like you a lot, but I'm a Trotskyite, as Trotskyite as you can get. He told me to go wake up Liliana. The two of them were killed in the same battle, and every time the date comes around I think of you, Mara, and I'm so happy that I held on to my ideals that day, to *my* way of seeing the Revolution. I think of you and your brother, and what could have happened if there'd been another blackout, if I hadn't had the presence of mind to say, okay, yes, he's very cute, he's a Monto, whatever; but this is about ideology, not about who's the best fuck.

Cris, Mara's mother, is still very pretty, and has decided not to remarry. She likes to say she prefers to have boyfriends who aren't so much "live-in" as "live-out," in the mistaken belief that "live-in boyfriend" is still something you say. Mara lost her virginity at the age of sixteen, a few months after writing the wolf poem, with one of her mother's friends. Crying made her more sensitive, and after each session of historical guilt and visions of the boots of brutes crushing the throats of beautiful young girls, it gave her an unnameable pleasure to prostrate herself, eyes closed, mute, imagining those huge hands at her waist, slowly removing what Henry Miller would have referred to as her "panty briefs." After that she dated a couple of punk rockers. And throughout that time, lying beneath those men, Mara occasionally lamented having been born at the wrong moment, having missed out on that dazzling whirlwind of courage and sensuality, because according to her fantasies—swaddled in quiet murmurs, panting and drool, along with earliest hypotheses as to what an orgasm might be—there couldn't be anything in this world more beautiful than working for justice and fucking in the name of the Fatherland.

Which is exactly what I'd been doing, as I'm about to explain.

9

I have so often feared for my life, and for the lives of those around me. Philosophy is Satan's playground. I can't explain why certain texts cause the golden down on my childlike arms to rise. The slightest mention of impending nightfall feels like the overture to a massacre. At times, when I am lost in those worlds, it seems to me that I can hear the clamor of criminal hordes as they advance, their mouths thirsty for the blood of the people. I can see them, stalking me through the interstices between paragraphs. Warrior games in the swamplands.

That night, the rain slashed against the window of my *pied-à-terre*, and the water in Yorick's fishbowl trembled as if in a hurricane. Montaigne Michelle figured out how to knock the fishbowl to the floor; Yorick, lord of fake seaweed, survived. The telephone rang; whoever it was hung up. The most sinister intuitions stalked me. Nature has an absolutely gothic effect on me. Frequently the sound of a twig snapping takes on terrifying overtones, and what meteorologists refer to as winds are in fact *eidos* for which there is no human name. Now the doorknob trembled as if something vicious were trying to force its way in. I clung to my thick black trilingual edition of Aristotle's *Metaphysics.* Dressed in double-thick winter pajamas, I put on my writing cap (a habit I've had since I first read *Little Women*—remember Jo?) and locked my only window. The storm sizzled outside, my thoughts now ominously italicized. Montaigne Michelle pricked up her ears and looked at me, worried. I raised my index finger to my lips, ordering silence.

It is well known that the experience of terror late at night is essential to a thorough understanding of political philosophy. According to John Aubrey's *Brief Lives*, Thomas Hobbes would sing at the top of his lungs each night in bed, because, "he did believe it did his lungs good and conduced much to prolong his life." This Galileo of political science lived in fear that one night someone would cut his throat; he sang to confirm that his throat was intact and to establish the deafening nature of the World. It would not be unreasonable to venture that Hobbes's intimate knowledge of fear did wonders for his mature work; his writing is permeated with an extraordinary glut of visual detail through which a sense of terror becomes systemic. Rousseau, too, suffered episodes of both classical and baroque paranoia. (As Augustus said hoarsely during one particularly emotional lecture throughout which he stared into my eyes: *The* Is *demand for mental unity can turn suddenly into the sensation of being surrounded by enemies.*) How to protect man from himself?

A cockroach scuttled along the edge of the room. (When

little Montaigne first arrived, Yorick and I were sharing our lair with an uncontrollable population. Yorick's fishbowl home kept him out of danger, but on several occasions he'd had the opportunity to observe that cockroaches, even half-dead ones, have excellent swimming technique.) I gave the order for Montaigne Michelle to set her ambush . . . Now! She purred toothily. The individual in question (a *Blatella germanica*) came forward a meter or so; Montaigne put it down with a single swipe of her paw. Flat on its back, its abdomen contracted in pain, the cockroach bent its antennae toward us. I believe that it sensed the formidable presence of its motionless adversary—perhaps, too, that of the impromptu Thucydides who sat nearby taking notes. Finally it managed to get back on its feet. And here is where this domestic tableau takes on transcendental dimensions: it was at this moment that, overawed by such brutality, irresistibly attracted to a power far superior to her own, the scene's victim *advanced voluntarily toward the Predator, and bowed down to her, in a sign of Reverence.*

I stayed there beside the fish bowl, wholly absorbed. How to explain the fascinating virtue of she who *perpetrates* her own devouring? Is there some voluptuous connection between Reverence, the Sovereign, and Death? I immediately began chewing on my pencil, my interior voice obsessively mimicking the insect's thoughtways, the *dictamen rationis* of that sesquipedalian voluptuary:

> *"As star witness to these violent acts, of my own free Will and in full Possession of my Chitinous Exoskeleton, I bow*

> *down before the Overwhelming Display of the One who crossed both Time and Space to show me her Strength. Spawned in the time of the Hordes, I hereby yield my life to the Admonitory Visage of she who has come to possess me. I find her Irresistible. I believe wholly in a Beloved Kingdom which—were I anything more than a small Dying Insect—I would gladly exalt to all the world: the Kingdom that is the Engine of all desires, even those that existed before rage, or cowardice, or War, or Language."*

I would soon return to the initial triad, the origin of my research: a First Person, born amidst predatory hordes, described as part of a metaphysically powerful scene, the *ad intra* forms of the inner voice. The story of the primate who undergoes the process of becoming human, who is pursued and captured by beasts; a theory toward an anthropology of voluptuousness and war, describing the maniacal system of Interconnected Persons that sends an irresistible charge through the Circuit of Will . . . My theory began to open out, a series of explosive bundles going supernova. I was present in flashes for a strange summary of the history of the world, a *grammatical* history, where each *I* is lost in a jungly void—but then something awakens it from its stupor. The *I* realizes that on the far bank of Being, groups of *Them* are playing with their peers. The *I* goes insane: it wants to cross the river, to go to *Them*, to touch *Them*. On the Island of Third Persons, there is a carefully maintained set of telescopes that allows *Them* to see across the river. "Hey, *You*, the one with your feet in the water." The heart of Little *I* rejoices: life exists, and has meaning. From this moment on he will do anything to maintain his status as a *You*, to *cardinally* approach that which fascinates him, to lessen the distance that separates his self from theirs. The *I* of the transmissions is identical to the "point of view" as defined by Leibniz: ubiquitous and individual, interconnected both forward and backward in time with every event throughout the past and future of the universe—that is, with *each and every person* who violates, suffers, inflicts. Let grammar be a four-dimensional historical model. The material causality that courses through each existence depends upon a Voice, upon a revelation that fills each gap in the human brain. This revelation takes the form of a Third Person who speaks (acts) like the reverse of a voice preparing itself for a mission: the reverse of the voice of Jesus activating his cronies by speaking directly into their minds; of Angela da Foligno, patron saint of those afflicted by sexual temptation, who received divine guidance in the writing of her *Book of Visions and Instructions*; of Joan of Arc accepting orders to attack the English; of St. Anselm, hearing in a dream his proof of the existence of God. For he who has never heard stories of gods, heroes or saints is unlikely to want or be able to transform himself into a hero or god. This god, stronger than me, who upon his arrival will prevail over me . . . is it *him*? The tip of my tongue takes a trip below the clitoris of my palate as my lips open and close ever so gently, *him-him-him*. I had the sensation that beings bereft of light hung nearby amidst the impalpable shadows; that a man was watching me in precisely the way prey watches a predator. Was this the call?

Is this the call? I asked aloud, dropping my muse, the *Blatella*, into the fishy maw of Yorick's bowl, watching as Yorick drifted up toward it.

The transcendental manifestations of my thoughts remained opaque, silent. Fear sifted through the air around me once again, and I shouted, *Vade retro*, you damned one! To clear my head, I turned the television all the way up, and at last my prayers to Kali were answered: I hit upon a James Bond marathon.

The entire career of this spy, fellow countryman of Thomas Hobbes, serves to show that there is no obstacle born of politics or love that can't be overcome if you can count on the cooperation of whomever designs the plot. *Dr. No*—purest balm of Bondian adventure—had barely begun when I started to look through my notes. As of fifty-two minutes and five seconds into *From Russia with Love*, just as James positioned himself to kiss the Russian spy (whose raffish title was nothing less than Corporal of State Security), I had begun polishing 2.1.2, an extremely important subsection. Exhaustion washed over me, and my gaze drifted up to the immense night. I collapsed, overcome, and had a magnificent dream.

It was the first few minutes of *From Russia with Love* and the white cat fondled by Number 1, the brain of SPECTRE, grew slowly darker in color—darker and darker, until she was suddenly revealed to be Montaigne Michelle herself. The cat continued to allow Number 1 to caress her, with a somewhat perplexed look on her face, as if asking herself, Why would someone fall *intentionally* into a trap? Because, responds

Number 1, a correct reading of the enemy's mentality shows that they always treat a trap as a challenge. He caresses the cat again. The cat's eyes fall half closed; the SPECTRE operative brings his wrinkled mouth to her tiny ear, and whispers: *A trap is an offer you can't refuse*. The operative continues speaking to the cat while observing a tank where a triad of fish identical to Yorick are swimming. He says:

–Siamese fighting fish. Brave, but on the whole, stupid. With the exception of the one we have here, who lets the other two fight, waiting until the survivor is so exhausted that he cannot defend himself. And then, like SPECTRE, he attacks.

At this point my memories grow hazy—there was something about the SPECTRE character using the *Lektor* (a code-breaking machine) as bait. I remember with astonishing clarity that I was obscenely aware I was dreaming—and that, when the roles had been handed out, to my sovereign surprise I'd been assigned to play the very *Puella Bondinis* in question.

No more doubts, no more sleepless nights, I murmured softly to myself in the half dark. This was the call, the dawn that precedes the voluptuous war. And here is the opaline message that I slid under the door of the Augustan office the next morning. An ode to devotion inspired by superior firepower, a sketch of unambiguously carnivorous appetites, I translate from the Latin (*ego velut linguam . . .*[4]) the invitation that is my secret, which I enclosed in a manila envelope along with a candied date:

4 . . . coeli.

I
like the language
am in his mouth the plaything of a monster.

Morituri te salutamus, Augustus!

10 Puella Bondinis

Agent Provocateur

Both within and beyond the borders of carnivorous Asia, the visage of the tiger is a splendor reserved for the gods of death. In the warrior cult of India, the nuptials of Kali and the tiger form a chapter in the story of the gods' appetite for the twin attributes of power and animality. The hybrid history of warrior transformation has perpetrated both psychological and graphical outrages, such as the stele raised by Ashurbanipal the Assyrian, which tells of the time following a great flood when lions and tigers roamed the Earth, filling it with their deadly attributes (the tiger is tiger to both man and tiger). Samson dealt death to a lion, and Heracles did the same to that of Nemea; both took home the bones. Jehovah sent tigers and lions against the Assyrians who'd occupied Samaria—but after the slaughter, Jehovah claimed invisibility for the cult that worshipped him and would unify his clan. Kali, in contrast, accepts as offerings the heads of his fellow tigers, and of the thousand soldiers torn apart in battle.

The Deer Woman, escaping from her fellow humans each night to copulate with antelope; in the Mahabharata, Rama calls on the gods to mate with monkeys and bears to produce superhuman warriors with the speed of the wind and the strength of the elephant: these are scenes from a secret threaded through all eras and all men. Thus, congress with savages is part of the core story of the Theory of Egoic Transmissions.

–Who is she that advanceth through the night?

1.

The area in question is an elegant neighborhood in the capital, known most recently by the oxymoronic moniker Palermo Manhattan. A summer night. The slight separation between me and the world consists of a black knee-length skirt, a green satin blouse, and short, badly scuffed leather boots. I never wear nylons, they discredit my skin. My underwear is of violet lace, and I'm wearing it only for the company—granting access of that type isn't part of the plan.

Timide à mes heures, all descriptions of my physical charms have thus far been superficial when not inextant. The reader must not allow the radiance described below to blind him or her as regards the matter at hand; instead it must shine a clear light on the importance of the drama to come. That is, I am now obliged to speak of my beauty.

My skeletal structure is flawless and persuasive, often inescapably so, at least according to the occasional desperate snouts of big boys, old men, and the sapphic. I am most elegantly distributed, my flesh unfolds in a soft, glowing imprecise skin tone between olive-gold and the lyrical ivory of Byzantium. My other parts yield commentaries of varied tenor and quantities of saliva pursuant to issues of innate distinction and Buenos Airean loveliness: my black hair begins its plunge into the void, then restrains itself with unction an instant before reaching my hip; my eyes are black and deep, slightly crossed; my mouth is orthodox, red. Seen from the front, the eminent twin towers rise spiritedly below a fine Doric neck, and the jawline of a lady carnivore. From behind, of course, matched anatomical glories, an intersection of feminine aesthetic and military deployment known, *per secula seculorum*, in the Biblical sense (mark well the customary insolence of the source). Thus the Singer pontificates upon the fascinating farewell of a lady: *Return, return, O Shulamite; return, return, that we may look upon thee. What will ye see in the Shulamite? As it were the company of two armies.*

The priceless resources at my disposal only acquired strength as they came to know the enemy by taking Communion with him, in an act of atrocious intimacy. Regarding which, Rodolfo Walsh once wrote:

> The main characteristic of enemy intelligence is structural analysis. The determinant factor is a knowledge of our own structure's political and ideological aspects and its spacial, temporal and relational organization, beginning always from the assumption that in knowing the objectives pursued by one's adversary, the strengths and weaknesses of their forces, their

> chains of command, the distribution of their barracks, their logistics and their communications, one knows enough to destroy them if one also possesses superior firepower and mobility.[5]

By this point the reader will have realized that the experiment herein described required making of my body a laboratory, and also a watchtower from which to direct an assault by land.

The building is early 20th century, with walls of stone. Inside, a large wood-paneled vestibule extends along a set of picture windows that give onto an interior garden of smoky greens. The light dims as I advance toward his dwelling at the end of the corridor. The buzzer sounds—the burp of a mockingbird. Across the hallway, the doorman shrinks back behind the counter when his fish-like gaze meets my sidelong glance, his deftly lipid behavior confirming that he knows he has been warned. He changes the channel on his security monitor; the screen now displays an empty swimming pool.

I hear hurried footsteps, comings and goings inside the apartment. I pull back, and find the perfect angle from which to see the face of my prey as he anxiously opens the door.

The physical reality of Collazo takes me by surprise. He is enormous. Much taller and brawnier than I'd imagined. Too, he is fundamentally uglier, is in fact so startlingly hideous that

---

5 Walsh, R., "Curso de la guerra en enero-junio 1977 según la hipótesis enemiga." 4. Descripción de la inteligencia enemiga. Ediciones de la Flor, Buenos Aires, 1994.

it burns your eyes, leaves you blinking. Did Collazo have a precursor? Naturally he did: this is why I prepared so carefully for this encounter. In order to find Collazo, I had to scrutinize Augustus's weaknesses; to analyze the encrypted messages, the hidden details, the reverse side of his sentences; to find, in the course of his classes, a few clues that would lead me to decide it was *him*, Collazo—him and no one else—that I had to seduce, to lasso with a noose made of women's hair, to bring in chains before the Old Man for him to gloat over—to take hostage.

Collazo says hello with a feigned indifference. He asks if I had any trouble finding the building; I invent a showdown between taxi drivers and picketers to explain my late arrival. I follow him up the hallway without a word. Dark shirt, knotty shoulders; pants tight over the crotch and at the waist, concealing little. He turns, slowly, to face me, and repeats a question I hadn't answered; up close, lit by the halogen lights, his face opens out, wider and monstrous. He stands before me, enrobed in the strange glamour common to all veterans of the Dirty War. A huge mustache stretches across his face. The nose, deeply etched; bristly eyebrows that seem to poke at whatever he observes, clawing at clothes, scratching at the skin of things. I interrupt my horror briefly in order to answer him.

He examines me lasciviously from top to bottom, focusing mainly on my middle third. My first clear sensation, separate from all else: the odor that lies in wait beneath his cologne, a layered, tuberous scent of semen enclosed in its mandrake coffer, rancid, sharp, writhing beneath his clothes. The left side of his eel-like mustache lifts to show sharpened fangs.

–Whiskey?

–With ice, thanks.

Collazo paws through a variety of liquors without taking his eyes off of me. He pours two glasses; his body is stout as a head stock boy's, but his arms can't be too strong at this point—I don't think you could say they've done much over the past fifty-odd years. He holds out my glass of whiskey; stepping closer to receive it, I sense his gently monstrous radiation. Yellow teeth, violent mouth. I hold my breath, take a drink.

–So you're in Roxler's class . . . What did you say it was called?

I go to speak but just then a piece of ice gets caught in my throat. I cough briefly. He seems amused. He asks how old I am. I blurt out a lie—twenty-eight, doing my PhD. Collazo hands me a napkin and a glass of water. The thought occurs that he's given me the napkin so I'll have somewhere to spit out the ice cube, and I stop coughing. He looks at my hands around the whiskey glass, and I realize it can't be hidden: I'm trembling.

–It's a little cold, isn't it. I'll turn up the heat.

Collazo disappears down the hallway and I slip into the bathroom. I lock the door. This bathroom in the center of the house is the lair *par excellence*, the den of dens. Like a mist swirling up from a lake in which monsters sleep, Collazo's odor is born herein, his aura, a red stain as seen through a thermal scope. Here he dwells, leaving behind flakes of skin each time he bathes, scabs stuck to the shower walls, spatterings of semen that a woman, someone's grandma, will be paid to come clean up. There are no thong panties hung like flags, and their absence speaks to a state of desperation, a certain degree of vulnerability that is essential to the success of my mission. I look through the medicine cabinet. A shaving brush, rusty nail clippers, bits of fur here and there (the beast chews at its own hair and spits), and a few colognes from twenty years ago, the bottles almost empty—an ascetic, leftist intimacy. The cracked wall tiles bear traces of recent damp, of rising steam, saliva in larval form. I close the cabinet door.

And there they are, my eyes, guileless, looking back at me from the filthy mirror. The long, long eyelashes, the arched eyebrows shining with determination, and lower, out of view, the labyrinthine organ for which he is willing to lose himself irretrievably. I don't mean to overemphasize the beauty of these features, but the mirror doesn't lie, does nothing but show what it sees: in these features, in the moral contrast they offer to the vile and contemptible brutality of Collazo, resides the key to what will bring him to a boil. There is no escape.

I walk quickly out of the bathroom. He's not in the kitchen; I cross the hallway, look for him in the living room, there's a small zebra-striped rug, I step onto it but it's a trap, I slip and fall to the floor. Collazo watches me fall. He comes slowly across the room, as if hoping to get a peek at my panties or something. I hold out one arm, let him lift me to my feet. His fingers leave marks; I show him the red prints of his huge hands pulsing at the surface of my skin. He says: "Very delicate, yes."

He takes my glass and sets it on a shelf. He smooths his mustache, as if enjoying a brief interlude before consuming me. He takes me by the waist. I try to maintain the distance between us, but it's futile: everything is saturated with his hideous radiation. I close my eyes, but even so his monstrous features hang before me haloed in blue. His rancid breath, the cologne mixed with sweat, the unconditional mustache, the echo of his eyes, malicious, wallowing about beneath my clothes, that nose pricked by Triassic insects, nostrils like holes in stone. *Enough*. I must not allow anything to stop me. I disentangle myself from his arms, let myself fall onto the sofa.

Seated now, my legs uncrossed, the heat begins to worm its way up past my knees, reshapes me, tightens, pulls at my mouth—leaves it hanging open as I stare at him. I must be bright red. I cover my face with my hair, peek out to spy on him, and a sensation rises from my stomach. Then I realize that I've landed on a cushion whose triangular corner is poking deeply, vilely, in between my buttocks.

Standing there like a shadow stretched over a victim, Collazo examines me in silence. The halogen lights zero in on his bald head like well-trained snipers; the mustache widens to both sides as he smiles. He's certain that the battle has tilted in his favor, and he ponders, all but obscenely, his theoretical control of the disputed terrain.

–Let's take a little walk through the woods, he says. The park's just right over there.

He comes forward, the dark fabric of his shirt filling the lens, a classic cinematographic fade to black.

1.1

Oh, Augustus! The first time you spoke to me under the words, I failed to understand. But you immediately noted my unease, and moved your head impossibly slowly, as if nodding in agreement. You think me excessively prideful, but I assure you that all this time I have suffered a great deal—and I have missed you even more. That is why, before launching my attack, I need to know your state of mind. Don't let obsessive thoughts bewitch you. Because what I want to say to you (what I howl so that you might hear) has more to do with protecting the courtly synthesis of your legacy than with my negligible, insubstantial, egoic role in the events themselves.

It is a strange world, yes. You must learn that you are alone, even when followed by multitudes. Perhaps, by the grace of Leibniz, there exists some other possible world where you wouldn't need me. Who knows? Not even Leibniz. Maybe in that other world, your theory and your words and the single arrow that is time would together have been sufficient; you could have pushed forward without my help, conquering spaces and times and it wouldn't have mattered to me in the slightest because given the rules in such a world, you wouldn't need me. But that possible world could never really exist; it would be self-contradictory. My new activities have nothing in common with the things I was doing before, which were themselves docile copies of the things I thought I would be doing back when I first entered our house of higher learning, and thus entered your theory, Augustus—your doctrine. Your doctrine, which has changed everything. If you only knew the wild paths my investigations have taken! The seditious spin of the steering wheel of my research! I was focused on baneful things, my dear. Perhaps *baneful* is not exactly the term I'm looking for, but it's an adjective that brings to mind the image of an eagle bearing down on its prey. I would love to bombard you with details. If you knew them—and it's unclear whether or not you're ever going to find out, still unclear—I know you would be proud of me. Don't ask me how, but I know. Would you like to know what this is all about? Of course you would. But I'm not going to tell you. Ha-ha, not yet. Don't get upset. Soon I will see to it that you know entirely too much—soon I will illuminate the dark side of your philosophy.

What were we talking about? Ah yes, that the world-without-me could never exist in any form whatsoever, because my presence is a *necessary condition* for your theory. It is true, of course, that I can't have been its efficient cause: you were able to formulate the initial phase of your doctrine all on your own, with no need for me to act directly upon you or it—or perhaps I did, but only in the world of dreams, my dear, where Cinderella theories dance alongside their fairy godmothers! In the world of things, however, things have changed a great deal. You must face this fact, Augustus. Because in the world where your theory exists, where it *truly* exists, in its purest, most revolutionary form, there too exists The Act—the act that converts your theory into action. The act is thus intrinsic to the doctrine; it is part of it. And if you were to ask how I know this, well, I would answer that I owe it all to you, *because I read it in your theory*, and in reading it I consummated a rite of initiation at once wondrous and absolute. You have given me a lever with which to move the world, and the only thing that matters to me is learning how to move that lever. I know perfectly well that you love us all equally—but I also know that some of us are more dear to you than others. Some of us understand what is drawing near, ravenous and blood-stained, the vertiginous tiger, and we fear nothing.

The greatest leaders perished precisely when they no longer knew how to revolutionize the revolution they had begun. And you don't want that to happen, now, do you, my dear? You want your name raised up above the supralunar clouds, where reign the perfect forms of thought, isn't that so? The change must come from within—from within *you*. You don't need much. You only need me. My eyes are closed, and the bubbles are up to my chin. His big gray hand rests on my tawny belly, while his other hand pushes my hair back, his fingers unable to let go. In your mouth I am the plaything of a monster. I let my thoughts swim in the darkness until I can't hear them any more.

In the afternoon I took position outside a bar called Platón, named for your favorite Greek, and waited for you there. My plan was to allow time to slide past in its usual fashion: faculty members would soon start to arrive individually, each in *his or her own form*, and sooner or later you too would appear. Every so often, someone who wasn't watching their step would slip on the sidewalk, their foot now smeared with dog shit. Two hours passed this way.

Over and over I envisioned your arrival, a succession of

silent films projected on the filthy white façade of the department building. My transcription:

> *Augusto García Roxler makes his way up the wet sidewalk, locked deep in conversation with his own thoughts. His gaze suddenly lifts, drawn to the presence of a ~~very pretty~~ gorgeous young woman sitting near the entrance to Casa del Saber. The Professor stops short. He recognizes her immediately: the enigmatic silhouette, modestly half-hidden, is that of none other than ~~his destiny his nemesis his Significant Other~~ his most deeply beloved student. Augustus clears his throat, thinks: Should I speak to her directly? He imagines that this exquisite young woman is probably furious because he ~~hasn't given her the time of day~~ seems to have ears only for the sycophants that surround him even though he knows that ~~she is the only one for him~~ he owes the most lucid elements of his doctrine entirely to Her. Augustus wants to go to Her, but ~~he's nothing but an old chickenshit~~ he fears being rejected ~~because he's such a chickenshit~~ and deep down inside he's secretly afraid of her and also because he's nothing but an old chickenshit who's lost his strength and lets himself be manipulated by the sinister sycophants around him. An unrecognizable voice resounds from off-stage—from within his brain—it shouts something that will determine the outcome of this nightmarish story. Augustus watches her eyes. She turns her swanlike*

> *neck, looks back at him. He roots around in one of his shadowy pockets, extracts a wrinkled copy of his notes on my comments in his class, whispers something that we can't quite catch but its meaning is clear—there are admiring comments penciled in the margins. He looks at her ~~overcome with passion he caresses her with his eyes lowers his glance and cries begging for forgiveness my love, I can't take it any more, I belong to you as well~~ with destiny in his eyes; he invites her ~~back to his house, and she responds with a mischievous grin~~ to join him at his regular table at Platón for croissants and a cup of tea.*

I waited, and waited, and waited, and you never arrived. Was it possible you were wearing a cape that rendered you invisible? Were you already inside when I arrived? None of the beings who prowl the halls of Philosophy and Letters truly exists before nine in the morning. I myself once tried to break this natural law for a few hours, but was abducted by Berni Bleizik from the priory of *Metaphysics*, famed for his somniferous gifts. After waking from his spell, I saw that my fist had clenched around my crispy butter croissant, crushing it to bits.

I gathered my papers, my books in progress, and crossed the street with my mind made up: I was going to intercept you inside. I almost slipped as I penetrated the department building. Thank goodness I was wearing these army surplus boots, ideal for bad weather:

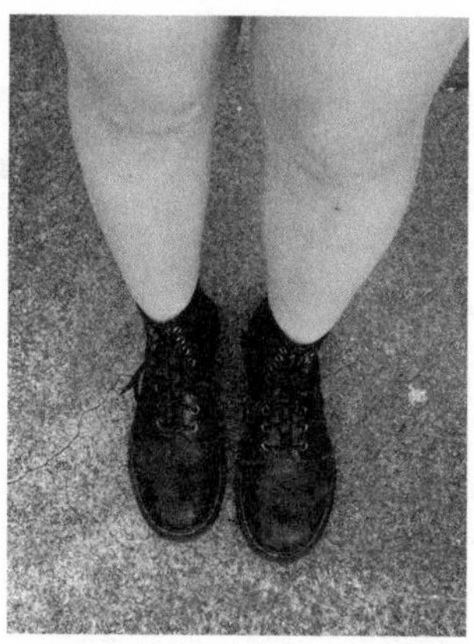

I threw myself up the stairs, and sniffed around the offices, the research units, the specialized libraries of the fourth floor. I circled through the main library, its reference area, the Periodicals section. I couldn't rule anything out, even searched for you up on the fifth floor, which was still under construction, thinking that perhaps you were fed up with the pale imitations of Duchamp that populate the faculty bathrooms. I sought you sought you sought you, and found nothing. Which is when I decided to change strategies. I would go to the pay phone on the corner, call the Faculty Lounge, and explain that a bomb was about to go off.

As this wasn't during midterms or finals, the threat would be taken seriously; it would create a true sense of danger, would foment panic, the building would empty, and you would come out of hiding. I would stay there at the window of your favorite bar, savoring a snack, trying out different Dostoyevskian facial expressions as I watched you escape out through the door to the right with your dear E.G., who's now a B.M. (Blubbery

Minion), the two of you holding hands as you ran, scared shitless. I so enjoyed imagining you vulnerable, frightened, overwhelmed by what had happened, caught in the sniper sights of *moi*, that I walked slowly to the corner and actually did it. Ha! Pay phones and philosophy have always been strong allies.

They exited the building a few at a time, much as they'd entered it: students, professors, and craft vendors abandoning the abode of the humanities, walking happily along, chatting with whomever happened to be alongside, smiling and laughing. Only the most nubile among them seemed at all excited or scared. Then suddenly I couldn't believe my eyes, and wanted to claw them out.

You were walking calmly, talking to *that woman*. B.M. was tucking a bunch of nerdy folders into their binders, and as he went to say goodbye, he likewise exchanged pleasantries with her. She smiled, and TOOK YOU BY THE ARM. The two of you had undoubtedly entered the building together through the parking lot, but had you come in the same car? She pressed a thin book (*How to Knit?* The dialogues of Foucault and Deleuze?) flat against her brown, knee-length skirt. She said a few words, and YOU APPEARED TO BE LISTENING. Instead of heading for Platón, your habitual watering hole, or Sócrates, your favorite redoubt for more elegant encounters, the two of you wandered over to the cafe on Directorio Avenue—one that isn't even named after a philosopher. And I followed.

As enraged as Achilles in full Greek rhapsody, I pulled myself up to where I could see in through the window. *That woman* wiped the tip of her napkin along her rat-like jaw, pretending to listen attentively; her erect nipples aimed at you like bolts on a pair of crossbows; she stared at you, her gaze insane, her eyes made for pretense and lies. She nodded tritely at everything you said, and raised her pinkie as she sipped her tea. And Augustus's lips moved—no, I'm not talking to you in Second Person any more, not now that you've distanced yourself from me—but I wasn't quite able to make out what he said. My fury was swallowed by my astonishment, but promptly clawed its way back out.

Every battle plan includes a vague but finite number of expected casualties. Wars begin on the day least expected, and thus a Roman with a Greek nose makes his way along some creek on January 10, 49 B.C.; he crosses the Rubicon, and unleashes a civil war. So it goes. One day you make a bomb threat, and in less than an hour you see how you've been betrayed. One day you plant, for example, a very special type of bomb (a symbolic bomb), and soon your most substantial contributions (adjectival, metapolitical) sink to their deaths at the hands of an unacceptable triad. Because *that woman* is unacceptable. From her immoral appearance, you'd think she just stepped off the stage at a cabaret; from her wouldn't-hurt-a-fly demeanor, you'd think she was some poorly educated housewife leeching off her husband for survival. She may well study Letters. I first noticed her existence one afternoon when I was wandering through the halls before my Special Problems in Ethics class. She had her hair up in a little bun, was wearing a little brown crochet jacket. She was sitting at a table in the bar on the first floor, surrounded by a scruffy little group of students and—I can hear her murmuring now—she was laying out a Tarot spread. At first glance that made perfect sense: with the consolidation of the internal market for handicrafts and bootleg videos, Tarot cards and Occultism wouldn't be far behind. I walked up, looking as dismissive as possible, and *that woman*—incapable of resisting the aura of domination that my personality secretes—invited me to cut the deck. The card that appeared was the Tower.

She looked at me, her little rat-like eyes filled with alarm. In her schoolmarm-from-the-capital accent, she said, "The Tower reprezentsh the paradigmsh conshtructed by the Ego, which iz the shum of the shtructursh built by the mind to undershtand the universh." Someone elbowed her, saying something about Kant, but she rambled on: the Tower represents those who are prone to visions and epiphanies, but when Reality doesn't conform to their expectations, the Tower is destroyed by the lightning, and they go crazy, become aggressive, tend toward evil. If the Tower is pointing downward, it is digging its own grave; if it points up, perhaps it's time for the Tower to change its attitude and ideology. (The table she was using was round, and it wasn't really clear which way the card was pointing.) The Tower symbolizes the passage from the alpha state to the theta state; in the latter, the information produced by the Ego overwhelms all external stimuli, creating what is known as a hallucination. "Which alwaysh impliesh defeat, deshtruction, and catashtrophe," she added, adjusting her bun.

I felt the same disdain for *that woman* that I'd felt for one of my first psychoanalysts, whom I'd held hostage in his office until he admitted that not a single one of the idiotic comments he'd made during our session was a properly formed sentence or meaningful proposition. What matters is welcoming each of the tests our fate has in store, facing them with strength and bravery. Here lies my own Rubicon, I said to myself; here between Puan Street and Pedro Goyena. The twenty-four kilometers between the spot where the Rubicon was crossed and the point where it empties into the Adriatic Sea are contained many times over in the immense asphalt skeleton that undergirds the city of Buenos Aires, home of my days, while the bit of world that stretches from Massachusetts to North Carolina corresponds to the Madrilenian lands that saw the first of the heroic deeds of Cervantes's man of La Mancha: such was the distance, such the trifling creek that separates destiny from Valor. In political philosophy, such occurrences unleash the violence contained in man's true nature. I looked down; there was water flowing along the gutter.

Do you like music? I bet there's a ventricle of your Old Man's heart that adores boleros. Perhaps a few Cuban classics will bring nearer some new variation on our theme:

> *Qué vale más, yo niña o tú orgulloso,*
> *o vale más, tu débil hermosura.*
> *Piensa bien, que en el fondo de la fosa*
> *llevaremos la misma vestidura.*[v]

And indeed, you will ask yourself, who is worth more? Darling: the answer is found in the extraordinarily delicate syntax that allows one to choose either an alliance between youth and power, or the solitude of the throne. Alone on the throne you will find yourself surrounded by inept fatsos; allied with the power of the novi, you can hold fast to me. The verse is repeated, emptying out into a subtle yet noteworthy conclusion: *vestidura* becomes *sepultura*. A very suggestive choice. (Note: there is cruelty in the sovereign nature of Veneration as well.) Who is worth more, a simple girl like *me*, or *you* so proud: you must accept the fact (*¡piensa bien!*) that your beauty is weak, that the grave is near. You must listen to me before it's too late.

I understand that at your advanced age you might think it best to play your cards close to the chest, to safeguard your power within the department, to act like the Roman *testudo* as they defended against, and eventually laid waste to, the vast human hordes.

Schilddach (Testudo). Relief der Antoninssäule in Rom.

But this is a trap, my dear one, a trap! You cannot and must not trust anyone in those environs. And that woman . . . frankly, I don't want to discuss her. Advanced age tends to give poor counsel—don't listen to it. If you do, it will make you feel weak, when in truth you should know that you are strong because you can rely on me. You must have trust in my youth. You think that the presence of that woman and B.M. will protect you, as their brains are nothing more than boils growing on your own. But you are swimming in barracuda-filled waters. I, who have used my own flesh to incarnate each part of your theory, am willing to take the next step, and as many subsequent steps as might be necessary. Do you understand? I know what your theory requires.

We live in such a strange world, my dear, a world so immeasurably yours and mine. Terrible things are going to happen! I will have to do terrible things. Your words have set in motion a secret, inexorable process. I have exchanged the loftiest heights of intellectual speculation for the testing grounds of the abyss. And I must proceed in thusly, Augustus, must seek out the brutality that exists within me, in order to put myself at the service of the Theory-World to which we both pertain. It would surprise you to know that I have one of you in hand. (It would also surprise you to see yourself reflected in his gauche caviar ways.) How I treat the hostage will depend on every word you speak, do you see, my dear? When I'm with him, I'm speaking to you.

I'll leave you for now with this syllogistic verse that I found myself composing out loud in English as I was putting on my boots to head out to meet my victim[6]:

> *All war is based in deception (Cf. Sun Tzu,* The Art of War*).*
>
> *Definition of deception: the practice of deliberately making somebody believe things that are not true. An act, a trick or device intended to deceive somebody.*
>
> *Thus, all war is based in metaphor.*
> *All war necessarily perfects itself in poetry.*
> *Poetry (since indefinable) is the sense of seduction.*
> *Therefore, all war is the storytelling of seduction*
> *and seduction is the nature of war.*

2.

"Friday, 10 o'clock, at Guido's." Perfect—and I had the good sense to arrive at 10:30 so as not to arouse suspicion. Collazo still wasn't there.

I decided to wait for him posed daintily at the bar. I kept myself entertained by rereading certain passages—not particularly well-argumented ones—from *Fetish, Fascism, and the Collective Imagination: the Masculine Myth of Nationalist Argentina*. The lighting was terrible and the background noise was very distracting. The *maître d'* kept looking at me with

6 remember: even when in his COmpany, i wiLL actually be tAlking [Z] to yOu.

that cheekily depraved expression men reserve for single damsels. I grumblingly gathered myself up and turned my back on him. Then I realized: *all* of the men were looking at me, their verbs left half-conjugated in their mouths. Suddenly I feared that I was on the verge of bouncing out of my blouse in full view of everyone. Paying close heed to the little libertarian glimpses my outfit allowed, I slowly caressed my torso until my modesty was once again intact.

I later learned that Collazo was already in the restaurant; the good-for-nothing had seen me arrive, and had made a bet with himself as to how long it would take me to go look for him at the tables on the terrace. I'm glad that even at his age he sees well enough to take pleasure in that kind of mischief. I mumbled an awkward hello (automatic courtesies are trivial) and joined him at his grimy little table next to a row of parked cars. He seemed amused to see me. Without wasting a second, he spoke to the waiter with a certain cold attentiveness that I have observed before in similar individuals.

After asking the waiter for a dizzying number of details and clarifications, Collazo leaned back in his chair and gestured as if proctoring an exam. I shrugged, and gave the kind of evil little laugh that the male libido will go far out of its way to hear as angelic. He asked me something about my thesis. I answered at length, looking over at him from time to time through the fog of my aversion. He fingered his thick mustache, at times softly, at times twisting it down to the corners of his mouth and nibbling at it, as if what he had arched above his mouth was a delicious miniature version of me.

The waiter poured the wine for him to try, a Poligny Montrésor, and Collazo nodded his approval. When he noticed that I was singing quietly along with the music, he asked for it to be turned up. It was a marvelous ballad by The Platters, and a careful look through the menu combined deliciously with our smiles.

The waiter divided each dish into two equal portions, but gave Collazo most of the parsley. The tender orange-and-ruby colored slices of meat slid meekly across the white porcelain, accompanied by glazed baby potatoes, almonds and capers. Collazo grinned at me, and I grinned back. I was afraid, of course, but I knew that I had to provoke him if I wanted to see the monster that the theory had in store for me. The Chardonnay was a murmur of pale gold in our glasses, and now . . . *en garde!* I gave a twist he could not have foreseen, plunging the dagger into the left side of his vanity.

Collazo calmly leaned toward me, his eyebrows stiff with

cruelty. I lifted my chin, my narrowed eyes now oblique to his pitifulness. Then I said something so evil that I prefer not to transcribe it here.

He looks at me coldly, as if intending to impale me. He knows that he can't let his gaze drop to where my cleavage awaits: if I'm able to capture his eyes there, leave him stuttering at the edge of that precipice, my ampleness will render painless what he clearly intends to be an excruciating silence. His face, naked, caught like a bug in glue. My fiery torrent has come calmly to an end at "and what then?" I can see the gray hairs poking out through his shirt front, and above, his wrinkled Adam's apple now erect. His self-consciousness betrays him. He laughs—it's just that I'm so funny.

This sort of back-and-forth is essential to my plan. I must provoke him until fury and fascination leave him completely blind, unable to think. That's when my thoughts will spill in through the syntactical holes in what is, theoretically, his free will, and there will be no saving him then, no escape. For now he sees only the water's surface, the reflection of his self-portrait as on-stage seducer rocking gently on the waves. He doesn't know (can't know) that this ocean is full of heads, thousands of them, heads from my collection (and a few from Augustus's), all laughing at him. As Sun Tzu once wrote, "if your opponent is of choleric temperament, seek to irritate him." If he is arrogant, encourage his narcissism. And if he's in the process of making a mistake (says Napoleon) don't stop him. In the end Collazo must be the one to throw himself on top of me, and I must cuddle up to him and bear it. I have to, even if it disgusts me so much I can't breathe.

For the moment, much to my chagrin, this supposed challenge isn't, strictly speaking, the problem closest at hand. For Collazo, the real problem is the interval (the density, the syntax) between my calm and his silence, one that requires a demonstration of proportional violence. He'll have to distill a shot of pure acid to wipe this expression off my face, and frankly it is in my interest for him to do so: otherwise that rhetorical burbling of a few moments ago could lead him to believe that I'm after some insignificant little triumph. To attack the argument that my momentary peace is mere solipsistic vanity, Collazo could employ any combination of bodily disdain + a line of reasoning other than the absurd path being laid by what we will call, for now, Impudence, that great maw-softener—if only in the interest of rescuing the delicate project of his own good mood from a nervous date's awkward outpourings.

Fingering his mustache, Collazo stayed calm. His fork flipped a caper back and forth. Then he punctured it, and looked at my mouth:

–I must say, I'm very impressed that you caught that hidden reference to Marx's *The German Ideology*. I didn't know that people your age (here he ran his tongue across his lips) were still reading things like that.

Of course I made light of the brilliance of my memory, politely minimizing the whole affair. But my hand, deep in my backpack, twitched against the cover of *Fetish*, with its frenzied photographic collage of *haute droite* characters. Oh, Collazo could never even imagine my piercing theories on 20th century nationalism! I gently explained that from the moment we entered university, all students were bombarded with the insights of a whole execution wall's worth of Commies, and that the complete works of both Kautsky and the ex-People's Commissar for Naval and Military Affairs, Trotsky, were listed among the texts that we had to memorize as we stood in formation during the school's patriotic ceremonies.

Collazo gestured for me to stop. He squinted beneath his bristly eyebrows, his face gone to stone like the solemn bust of some *gauche caviar* prince. He let his gaze drift into the distance and said, very slowly, the words of another, phrase by phrase as they flowered in his mind:

–"These innocent . . . and puerile fantasies . . . of the philosophy of the young . . . whose philosophical bleatings only mimic the opinions . . . of the German bourgeoisie, these sheep . . ."

–"These sheep who take themselves, and are taken, to be wolves."

–It's been so long since I've recited that, he said, taking a bite of glazed potatoes, nodding his thanks. What a great quote. One of my favorite books of the period.

I took advantage of the fact that he was chewing, and added that ever since the Knowledge Industry decided to proclaim itself *critical* (i.e. since the *dernier cri* of its blusterings is to fancy itself a critic), humanism has been reduced to the republican version of intellectual purity; in the end, product differentiation is as important for (and within) the academy as it is for the capitalist corporations that academics love to hate. My disquisition, though perhaps a bit nerdy, appeared to have gained me a new, mustachioed adept. I blinked several times and added a few anacoluthons, feigning self-doubt so that he wouldn't feel diminished (and thereby emasculated) in the face of such a powerful demonstration of argumentative mastery. He acknowledged my commentaries with a laugh.

We were about to start our conversation back up (I'd made a silent bet with myself that this daring warrior would be on the watch for any opportunity to destroy me; only then would I show my fangs) when a profoundly secondary character caught our attention. At the table next to ours, a bottle-blonde with a swarthy past couldn't quite decide between the suckling pig and the octopus *a la gallega*. Her pronunciation revealed an accent that would tear itself to shreds on razor wire if the authorities ever found the time to build a fence around Buenos Aires. Given that Menemism had been banned on aesthetic grounds, any excessive yellow in one's pileous hue was now seen as shameless, and the woman's blatherings, which included scattered capitalistic semiwords like "AmEx," dissolved in the air like smoke signals emitted from some dismal raft of bad taste adrift on the current of time.

Collazo muffled an improvised chuckle with his napkin. The moral distance between our table and theirs led naturally to the forging of a sort of allied front between Collazo and me. It was then that he took advantage of my distraction, intrepidly captured my hand, and kissed it.

My first steps into adulthood have left me ill-equipped to differentiate between fury and other sources of heat. His mouth was still pressed tight against my hand. Then something fluttered beneath his preputial eyelid: it was passion, rumpled and lethal, capable of blowing the human heart to pieces (cf. Rucci's Murder by Montoneros, 9-25-73). Collazo was (is) a horrible man, but that doesn't make him any less attractive to my eyes. The little beast of hatred I carry inside quivers every time it hears his name.

–Mr. Collazo, can I bother you for a second? Would you mind signing this? It's for my great-aunt, she's been wanting to read your books since forever, a man said, leaning next to our table.

As he kindly leaned over to accede to my request, stretching out the moment with a question full of feigned attentiveness and a long pull on his cigarette, I got a clean look at his bald head. The sight took me back to Episode Zero. My blonde friend Ilona and I were looking down from our balcony seats at the award ceremony for the most important prize in Spanish literature. On the brightly lit dais far below glowed the bald heads of a bunch of fat emeriti. A fiery applause swept the great hall, advancing like napalm up to the ankles of the writerly tribunes holding court. And the prize goes to . . . A name, and a new wave of napalm flowing from the tireless palms of three thousand overly wined and overly dined attendees; spoons are left suspended in midair as waiters turn to look, and even the restroom attendants peek out of their holes. The Man of the Evening strides athletically up to the podium and smiles—not even the smoke from all this clapping can throw him off his game. He taps the mike with two fingers, brings his most powerful orifice up close to the metal protuberance.

–Good evening. I would like to thank—

–*Who is this guy?* Ilona asks me in English.

Her pale hand flails in frustration—if only she had binoculars. Her teeth are stained purple, and apart from her violet silk dress, she's wearing nothing but a ring of Russian amber; a champagne glass trembles in her fingers. She is gorgeous, her gray-green eyes gazing out into the distance as if catching sight of foxes in some scene from Tolstoy (*lupa homini lupus*). Down below, several men in suits stare up at us, their posture that of hunters. Ilona glides up tight against the balcony's golden rail, and one knee slides sinuously into view. The air is impregnated with pheromones. I grab her around the waist; it is my duty to inform her that the men below are waiting for us to fall so that they might gather us up. She ceases the mermaid act, sticks out her tongue and laughs. We are utter tourists at a party that has nothing to do with us.

–*So who is this guy again?*

–*Some left-handed writer,* (and then almost cooing as we sway softly there at the rail), *the kind of guy whose life I wouldn't mind ruining.*

She kept laughing, clicking her teeth against the edge of her champagne glass, not caring a bit. It isn't that she'd become accustomed to this type of high-flown celebration. (You can always count on one witness and one victim to bring forth a realist prose.) As for Collazo, it wasn't hard to get him excited about the possibility of adding his books to the departmental syllabi. The prospect of hearing his own name pronounced in professorial tones, and of a row of full-figured students murmuring it, taking their pencils out of their mouths to jot it down, was enough to guarantee his cordial devotion. I wish he'd hold his mouth still; he often grimaces in a way that inadvertently shows his teeth, rabbit-like.

We said our goodbyes at the door of the restaurant. The street was empty. Just as I turned the corner, I realized that he was following me, half-hidden as he snuck along toward me. A beam of dim green light made and unmade the street-side shadows. I walked quietly, tight against the wall—a public zone reserved for women and those marked for death. The faint gleam filtering down through the treetops was now at my back, as if pushing me toward the cone of darkness ahead. And now Collazo sprung his ambush, came tight along my flank to intimidate me, a rapid maneuver that took advantage of the scarcity of light. I kept my eyes on him as I retreated, and my knees cracked against the side of a flower box. He lunged forward. He had me precisely where he wanted me, akimbo there on the sidewalk. His broad silhouette blocked out the light. I couldn't see anything but the chest hair poking out through his shirt, and above, that mouth, that threat.

–You know, I had a really good time with you tonight.

His eyes traced me up and down as he spoke, his thoughts as clear as any slogan: *I'll calm the little kitten, let her know that I'd like a little something more*. I didn't say a word; my back hunched as if skinned like an animal. My triangle of love had swollen in all three dimensions. Collazo brought his hand softly to my coccyx, pressed down the way one does to get a dog to sit. A whimper escaped me. He looked me in the eyes, kissed me on the forehead, and let me go.

2.1

Individual consciousness boils down to vanity, whose applications form an interface around the body. Because love is a subtitle for something much more specific, more sidereal. Individual consciousness can only relate to others through itself, using the language of vanity. The Theory is unequivocal: it affirms a plot of divine manners lurking under the form of human interest. It unfolds the excess, the intimacy of being in the First Person, while knowing full well that there are Second Persons and Third Persons whose existence *with mine*, and only *through* me. The hierarchy of thought imposes a hierarchy on the order of things. The seductive powers of syntax (for those who observe its rules with both pomp and modesty) grow ever stronger by subjugating those gathered around the one who organizes the verbs.

I have plans for this man.

2.1.1

Thinking of Collazo's old, monkey-like eyes, I stroke Montaigne's white fur in the hope she will meow in understanding. The little one purrs beneath my hands. With her eyes half-closed, she watches a cockroach walk calmly toward the kitchen, much as one watches the world pass by from aboard a train—impassive, both of us watching. Holding that thought, I glide over to the flamboyant centerpiece of my library (the secret altar I have raised in honor of Hobbes) and catch sight of the question that now rises up through the cat hair: *How does one ambush human beings?* Back in the pavilions of past time and forward into the encolumned future, *syntagma* is the term used for a military formation that was invented in the 4th century B.C. and involves two hundred fifty-six warriors:

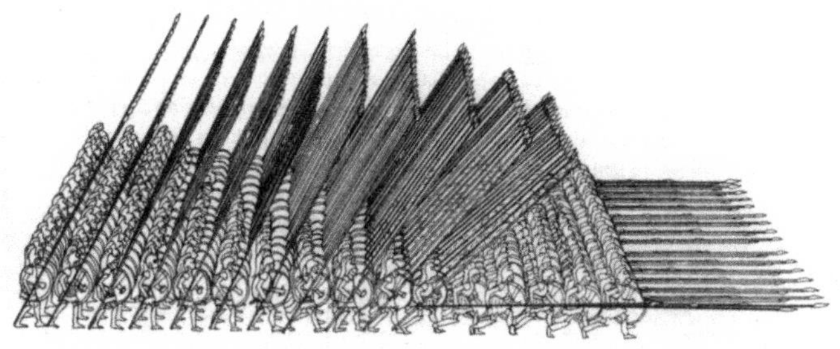

Other formations included the *tetrarchia*, made up of sixty-four men, and the *taxiarchia*, of one hundred twenty-eight; two *taxiarchias* formed a *syntagma*, and four *syntagmas* made up a *chiliarchia*, which had a total of one thousand twenty-four men. The *syntagma* prevailed as the most maneuverable of these groups, much like the Roman *centurias* born of the Marian reforms. When combined with the new weapons and tactics developed by Philip II of Macedon (most notably the sarissa, a long shaft with an iron spearhead at one end and a bronze butt-spike at the other to provide balance), in 338 B.C. they decimated the most prestigious military corps of the ancient world: the Sacred Band of Thebes. This decisive battle, which took place at Chaeronea, led to a crucial change in the very conception of war.

The Thebans utilized the first and only military formation ever inspired by a Platonic dialogue (Plutarch specifically cites the speech of Phaedrus in the *Symposium*), and had triumphed in what Pausanias considered the most significant conflict pitting Greeks against Greeks, the Battle of Leuctra in 371 B.C. Their elite corps was composed of one hundred and fifty pairs of homosexual warriors. In the flirtatious conversations at the banquet described by Plato, the one at which Phaedrus spoke, it was posited that homosexual warriors were preferable to heterosexual ones, because fighting alongside one's beloved was an incentive to unfurl one's courage and other virtues of war.

When the *syntagmas* of Philip II crushed the brave gay duos of Thebes, the Macedonian style of fighting came to predominate, and the theory of war popularized by the author of *The Republic* was reduced to ashes, along with the final pyres whereon laid the bodies of the valiant sodomites. Philip had trained his men to form themselves into a uniquely lethal beast; as distinct from earlier combat (and combat theory), where the possibility of winning honor stoked the *individual* strength and courage of each warrior, the Macedonian model entailed soldiers uniting to form *a single body* composed of infantry, archery, cavalry and siege weapons. Strictly speaking, they were *a single hand* of implacable fingers closing on the enemy's throat. Greek military homophilia had been definitively displaced by a theory of war that sought to revive a lost herd instinct, invoking the figure of the supreme predator with a beast built of thousands of men. The fact that the number of warriors involved in each of Philip's formations was a power of two no doubt stoked the formal appetite of Johan van Vliet, who saw in the Macedonian *syntagmas* a milestone in the technical transformation of men into beasts, later perfected by the pact between masses and State known as the republic (where the pact of conquest is the sovereign's secret).

One of Philip's tactics was to provoke the enemy all the way to the bitter end.

2.1.2

The purity of the horror involved should not, must not, be assuaged. I must act upon him so as to inspire *armies of organized brutality sent vectoring toward me*. I muse upon my options: 1. To cause him to throw himself upon me like a wolf, voracious, brutal; 2. To watch him sniff and salivate at my nymphean estuary.

The blow cannot fall in vain. I must swap out his venereal appetite for the blood-stained excess that is at stake. It isn't enough simply to arouse his desperation, his unconditional surrender to my delicious parts. I have to make him gather every ounce of strength and brutishness, make him reveal to me the purest form of the monster of dominance and destruction, because only then . . . The night does not flee from the wolf of the night: deep in the silvery foliage of the world, it lets the wolf lick its throat, hides the wolf beneath its mantle, and waits. It doesn't matter if disgust causes my skin to crawl; he will throw himself on top of me, and I will quietly resist. The worse it is—the more strongly, the more violently he takes me—the better. Yes, the worse it is, the better. To distance myself from the horror, I try to focus on the fact that though

I must yield in the name of his pleasure, he—*we*, Augustus—we serve in the name of justice. It isn't enough to dangle a delicious *fruit vert* before his eyes, and watch him prepare to gorge. I must produce, indirectly, *through* him, *into* me, the bloodbath whose repercussions will be felt in the System of Persons. I must work through him, and yet not: it's like hypnotizing a lion.

Collazo (like Augustus) has long, stabbing, beautiful hands. They scratch and stretch everything they touch. The thought of them reaching for me makes my hair stand on end. In the words of Pasteur, that genius of evil germs, *le hasard ne favorise que les esprits preparés*, isn't that right, Montaigne, *ma petite chat?*

2.1.3

I'd imagine a train. The blood-curdling nature of a straightaway. The dark spill of a tunnel, the weight of the eyelids, this darkness. The streams of lava, their halting flow; the black earth shuddering beneath the thunder's throat, stained by this glowing red saliva. My mind would return to me, if only to hide beneath my fist for a few brief moments; a sigh would be heard, and a princess, weak, sallow and feverish, would be seen falling from a fog-laden tower toward the erect lances eager to impale her. The hand of the fog would tighten lasciviously around the curves of her body, licking wildly at her secret rage. I would paint a picture of a train destroying a village, the devastation reaching both forward and backward in time—first out on the plains (floating pollen, tranquility, distant hills) but the noise grows, becomes deafening, implacable, time and space inverted, so loud one must clench one's eyes shut. Avenues of fire; at the outside doors, asphyxiation. I would paint the lava streaming down across the black earth, lava from the sky that hides wolves and maidens beneath that same stain of fear, an explosion of blood set free—warning bells and clouds would destroy the remains, the echo of insane gunpowder and silent visions, and the rhythm that has set the world atremble would swallow me whole.

2.2

At times I think about the hidden life of certain harmful thoughts. It seems to me an enigma: the second name their presence acquires. I know of a relevant interpretation of the myth of the Cretan labyrinth. Minos is having nightmares in which Asterion becomes disgusted with having to eat those who have come to usurp the throne. The youths who owe their lives to that disgust hide behind walls of fury; they conspire together there in the bowels of torment to create a new race. Power consists in terrorizing fear itself, thinks Minos. These walls exist to multiply my strength; terror is the stone that gives form to and divides our thoughts. Minos can't stop thinking, his thoughts reflecting the silent struggle that in time turns men into marauders. His wife, Pasiphaë, watches him silently from where she leans against an onyx column. She forsook her taurian loves the moment she saw how others fled at the sight of her little one; her blood has emptied out in the ensuing wait. The myth's one empirically significant detail is that Pasiphaë likes "brute access," a phrase derived from the Greek meaning "sex in the rear."

Minos doesn't yet know that the conspiracy for which this magnificent labyrinth was created is itself a form of thanks offered by the partisans. Nor that in order to get them to leave their holes and abandon their weasel disguises, he must make use of the ferocity from which his strength derives. He intuits, thanks to this apocryphal sect of thought, that his analysis of that ferocity, that dark figure of suspicion, has at last obliged him to rise up in a pure form of physical domination and destruction. It isn't enough to have sacrificed a bastard child for the cause. (Asterion, fruit of the queen's desire, of her lust for both animals and men, has no cause of his own.) The strategies of Minos's army must be determined by its physical structure. Meanwhile, throughout the labyrinth, from its center out along its tunnels and days, in each nook and corner the walls pray: *When the State feels itself obligated to rise up in a pure form of physical domination and destruction, the conditions are ripe for the triumph of the revolution.*[vi] The walls pray, but no one else does, as everyone else is dead.

2.2.1

But:

Can Collazo be considered a *Person* in the strict sense of the term? I watched him nestle an ashtray in the graying hair on his bare chest, the way men do when they're accustomed to surroundings organized around them.

I made his gaze climb onto mine.

2.3

He walks alongside me, a heavy shield, or a giant ogre. An ominous moon hangs overhead. We cross Libertador Avenue, head toward the dark woods of Palermo. The wind hisses softly through the foliage, and there are glints of blue in all directions. We can just make out the burbling tumult of a distant underground stream. A bird grazes me as it flits by, but no, night has fallen, these are bats. The trees are prototypes for demons. Our feet sink deeper in with each step; the trees and the signs are links in a single chain. I turn back to look at the avenue where beastly quadrupeds roar in a river of lights; here inside, in the forest, I catch the scent of the snares of bushmen. The drooling apostles who spread revealed truths with dick and dagger much as one tears something out by the roots—the vine that bears the fruit of a curse, or of a slaughterhouse, or of a brothel—I can see them coming. Don Juan Manuel Rosas and his mazorqueros are here, are roaming my body.[vii] I cannot cover the page with my body, must keep walking, but I can feel the greedy mouths twisting livid deep in the porous black soil, down near the chorus of serpents, their infinite girth, infamous executioners, their fangs, the rites of a horrifying colossus, devourer of hymens and men. We'd felt the roar of this darkness as far back as the edge of

Libertador: the gray ghosts from the time of Rosas still stalked the paths along the canals.

I think Collazo sensed my fundamental terror, and spoke as if to calm me. He talked of the *corridas* of doña Laurencia, of her many appetites, her crepuscular lover. He said that she was kidnapped, taken to the domains of Don Juan Manuel to be abused, forced to submit. Whispering directly into my ear, Collazo repeated the part about "the custom, here in the delta of the Río de la Plata, of the right to rape," his massive hands leaving marks on my arms.

I looked up at the sky, terrified, and thought of Augustus, of the quote from *Prototype for Approaching the Victim* where a motive for the existence of armies is proposed: "Only within a plausible psychological theory can human wretchedness, organized to function as antidote, persist." If you can't beat them, I thought, you can at least confuse them. I recycled a series of poisonous opinions about a historical novel based on the life and times of Rosas, a book I'd never read, but I knew the plot fairly well. I spoke quickly and vehemently; carrying on that way for quite a while, I basically destroyed the author. Collazo said nothing, perhaps impressed. Later he asked me if that author, too, was listed on syllabi in my department. I laughed, and so did he. Striding along, dodging my solemn pronouncements, Collazo returned to the task, declaring himself fully prepared to defend the theory that one summertide afternoon, Manuelita Rosas must have snuck away with that contrite poet (what was his name?) to listen to a few strains of the national anthem that Vicente López y Planes would one day inherit. Collazo pointed to a plot of sunken ground in the middle of which a rusty iron spike stood erect.

–Right here. He had her by the arm, wasn't letting go. She was crying uncontrollably, whimpering and wailing like a snot-nosed little girl.

He squatted down to inspect the ground. The dying light fell across the back of his sweatless neck. Up ahead there was a small abandoned fairgrounds thick with weeds, inhabited at present by a sect of spooky-looking merry-go-rounds.

With a quick right hand, I pulled open the two buttons of my blouse; I stood motionless, my legs spread, my boots sunk into the earth. All it would take now is for him to turn to say something, and I, swathed in this tenebrous ardent light, would look into his eyes, ready to unveil the artistry of my pitiless verdict, to perform my duty in the name of all, *terribilis ut castrorum acies ordinata*.[7]

A shadow slipped past, was now behind us, and whatever the man said ended emphatically: The money, give me all the money, now.

Collazo was still hunched down. Maybe they hadn't seen him. Maybe he was planning the perfect strategy for taking the assailants down with two or three blows. He would rip the rusty spike out of the earth, throw himself at them like a master samurai, spit that cyanide-laden Montonero tooth with the precision of a ninja's dart. He gathered himself up, his face deadly serious, and took a step forward. The violet

---

7 "Who is she that looketh forth as the morning, fair as the moon, clear as the sun, and terrible as an army with banners?" (Song of Solomon 6:10).

branches of the trees stretched out overhead. He shot me a wink, looked one-eyed in the dark.

–Leave this to me, he whispered, rooting around in his front pocket. Boys, here you go, ten pesos. He pawed again through the contents snug up against his balls. Hey, look, that's twenty altogether. All yours.

–Son of a bitch, give me everything you've got, this isn't some scene from *Tumberos*.

One of them brandished a knife. With a brief sigh, I opened my little backpack and brought out the French edition (1934) of Trotsky's *History of the Russian Revolution*, *Naufragios* by Álvar Núñez Cabeza de Vaca, *De Civitate Dei* by St. Augustine (the Migne edition, bilingual, with the disastrous Spanish translation), *Storie italiane di violenza e terrorismo* (a fascinating analysis of Potere Operaio, cradle of the Red Brigades), and a small anthology of Catholic poems (very funny) by Péguy. Collazo and the two socio-political outcasts watched as the books piled up. It was then that I realized, thanks to the roving eyes of the muggers, that the buttons of my blouse were still open. Oh my god, I thought. I didn't want to make any false moves, so I left them open.

One of the two correlatives of capitalist perversity took a deep huff from the plastic bag in his hand, and stared at me. Loki was thin, light on his feet, with coarse skin stretched tight around his proletarian bones. He now showed us the angriest facets of his earthly *I*.

–Give me your cell phone, your wallet, your credit cards—both of you, right now.

Cacha, the other inheritor of social injustice, began poking at the pants pockets of the ex-guerrilla, who raised his arms. Leaning sideways against a tree trunk, Collazo furled his tiger's brow and murmured:

–Nice and calm, I'm unarmed.

–Hey douchebag, who said anything about you being armed. Let's see if you've at least got some cash.

He opened Collazo's wallet, started flipping through the credit cards.

–Visa, Mastercard, American Express, cool. Nothing gets canceled until tomorrow night, you feel me?

I lit a cigarette, and took a step forward.

–Loki, Cacha, wait a second. Let me say something to you guys. This person here in front of you, whom you've disrespected, he basically dedicated his youth and his life to a cause that included saving indigent slum-dwellers like yourselves, and everyone else who wasn't born where they might have liked, who's been treated like shit by Fate. Your families, your loved ones. The socialist fatherland wasn't merely a dream. There were years and years of underground struggle, of getting insulted in the streets, of books that no one wanted to publish, of taking your head in your hands at the Bar La Paz and shouting, "No! Enough! This is not how things should be!"

The three men stood stiffly for a long moment. I kept talking; I don't even want to remember what I said. Loki walked over to where Cacha was standing beside the ex-militant.

–So you're a politician? he said to Collazo. Are you? Are you?

Collazo tried to duck but Loki's hand caught him full in the face.

–Answer me! No? Nothing to say? You motherfucking thief!

Now he started punching Collazo, and in my stubbornness I shouted, No, no! He's not a politician at all! He's just a leftist intellectual!

Cacha and Loki looked at me, looked at Collazo, and started hitting him even harder. There were no more arguments worth making; history had ruined all hope of discussion. My tone had been appropriate, and even my sentimental choice of certain terms, but what perverse idiosyncrasy—so harmful! so fruitless!—had strained my common sense to the point that I tried to make Collazo seem heroic? Are good intentions enough to make someone a hero? And what must his good intentions have been, exactly, if they were never to become anything more, or if in the process of transforming them into actions he'd done some horrible things, and if the very ineffectiveness of the transformation demonstrated the incoherence and criminality of this hardly ideal situation? What's more: what absurd aspiration had led me to intrude upon the natural right of a poor man to mug me in the forest? Dignity? What dignity could there be in this old bag of ideologemes lying in the grass, bleeding from the nose? Analyzing the situation now from a metatheoretical standpoint, how could I have hoped to convince them with the pathetic irony implicit in a situation where one monkey holding the knife of possibility faces off against other monkeys holding knives of . . . actual knives? I sighed. The expected recipients of revolutionary benevolence kept kicking Collazo there where he lay. I had committed the sin of atavistic condescension. I was on the verge of losing my earnestness and starting to cry.

–Enough, enough! Please leave him alone!

Loki shot a sign to Cacha, his twin in structural poverty.

–Tie the fat girl up and make her quit yelling.

Cacha advanced on the *fat?!?!?!* girl with a roll of sisal twine. I still had my lit cigarette, and buried the burning end indignantly in his arm. He smacked me in the face; then, with amazing precision, he tripped over the iron spike, his foot striking it so hard it made the earth shake. He hunched over, mute with pain. Then he limped to his partner, who was punching the prone Collazo below the poverty line.

–Loki, come on, we're done here, let's go.

–You got everything?

–Yes, come on, time to bail.

These two, long pillaged by the system, bundled up their booty and took off toward the dark circular drive too small to be called an avenue. I ran to the wounded-in-action.

–Did they hurt you?

With a certain agility, Collazo rolled onto his side in the grass.

–A little, yeah. But I played a lot of rugby when I was young—my stomach is still hard as steel.

–Really? Can I see?

–Sure.

He opened his shirt. There were a couple of red marks, a few bruises; the stingy light made it hard to see much more. My hand drew close to the grainy skin. Scars, offered like a harem of thirsty mouths, the toothy topography of ancestral sharks, the palpitating cartography at the mouth of the slough. The red, the black—the *fur*. I closed my eyes, being not quite ghoulish enough to carry on.

–I'm really sorry about your American Express card, I said as I helped him up.

–Don't worry, he answered, brushing the dirt from his clothes.

–But they took the books!

–Maybe they'll help raise awareness . . .

We laugh a little. Then we walk for a while without saying a word.

–Should we follow them?

I could hear the disappointment in my voice.

–No, let it go. They took some money, they beat me up a bit, but nothing serious. Look!

And there was my poor old useless history of the Russian revolution, abandoned in a pile of dead leaves. I brushed away the dirt with my hands, scraped off the edges, paged through quickly as I hefted the book to make sure its spine wasn't broken. I held it up high and inspected the cover, searching for signs of human meddling. Then I tucked the volume deep into my backpack.

–Of course they kept the Péguy, I murmured bitterly.

–At least the police didn't come. They'd have confiscated the book, and nobody'd ever have seen those poor thieves again.

–Did you know that police officers and thieves tend to come from the same social class, and have exactly the same disdain for anyone who got the education they never received?

I would have kept talking, but I was exhausted.

–Are you okay?

–I don't know.

I kicked at a loose leaf.

–They called me fat.

–I thought they said slut.

–Um . . . Are you sure?

–You like that better?

–Well . . .

For a second I pretended I had something caught in my throat.

–At least it's good to know that their nutritional shortcomings haven't damaged their vision too badly.

The son of a bitch said nothing. Nothing! He just let my sentence hang there in the air until it finally floated away.

In the ice cream parlor on the far side of Libertador, the middle-aged guys and the young girls were like separate voting blocs in Congress, not obviously at odds but definitely from different camps. We explained to the guy behind the counter what had happened, and he consoled us with some free almonds. I ordered Nero chocolate with the works; Collazo had a mango and strawberry.

I looked at his forehead. His bald pate reflected the street on all sides. I sighed. From then on, every time he saw me, the word "fat" would be hanging from my neck like a cowbell, right there *in medias res*.

But just now Collazo didn't even see me. I wasn't there at all, or it was time to go.

–Should I call you a taxi?

–No, that's all right, I'd rather walk.

I headed out along República de la India, impregnating myself with the nauseating odor of the zoo, the dogs' excretions, and my thoughts.

2.3.1

I simply can't understand how it's possible that they *didn't even try* to throw me down in the mud with their muddy hands and decivilize me from behind. And me, on my knees in the mud, *comme un chien.*

Now that dusk has fallen, (now that Yorick of Minerva emerges to splash about in the swamps of the world,) I withdraw into my chambers. It's been a long afternoon of not wanting to think about things. I opened a soft drink and looked at Yorick, swimming calmly around in his bowl. Lucky fish, who doesn't have to struggle against scale-lined reality or its doppelgänger minions, these thoughts. "We will triumph!" I muttered. "They'll see!" The kitten Montaigne tensed up and ran from my sight; predictably, she had omitted defecating in the litter box.

Poor Augustus, he doesn't fully realize how serious the problem is. He's very busy walking up and down the labyrinthine hallways of the Department of Philosophy and Letters, distanced from the world of concrete facts, as if nothing was going on with *that woman*. Little by little, his power fades. Up on the fourth floor where the research institute is located, there is a hive of tiny and deviously well-hidden offices and classrooms. Attacks by ineffable assailants are far more common than necessary (although perhaps the number of such attacks is coincidental, and "attack" and "necessity" harbor some mysterious semantic bond). There went the two of them, followed by B.M., a.k.a. Fat E.G.

I watched them, my earphones on, manifesting, through my vestal stillness, the deadly implications of the spatial syntax that had been perpetrated; I stood like the *I* that rises up at the beginning of a sentence, on the verge of throwing itself upon a verb and an object, of ruling over them, possessing them, or remaining tacit, not quite revealing itself—and yet in control of events. As a sort of reply to the tenor and quake of that scene, here is the song I was listening to at the moment—here we go with the guitars and the lyrics:

Se te olvida
~~*que me quieres a pesar de lo que dices,*~~
~~*pues llevamos en el alma cicatrices*~~
~~*imposibles de borrar.*~~
Se te olvida: que yo puedo hacerte mal
– si me decido –,
pues tu amor lo tengo muy "comprometido",
pero a fuerza no será.[8]

8 I'll take the liberty of arguing down the seventh line—the potential end of the sonnet. I propose the word "oh:" "Que a fuerza Oh será." In exceptional cases, both in politics and in love, a narrative's sovereign entity—the First Person, the one who organizes its desire—rules over the lives therein. I

~~Y hoy resulta que no soy de la estatura de tu vida,~~
~~y al dejarme~~ casi casi se te olvida
que hay un pacto
entre los dos. [viii]

3.

The sunlight turns the brownish waters green, blazes out from behind the silhouette of Collazo, who stands upright in the boat. He's wearing a wide-brimmed hat, a white shirt open at the chest, black trousers. Willow branches caress the surface of the water; the vines open before him like an endless succession of curtains. He leans against the rubber-lined edge, tests the hand-forged blade of his knife on the swollen lobes of water hyacinth that float alongside. At times the light goes dark, and his face, his eyes are hidden in shadow; his dark mustache glows sweatily above his mouth. We have a dog, a Winchester, and the knife that Collazo now tucks into his belt.

The boat glides slowly across the water. The roots of the trees are submerged; the weighted air molds itself to the gold and black forms that enclose it. The bromeliads twist in on themselves, swaying softly. The riverbank shows the rough lay of the land, the broken line of treetops. Branches lean out over the river, observe the water's flow, see it quiver beneath them. Black birds circle in the sky. The branches trace endless

---

shall carry on with my plan.

paths on the mirror between us and the mud and rot that lie beneath.

I have the feeling that Collazo's enormous hand is about to grab hold of my thigh. I say nothing. I lower my gaze. Vertigo criss-crossed by chasms, the air ceases to move, the ferocious sun covers everything in white. I fear only that my obsession has been revealed, that the monsters have made me translucent, can be seen through the cracks.

From time to time the water goes totally black. The sun disappears, and we hear a quiet hiss, as if something were catching fire somewhere out of sight.

Collazo stands at the edge; my eyes rest at the height of his belt, or a bit lower. He looks down, and there I am. He looks at me and grabs at himself, his hand tracking across the zone. Beneath the cloth waits the red spear, the mute inhabitant. She (I) pushes her hair back from her face, turns her head to look toward the trees. Collazo slides his hand slowly along his critical apparatus, and shifts it to one side of his fly.

–You see? This is what they mean by "packing." Everything off to the side.

She (I) looks closely. The mountainous chain hangs well down his thigh. She waits for a few seconds, takes a deep breath, looks him in the eyes.

–The left side, she says.

Collazo smiles. Of course, from her perspective it's actually off to the right.

–And that tells you quite a bit about a man, doesn't it.

Collazo is behaving magnificently.

–Do you always pack to the same side?

–Me, always.

Collazo rubs his hands briskly up and down his body, shooing away the stubborn mosquitoes that have come to appropriate his blood. We pass below some branches and his face falls into shadow.

The heat grows. Our clothes stick to our bodies, and the air is dense, filled with bright flecks. Collazo's white shirt is open down to his solar plexus, the valley through which knives enter; the grayish fleece on his chest shines with sweat. Collazo slaps his arm for the Nth time, and looks at me.

Any moment now. Any moment and he throws himself on top of me. His huge horrific hand takes me by the back of the neck—I feel an inverse wind, a momentary tornado of heat and teeth—I release my breath, squeeze my eyes shut, and whisper to throw him off track:

–Have you ever hunted for white-eared opossum?

The light shines on Collazo as he lets go of my neck and grabs a handful of cartridges.

–They're an appalling animal, he says. Whenever they feel trapped by a predator, they spray a defensive secretion out of their genitals, this revolting yellow liquid. And if the threat is inescapable, they lapse into a coma and go completely still.

As he speaks, he puts the cartridges in the shotgun. The river gathers speed—I can feel the current humming in the tips of my toes. My body, a vessel full of blood on the verge of spilling over. I run my tongue across my lips.

Collazo looks at me.

–They love to play dead, he says. To play dumb.

He bites down on his cigarette, and comes down off the edge. Then he hefts the shotgun, presses it against his temple. I treasure the moment intensely. A few sparrows twist and turn against the sky, and Collazo aims, tracks them in his sights, breathes, the seedpods around him yellowed by the heat. At the other end of the boat, the dog chews on Collazo's overshirt. The dog came with the boat, I don't know its name. Collazo lowers the shotgun and looks at me, his brow suddenly furled. Everything goes dark.

(Silence. Collazo, fear and trembling.)

As we come out of the tunnel, the light returns like an exclamation. There are countless golden flecks suspended before our eyes. His long calloused fingers spread suddenly against the foreshortened mirror of black water, move lightly across the surface of the swamp amidst the chirring of crickets and the creak of wood as it begins to break.

Then he brings his hand to my ear. I jump, startled.

–Relax, he says, smiling, wetting my ear with water. It's just a little shit.

I let loose a bored sigh, and take my comic book back up—a *Nippur de Lagash*. The Man of Lagash has fallen in love again, this time with Karien the Red, queen of the Amazons, with whom, several issues later, he will engender his three-eyed daughter Oona. In the issue I have here, the Wanderer meets Hattusil, the Hittite hunchback considered to be the greatest warrior on the planet, who will become his best friend.

I watch Collazo out of the corner of my eye. He doesn't notice. My mind wanders silently through the swamp, shimmying along as it awaits the sudden appearance of a supernatural anaconda.

Then Collazo coughed. He gestured at an opening filled with scrub. The grayish bank was covered with hills of garbage rising to the sky. He said that at 6:30 one evening, just as summer was beginning, his organization had launched an assault on the *Itatí*, a yacht that belonged to the Commander-in-Chief of the Navy. An underwater mine of ammonium nitrate had been laid by a team of divers formed in Cuba in the late 1960s—the same team that had blown up Villar's yacht in some other inlet here on the Tigre Delta. They knew that the admiral would not be aboard—armed Peronist left-wing loyalists by profession, what they actually sought was an unwitting ally in the Armed Forces. They'd shot up a police helicopter to facilitate their getaway; a few days later, they went up against the last of their targets on the Peronist right wing, Alberto Campos, political and military enemy. Just beyond is the Reconquista shipyard; they'd occupied the entire facility, and posted a sign to serve as warning and prelude, *Danger: Dynamite*. Nearly a thousand vessels were blown to bits, and the oil from their motors covered the water with black, and the fire floated on the water. It burned until morning, and the attackers flowed south across Buenos Aires; the combat platoons blocked Libertador Avenue and took over the public transportation system. The din was deafening as the magnificent youths advanced along the city's main arteries, slamming their vehicles into banks, smashing windows and storefronts. More than fifty cars were set on fire, as well as businesses, concession stands and police vehicles.

This was followed by a wave of hand-thrown bombs, and banners filling the air, and bursts of gunfire to which any number of meanings would later be attributed. All of this was in 1975—two years before I was born—and timed to coincide with the anniversary of Evita's death.

Occasionally Collazo looked over at me to make sure I hadn't taken my eyes off him. His Panama hat burnished by sun and sweat, his wrinkled skin, and the blackened tips of his mustache; beams of sunlight, insects; a Colt Commander .45 with a grip safety, the bombing of the Army Information Service headquarters in Buenos Aires, the theft of sanitary materials, stalking and assassinating a union leader, machine-gunning the facades of the Fiat and Ford plants. The clarity of these acts went beyond what is required to send a message. It assumed that all the corpses and threats formed a ritual path leading to exemplary ends: the negotiation of exclusively political objectives, and, rather greedily, the provocation of a new coup d'état by the army. It was believed that the masses would then rise up voluptuously to resist the ferocity of the State, thereby automatically strengthening the armed organizations' political wings, which would assume power once the victory was complete.

Collazo stabs his pole fiercely into the water and we pick up speed, impelled toward the triumph for which his determination, his very nature, had destined us. I lie down on the bench so as to be looking up at him. His eyes, coffee brown or dynamite red, they pierce me. I know that he's on the verge. He will throw himself on top of me, will not be able to control his teeth, his filthy claws will send shivers down my spine, and

I will lose consciousness. I close my eyes the better to resist. Collazo pins my arm behind my back, his breath is in my ear, thick, cavernous. He puts all his weight on top of me, and I gasp. He paws at his zipper, trembling; he bites my hair, right behind my ear. I cannot breathe. He is apparently subduing me. In the thinnest of voices I say:

–Are you going to sing or not?

I push my hair back, scrutinize his face. I feel like shouting *I will neither collaborate nor surrender!* (quoting Norma Arrostito, legendary Montonero leader) but I'm afraid of ruining this parodic bliss so I keep quiet. I can hear his breath at my ear. He doesn't move. He doesn't speak, neither do I, and there is no sound around us. Suddenly it is as if the spell were broken, and in place of the Beast, an old man stood up only to sit down again, tiredly, on the bench, resignedly:

> *No somos putos, no somos faloperos,*
> *somos soldados de FAR y Montoneros.*[ix]

I rise up before him, my face alight. I find it irresistible that he would agree to sing, I can't help it. Behind my eyes I confirm the presence of a feeling so powerful I want to bite him: his very being exudes a vulnerability so unpleasant that it makes me dizzy, rivals the strength of my patience without rising to the level of my disgust. But enough. Let us return to the scene. I have no desire to distort a rigorous political theory such as has been established in this book just to make of it a simulacrum for some monstrous sort of love. I shake my head. I speak softly but firmly:

–The rhythm was a little off.

In fact all he'd done was recite the words. My dear Collazo then did something absurd—*he demanded a kiss first*—and I, all but creating the objective conditions (back arched, tender breasts offered in lascivious salutation) which would enable him to obtain one, I said no. The fact that instead my spine stayed straight, that the shape of my body did not form a hollow in which he might take shelter, must have awakened in the old soldier some instinctual urge to obey.

Ni votos ni botas / fusiles y pelotas.

Brujo vení, vení Brujo vení / te va a quedar el culo como el Tango de París.

Rucci traidor / saludos a Vandor.

El pueblo te lo pide / queremos la cabeza de Villar y Margaride.

Duro duro duro / éstos son los Montoneros / que mataron a Aramburu.[9]

Cinco por uno / no va a quedar ninguno.

Mugica, leal / te vamos a vengar.

Qué lindos son tus dientes / le dijo Rucci a Perón / Perón contestó sonriente / ¡Jaja! Morirás como Vandor.

Con las urnas al gobierno / con las armas al poder.

Fumando un puro / me cago en Aramburu / y si se enojan / también me cago en Rojas / y si siguen enojando / me cago en los comandos de la Libertadora.

---

9 To which the unionist right wing responded, from the other side of the plaza, "¡Duro duro duro / la patria socialista se la meten en el culo!"

Fumando un pucho / me cago en Santucho / y si se enojan también en Estrella Roja / y si siguen enojando / me cago en la zurda y en todos sus comandos.

Vea vea vea / qué cosa más bonita / peronistas y marxistas / por la patria socialista.

Vamos a hacer la patria peronista / vamos a hacerla montonera y socialista.

Vamos a hacer la patria combatiente / en su medida y armoniosamente.

Si éste no es el pueblo / el pueblo dónde está.

Abal, Medina, ¡queremos cocaína!

No rompan más las bolas / Evita hay una sola.

Luche luche luche / no deje de luchar / que a todos los gorilas los vamos a colgar.

Con los huesos de Aramburu (bis) / haremos una escalera (bis) / para que baje del cielo / nuestra Evita montonera.

Qué pasa General / que está lleno de gorilas el gobierno popular.

Conformes, conformes, conformes General / conformes los gorilas, el pueblo va a luchar.

Qué pasa General / no alcanza para nada el aumento salarial.

Yo te daré, te daré / Patria hermosa / una cosa que empieza con P

Se va a acabar, se va a acabar / la burocracia sindical.

Aserrín aserrán / es el pueblo que se va.

Juventud, presente / Perón Perón o muerte.

No es hora de votar / es hora de luchar.

La sangre derramada no será negociada.
Si Evita viviera sería montonera.[x]

I sat back down and crossed my legs, the better to question him:

–Why did you stop singing? Just for dramatic effect?

–It doesn't make you better than us, the fact that you weren't on the wrong side. Everything about you shows how arrogant you are. You would have done anything to be the least bit like Evita, to be a montonera.

You should have seen me, Augustus. My thoughts slid furtively forward, hunched down in the brush, in italics; the roar of Collazo's prerogatives in my mind was quickly silenced. The game was mine in every sense. The victim belonged to me.

We tied up the boat. Collazo stepped onto shore, and used his pole to clear a path through the piles of garbage. The bank was quite narrow; only a few steps away was a thick grove of coconut trees and other palms, so dense that it was impossible to see through them. The dog, tired of being held captive on the boat, threw itself excitedly into the bushes. Watching it flee, Collazo gave me an unfathomable look, and tossed the gun at my feet, where it landed in a pile of dead leaves.

I walked behind him, swaying as if in drunken euphoria. I look at the shotgun in my hands and can barely restrain my laughter. Collazo is several meters ahead now. Noises filter through the forest: the trees strangling one another, quebracho branches snapped by the wind and baring their bright red hearts. I imagine his ash-gray neck twitching in the leaves, he disappears in the dark, reappears, and the scene is so powerful that to continue building it I picture myself digging my nails into his throat, firing shot after shot at close range. The sky changes color, and scatters mournful, sallow shades through the trees. Either a storm is coming or night is about to fall. I'm following Collazo and although he can't see me, I'm not actually hiding. The wind splinters and swirls, blows hard across my face, whips leaves into my face. I nearly scream but hold myself back, and laugh. I think I'm going to kill this idiot. I'm going to kill him because I have the compassion and nobility of spirit required to choose my victims for reasons that are strictly personal.

Part Two

Part I of this treatise explores the ways in which the voracity of beasts formed the earliest pedagogy, and prepared the ground for the invention of war. In Part II, the odd-numbered paragraphs examine the coded prehistory—carved in stone, inscribed within the human skull—of men who shared carrion with animals, of newborns kidnapped by eagles, and of other such scenes that crystalized the shapes of what would later become the fear of God. The invention of the spoken word as a chapter in the history of chewing meat; the pacts between beasts and human hordes that had to be established before the visible could be given names. According to Johan van Vliet, these scenes of Preclassic terror are the trace remains of primordial memories: the adventures of an early primate who, in the process of becoming human, spent thousands of years as prey.

The writings of Van Vliet defined the project of creating an ontology of human acts: a Theory of Egoic Transmissions, model for an anthropology of voluptuousness and war. Like other scribes of political ferocity (Hobbes, Luther, de Maistre, Bossuet, Stahl), in Van Vliet the natural evil of humanity is axiomatic; the beastly is the critique and the dogma. His attempt to reject fear-based stratagems co-exists in strange consubstantiation with them.

Never before in the domain of human thought had a voice resounded with the notion that the purpose of human existence was to serve as prey, or claimed that a prehistoric scene—the little monkey-man pursued and captured by wild animals—was being ignored in the name of human pride when in fact it should be serving as a magnifying glass. Anthropological explanations of brutality and war tend to blame humanity's fallen nature, gloating over our accursed fate. After all, God protected Cain, evil exists, the Huns triumphed. But all these histories of the birth of civilization begin, suspiciously, with tiny nomadic encampments wherein the Neanderthal family is already the stem-cell of the fatherland. By this account, inherited roles—the hunt/male, the hearth/female (cf. García Roxler, *the hunter/gatherer paradigm nourishes national infra-infancy*)—go hand in hand with the invention of weapons and fire, and are the most notable characters in a well-known script, one already possessed of a system of social classes, genders, and domestic rights and obligations that have persisted in various forms to the present day. This is the hunter hypothesis against which Van Vliet fought early in the 20th century, and which Augusto García Roxler came to solidify, and over-write.

How to assign a date to the birth of fear? How to explain humanity's obsession with fighting both the beast within, and the enemy within the beast? The primordial war between prey and predators functions like water poured or spilled into a rat maze, drowning the creatures; in the words of Van Vliet, "it is the substance that invades the memory-space of thought."

According to his theory, the entire external world postulates the existence of an invisible theater of war inhabited by visible actors. Leibniz hypothesized a matrix of points of view that built and completed the universe; Van Vliet in turn hypothesized that these monadic points of view are the ineradicable ghosts of future actions. There are cells in space-time that store memories of specific places, intentions, game-piece positions: history accumulates in these cells, and is transmitted to the actors through attractions, thought-ghosts, reincarnations, untimely calls from third parties: i.e. through egoic transmissions. These are indelible marks in the syntax that organizes interpersonal relationships in the universe, wrote Van Vliet: "After millions of years spent fleeing, escaping, surviving as a minor item on the menu of wild beasts, humans achieved their first incursion into the realm of predatory power through the invention of weapons." Thus, the history of technology is written into the ecological horizon of man against beast, with man overcoming beast, becoming the predator. This paradigm shift is only one landmark on the map of thought; it is Van Vliet's spatial syntax which connects it to the production of history. *Once the* I *enters the coordinate system of a syntax of prey, escape is impossible.* The *I* advances across a space dense with ghosts and purposeful geometries; this is the structure of the world, the totality of past and present points of view that pierce through space, and one another. The world is a field mined with points of view. Death—the problem of death—enters the world the moment one screams at seeing one's sibling disemboweled. Until then, humans only slept, and changed colors as they rotted. Our hearing is such that at night we can whisper to avoid drawing the attention of the beasts; when one shouts, the very volume of the voice is the spectacle that causes or leads to death. All possible pasts can be explained through the brutality inscribed in the world's governing syntax. To approach another, and start to tremble; to catch a subtle glimpse of the plan of attack, and count down the seconds to ambush.

Thus it is that no young male Masai is allowed to touch a woman until he has darkened his spear with human blood. The Naga warrior must return home with a piece of human scalp before he can be admitted as a lover. The Karamojo youth must distinguish himself in combat before being allowed to marry. Amongst the natives of the Gulf of Papua, only warriors have the right to sex. Verbs having to do with war (hunt, kill, bleed, fight) speak of prelude to sexual relations: before penetrating the flesh of one's own tribe, one must first penetrate enemy flesh. In this same remarkable vein, Hussman notes that the enemy scalp is of vital importance to the Cocopah warrior. He takes it to his hiding place, where he spends several days in communion with this piece of the enemy. He speaks to it "especially at night" of how to become a great warrior, and of certain special powers that he plans to bestow upon it; the interaction is "not in the form of a monologue, as he also falls silent, so that the scalp might respond." No one is allowed to observe these ceremonies: the intimacy between a killer and his prey is incomprehensible for those who have not been initiated into these rituals. The foundation of fear and the image of humans ceaselessly devoured together propel us toward the creation of pacts in the most intimate sense of the word, wherein one lies down with the beast, wherein pieces of the enemy's body join a conversation inherent to war.

In his trembling handwriting Van Vliet wrote, "*Scheisse*, I believe that I can reconstruct the cognitive evolution of the first moments of our species, when humans wandered the earth seeking shelter from wild beasts." He adds that, according to the beliefs of the Fon, all people are descended from a common ancestor who is half-animal, half-human. In the Fon initiation rites, each person enters into contact with his or her *vodun*, which possesses him or her completely; from then on, that person's survival depends upon the relationship between the *vodun*'s animal and human counterparts. "Prior to the history of weapons and technology lies the silenced prehistory of blood pacts between men and beasts. The prey-predator pact marks the first strategy of war; the first theory of war involves damsels married to beasts." When Zwa penetrated into the lands of Anzuru, he found nothing but God, tigers and the bush; then a tigress prostrated herself in front of him, and offered him her womb. Mating with savage animals has thus long had a starring role in tales of strength: only a pact with a beast guarantees survival.

The *Diary* of Van Vliet ends with a section entitled *Red Moon of Fon*, written in or around August of 1917. In Fodder's expedition journal we find: "The Fon were shouting as they entered our tent. They knocked things over and threw our equipment to the ground. Professor van Vliet stood motionless, watching them. The men drove him outside at spearpoint. The Professor stood with one foot in camp and the other in the black jungle. All was silence. Fischer and I covered ourselves with a dark blanket and crawled into the bushes. The Professor didn't seem to see us. We threw a few acorns at him to get his attention, but missed. The Professor was extremely tense, scrutinizing something that we couldn't see. Fischer slipped out from under the blanket, crept forward on all fours, tried to tackle him to the ground but the Professor would not budge. We pleaded urgently with him, *We must leave camp tonight!* The Professor ignored us. He stood stock still there at the perimeter of camp and said: *All forms of understanding are psychological calcifications of our first encounter with the beasts. The shape of the space within which human beings move corresponds to the positions of invisible warriors. Parenthetically, I believe I now understand why my sweat production rates are so variable: these Fon are sick of us, and have decided to kill me. This result does not render my previous results invalid. My theory is* progressively *true.*

When Fodder and Fischer abandoned the Dark Continent, they took with them both Van Vliet's *Diary* and the main log book holding the results of the experiment. In their opinion, Van Vliet was committing academic suicide. The only other possibilities were that the Professor truly believed the Fon would not allow him to escape, or that the tropical vapors had finally driven him mad. In any case, the two men knew that Van Vliet would never have liked the cold environs of

Cambridge, where they had met shortly before the war broke out, and that he was too surly a man to enjoy the company of his peers, so perhaps it was best this way. They would flesh out the theory, make it legible in the eyes of the world. But leaving years' worth of work in the hands of aboriginals who were obsessed with matches and thus potentially pyromaniacal was out of the question. The disciples decided to filch the master's private papers on the last night they saw him alive.

While going through those papers, Fodder felt the thin red hairs rise on his arms. Van Vliet's notes on what would become known as Egoic Transmissions went well beyond the scope of both the experiment itself and the information he had given them before they set off—the information that had led him and Fischer to join the Dutchman as disciples in the first place. Van Vliet appeared to have compiled a list of all extant bibliographical sources regarding fatal encounters between humans and wild animals throughout the history of Africa and the Orient: records of lions besieging the Fon and their neighboring tribes for months on end; statistics on children torn apart by wild beasts; reports on the customs of the Leopard Men sect in South Africa and the military strategies designed to eradicate them—and the Crocodile Society, and the Society of Tigers—cults that had erupted throughout the continent, their members claiming to be able to turn themselves into wild beasts; chronicles of collective psychoses written in first, second, and third person; notes on children who, believing themselves to be wild animals, attacked their mothers; on women in prison who howled like wolves; on female wolves who were taken by men as concubines, and who then killed those men and escaped back to the forest to give birth; cures for those with an innate desire to devour human flesh; an inscription from the 7th century B.C. wherein a monarch declares, "I am Ashurbanipal, King of the World, King of Assyria. For my pleasure, and with the help of the god Ashur, and of Ishtar, goddess of battle, I penetrated a savage lion with my spear"; the totem from the kingdom of Amenhotep III which bears a carving in high relief narrating how the king killed a hundred and two lions; the story of Colonel Chesney, attacked by a lion he found drinking at the banks of the Euphrates in 1830; of the ten Indian soldiers attacked by a group of hybrid ligers along the northern reaches of the Karun River where it flows through the Zagros Mountains; of the one hundred ninety-three cases of fatal *Panthera tigris* attacks on the Maldharis tribe; reports from hunting grounds on the tundra in northeastern Russia of foxes more than two meters in length that weighed a hundred kilograms apiece and devoured intruders; tales of the sumptuous hunt of the Nawab of Junagadh that ended the life of a prince; a daguerreotype of lion-crowned Aizen Myō-ō, god of love in Esoteric Buddhism, he of the fire-red body, his six arms holding elements both human and divine—bow and arrows, bell and vajra, a lotus flower still closed tight, and in the sixth hand something invisible, known only to the enlightened; transcriptions from *The Man-Eating Leopard of Rudraprayag* by Jim Corbett, who only killed man-eaters, including the Mohan, the Thak, Talla-Des, the Panar, the tigress Chowgarh, and the terrifying leopard of Rudraprayag; an engraving of the profile of the tiger Champawat, responsible for four hundred thirty-six deaths;

details on the elderly men and women who go to the edge of the village to die, so that the beasts won't need to enter it to claim them; on the device, patented in Mumbai, that electrocutes tigers; on panthers who specialize in stealing sleeping children; on the army of stone lions carved to celebrate the final defeat of the Yuan Dynasty's Mongol empire, the eunuch hero who gave the order to build them dying far from home, confident that he could reclaim his earthly glory in the Great Beyond; on rites of passage that include ritual transformation into predators.

Throughout western Africa there is a belief that each human group contains a caste of members capable of transforming themselves into wild beasts: men who gather, take the form of lions or leopards, and chase their enemies, driving them into ambushes, leaping upon them as the sun sets. The Leopard Men cover themselves with animal hides; the members of the Crocodile Society await their victims near rivers and waterholes, hiding beneath crocodile skins. They mutilate their victims—the skin slashed open, the bodies disemboweled as if by some ravenous predator. A meticulous examination of the wounds reveals them to be clean, parallel cuts made with knives bound together to simulate a claw, and the liver and other coveted organs have been carefully extracted, with no damage done to the surrounding tissue. The delicate touch implied reveals human calligraphy made to pass for the handiwork of beasts.

Formal records, chronicles, obituaries—Van Vliet held all forms of information in high esteem, believing each to be part of a single unifying Act. His diary was dense with bibliographical references, many of them scribbled down hurriedly during the walks he took around the encampment, or so Fodder and Fischer deduced from the sloppiness of the handwriting. Given how casually the references were dropped into the text, Van Vliet must have known them by heart.

After a few months in Seville with no word at all from the Professor, Fodder and Fischer threw themselves across the Atlantic. Keeping their scarlet antecedents tightly under wraps (in college both men had flirted with the socialism of Shaw) they sought political asylum on the east coast of the United States; no sooner had they been reborn as Americans than they were separated and sent to obscure universities in upstate New York and central Virginia, respectively. They stayed in touch during the interwar years, each keeping the other informed regarding echoes of the master's voice they had detected—echoes which from the beginning were already growing faint. They also put themselves to work finding a publisher for *Moonless Writings*, that being the English translation of *Maanloos Geschriften*, the only text of Van Vliet's that would ever be made known to even a minuscule part of the Western world.

In the course of their correspondence, Fischer discovered what he thought was a way to pull Van Vliet's theory back from oblivion. He saw that the Theory of Egoic Transmissions could be organized around a "childhood trauma" the human species had suffered, a primordial experience long since repressed. The persecution suffered by the earliest hominids lived on, carved in the depths of the species; it had influenced the evolution of the human brain, and thus the organization of culture as a celebration of the passage from prey to predator. (For Fischer, the very existence of *fear* as a mental phenomenon had guided the physical evolution of the brain.) This primordial trauma—not that of having been predators, as Freud had recently suggested in *Totem and Taboo*, but that of having been prey—explained the human fascination with transforming ourselves into predatory beasts, as well as our instinct for war and our talent for violence. The theory could now, at a single blow, both (1) present itself as a novel approach that would refute part of the theory of psychoanalysis; and (2) posit violence as a positive human attribute, and fear as the biological root of human behavior.

Fischer was exultant as he finished his letter to Fodder. Sadly, his intuition did nothing more than speed the project along toward its inevitable end. Why did Fodder grumble as he read and reread his colleague's proposal, unable to believe his eyes? To answer this, one must look to a line of bordellos located on rue Dauphine in Paris, where Fodder and Fischer began their *éducation sentimentale* in the year 1913, back before the prohibition of absinthe. Like other intellectuals of their time, Fodder and Fischer enjoyed the art of bordello conversation; they mocked the theories of the father of psychoanalysis and his attempts to create a new god consisting of sex. Perhaps if the phrase "childhood trauma" had been put in quotation marks, Fodder's reaction would have been different, but what occurred in Fodder's eye now was the twitch of one who sensed a betrayal. "How does this strike you, my dear friend." (Dear friend! The very phrase made Fodder squirm.) "Borrowing the notion of childhood trauma from the Freudians would thrust our ideas into the theoretical context that is currently on everyone's lips. It would excite the interest of the Freudians themselves, and even more so that of their detractors, guaranteeing our theory both enlargement and stamina."

Why was Fischer's solution such an obstacle for Fodder? After all, Fischer had found a market where the consumption of their theory could take place. The size of that market would grow thanks to the insertion of the subject of sex as its medical *pièce de résistance*, accelerating the theory's rate of adoption and thus swelling their share of the intellectual field.

Fodder didn't answer the letter. Instead, he simply waited for his disgusted look to project itself into the deck of possible Fodderian reactions that Fischer would be shuffling through. After several weeks Fischer sent a telegram: "Joining forces with an extant (if incipient) theory is exactly what we need. In memory of the Professor." Fodder threw it in the fire and ranted about Fischer throughout dinner.

For Evelyn—Fodder's wife—theories such as psychology-as-prehistory and the cyclical ritual transformation of humans into wild beasts (wherein it was beyond dispute that the gods created by religion represented the trace remains of the animals with whom primitive humans formed pacts in order to survive) were of little interest; she made a show of agreeing with him completely, trusting that this would be enough to get him talking about something else. Emboldened by his wife, the following morning Fodder sent Fischer a telegram: "You're asking me to make my tiny sect part of a sect that's even tinier. To what do I owe such an honor?"

Fischer responded immediately: "So what? At the very least we'd be having this argument in an auditorium that wasn't totally empty." Fodder replied: "No." Fischer answered: "My seminar on Van Vliet was just canceled. I have lots of spare time." Fodder invited him to come for the weekend, and Fischer caught the first available train.

The argument lasted all afternoon. Every so often Evelyn came into the study with coffee and plates of scones. She heard her Manfred say furiously, "But why should we choose to become vassals of an empire so small that it barely exists? Why don't we develop a theory that truly reaches back to the beginning of time? I didn't catch chronic colitis on that African riverboat just to see our results torn apart at some flea circus!" This sent her scurrying back to the kitchen to check on the turkey. Fischer stared out the window in silence—the elms, the conifers. Fodder collapsed into his overstuffed chair, still enervated by his own arguments, and Fischer began to speak: "When the subjective conditions are insufficient to prove to others the necessity of a given theory, a small nucleus must undertake actions that at first glance might seem unthinkable, so as to spread their ideas and bring down the regime (e.g. the other theory) in which they are embedded." Fischer spoke calmly without ever looking over at Fodder. "It's just a strategy, Marvin. That's all it is." The two of them continued on in this vein until six o'clock in the evening, when the turkey was finally ready, as were the respective decisions of the two academics.

After the turkey with its potatoes and currants, there was apple pie. Fischer praised Evelyn's culinary gifts, and looked with nostalgia at his old classmate, his partner in adventure, who was silently scarfing the food down. Little Jake began to cry in the next room. Not much more was said, and Fischer left the following morning. Long afterward, *Moonless Writings* was published by a small university press. Fodder and Fischer exchanged a few more letters, but their divergent ideological destinies multiplied the physical distance between Ithaca and Charlottesville many times over, and they never saw one another again.

Twenty-three years later, in January of 1949, a pilot flying his Auster J/5 monoplane along the 23rd parallel over the swamps northeast of Johannesburg saw a Caucasian man running naked through the jungle. The little white stain with arms disappeared into the foliage; in spite of the pilot's efforts to keep the man in view, he lost all sight of him. Returning to his base, the pilot, Manners, reported what he'd seen to his commanding officer, Lieutenant Owen, who furled his brow, used the tip of his boot to pull open the drawer where he kept his fountain pens, and asked Manners to fetch him the rubber stamps on the shelf. A series of aerial patrols were sent in, confessions were extracted from the inhabitants of the "black spots" where only natives lived, and a reward was offered for any lead on the whereabouts of the lost white man—all without success. One much-discussed hypothesis was that the "white Bushman" had been kidnapped by one of the local tribes, and that Manners had seen him in the final hours of his life, cruelly hunted down in the course of some beastly ritual. Thus it was that Professor Johan van Vliet, pioneer in the area of psychological experimentation, once more dodged the opportunity to return to the world of the living, white version.

The previous such occasion had taken place in southern Bulawayo, currently part of Zimbabwe, in the fall of 1942. The heat weighed heavily on the bush lands, trapped inside a yellow fog. The nearby swamp emitted a sweet aroma which drifted slowly through the foliage; insects buzzed and crackled in the air, a deafening din. A group of archaeologists was excavating a number of sites in the area. New World specimens, thought Van Vliet, smiling as he crouched in the scrub, his thick eyebrows arched over the eyepieces of a set of binoculars he'd bought in 1912 or thereabouts at a quayside market in Bremen. For the next few weeks he watched the scene develop with great interest, and once he'd established that they were looking for human bones, he decided to introduce himself. He hid his tattoos and other bellicose symbols beneath old linen clothes he hadn't worn since leaving his own encampment. As a final touch, he donned a khaki pith helmet, that essential element of the Commonwealth summer uniform; the Fon, traditionally fond of saving the skulls with which war provided them, had once kept this helmet as a souvenir. He stayed hidden until sundown. Then, in full view of Dr. Tom Monroe and his assistant, Dr. Lindsay Erron, Van Vliet stepped tall and straight from among the trees, surrounded by silence.

With an authoritative elegance foreign to the century from which the others came, Van Vliet explained that he was conducting research on the far side of the river, that his name was Marvin, Marvin Fodder, and he was working with a team from Utrecht University. He looked from one surprised face to the other with a delight he was perhaps unable to disguise. Lindsay Erron was of slender build, with alert gray eyes and a soft voice that she used now to note with a smile that they hadn't heard of any other scientific expeditions at work anywhere within the radius of their research zone. For his part, Tom Monroe—tall, dark, thirty years old or so—felt a tremor in his leg, a sensation he tended to get whenever he knew *exactly* which horse to back. He also felt the venom rising, afflicting his conscience; he knew that it would be worth his while to invest a few bottles of scotch in this alleged Martin Faber, and so, preempting Lindsay's womanly courtesy, he invited the man to stay for dinner.

Dr. Monroe drew back the mosquito net on the main tent. The floor was covered with rugs and weavings; there were maps and glass bowls, kerosene lamps, tables overlaid with white cloth to hide the bones they held. A plank balanced on a pair of sawhorses served as the main work desk. There were two microscopes of different sizes, and many other strange instruments which embedded themselves in Van Vliet's memory as he examined his surroundings. He headed instinctively for a stack of old books bound in bluish imitation leather—in the amber lamplight they were even more beautiful than he remembered. He caressed their spines as if mistaking them for the beloved backsides of the girls of Pigalle: *The Book of the Sword* and *Two Trips to Gorilla Land and the Cataracts of the Congo* by Sir Richard Burton, who'd baptized the kingdom of Dahomey with the fond nickname "little black Sparta," and *The Evolution of Culture*, a collection of Pitt-Rivers essays combining the history of warfare with Darwin's *Origin of Species*. Tom Monroe could not help noticing the murmur that crept from the lips of his guest.

A Zulu servant came into the tent carrying a tray of glasses; seeing Van Vliet, his face froze in horror. Monroe muttered a *ngiyabonga* of thanks, stretching out the vowels clumsily as Americans often do, and snapped his fingers to make the man disappear. He leaned against the precariously unstable desk in the classic pose of explorers, cowboys, and suave leading men from movies Van Vliet had never seen, and lit his pipe.

–I am in a position, he said, to confirm that we are currently excavating a site that will make history. Yes, my friend: history. We have encountered trace evidence of the funeral rituals of an *Afarensis* tribe: a communal grave that holds the bones of two small hominids, as well as those of a cheetah or some other mid-sized feline. The skulls of the children show signs of puncture wounds; we believe they were taken in their sleep and slain using a weapon made of animal fangs. The site's configuration showed no traces of religious significance, nothing staged to honor any deity. There are no gods here. In this tribe, the hunters not only warded off predators; from the very beginning of time, they were murderers as well.

Van Vliet looked out the tent at a clearing where a pair of sturdy, bare-chested Zulus were starting a fire. Beyond them he could make out a wooden structure of some kind.

–I hired several natives to work on the excavation while Dr. Erron and I analyze samples. Apparently we pay quite well—they've brought their relatives for us to hire too.

Monroe shot a wink at the clearing and smiled. Van Vliet

drew close to the covered mass on the table, and Monroe pulled the cloth back so that he could have a better look. The case of Monroe could inspire an entirely different theory, one that depended on the relationship that he sought to establish with the man he considered his precursor, and on a few empirical facts held hostage. Lindsay, her legs pressed tightly together and her hands on her knees, noticed that Van Vliet was ignoring the bones; rather, he was staring intently at her. Embarrassment rose in her cheeks, dilating the blood vessels around her nose. Her translucent eyelids licked down across her eyeballs; when she opened her eyes, exposing them to the elements, the green around her pupils went incandescent, then settled to a quiet glow. A slight quiver of the lips; her ears pinned back against her skull, a bit pale but with a slight bluish tint down toward the lobes. Van Vliet remembered the series of questions Darwin had asked about the facial vocabulary of the Chinese. When a person becomes indignant, do they straighten their necks, square their shoulders, close their hands into fists? If they encounter a problem, do they furl their brow, wrinkling the skin beneath their lower eyelids? When one attacks another, does the attacker furl his lip, showing his canine tooth on the side facing his opponent? Can expressions indicating guilt, dishonesty or jealousy be observed? Van Vliet raised two fingers as if he could reach out and touch Lindsay's skin.

Lindsay let her eyes fall half-closed; something about Faber seemed familiar, but she couldn't say what it was or where the feeling had come from. Monroe stared through the smoke of his pipe at Van Vliet, and lifted one authoritative finger. He ran to the far side of the tent, set some sort of machine to work, and the strains of Glenn Miller's "Moonlight Serenade" began to sound.

–Professor, do you like Glenn Miller?

Van Vliet's attention to all else suddenly collapsed. He lifted his hands to his face, and began to weep. Lindsay went to him, not knowing what to say. She held out her hand, and led him to a neighboring tent where he could spend the night. They never saw him again.

Part Three

1

In a little refrigerator, beneath a red tungsten gleam, a brain-versus-heart poster floated above the fliers and chewy candy. The caption read: *The Thing inspires respect, and perspiration—the Thing is Queen. The Thing—that which shall heretofore be known as the Thing—is the Sublime Attractor of Pure Sensibilities.* (The email invitation had chanted *Zarpe Diem. Cumbia Loonática vs. Chancho Malo and Organitos back-2-back. ArteRadix, Q'lo negro, Choris Cósmicos Kalenchus. Special Guests: Tumitumi + Gadortxa Full.*) The illustration was of a geronto-masculine profile whose curly beard formed a political map of South America. Andy confirmed that the proceedings in question would not include a poetry reading. (The *laissez faire, laissez passer* attitude of contemporary Buenos Aires obliged one to tread warily; there was always the chance that young women would venture onto the stage to share free-verse intimacies, pornographic outbursts, scattered rhymes in the local dialect.) And Kamtchowsky wanted to dance. She had always thought highly of the solvent rhythms and corpuscular-undulatory character of cumbia music; in the end, the eye of progress (its acritical, Phoenician voracity) drew near for a sybaritic feast, as if the phenomenon of spontaneous regeneration had suddenly sprung into existence, its very spontaneity consisting of a chic degeneration of the inadmissible.

Zarpe Diem took place in a synagogue that was clearly in the process of collapsing. Strings of tiny Felliniesque lights and colorful streamers dangled down from a ceiling pocked with mildew and grime. The walls were covered with florescent arrows pointing at the cracks that ran in all directions. A green-and-red sign warned that there were no emergency exits—it was of course completely natural for a synagogue to advise against diaspora. Another sign annotated the scene with the order to "Eat your partner."

An insidious, rhythmic bass line peppered with cosmic sound effects could be heard—the rhythm was explosive and disconcerting. A kid wearing only underpants and a soaking wet bowler hat was pounding away at a little toy piano; nearby were several laptops and metal boxes covered with phosphorescent decals. On stage, a kid with a tie around his neck and a feather headdress was acting out the role of a native—olive-colored skin, highland facial features, the feathers themselves. On the screen behind him, images appeared of this same kid, his hair slicked back with gel, using a garden hose to water the animal innards that filled the engine compartment of a car. A girl was squeezing a tube of red tempera all over the viscera and the open hood, a theatrically robotic expression on her face. Behind the stage, a young Carmen Miranda (with the requisite headpiece of bananas and cucumbers, the dark hair and exuberantly crimson mouth) crouched down to check the cables.

Otto and Pebeteen donned motorcycle helmets and walked up on stage. Each had a keytar strung across his chest—a common cumbia instrument. Pebeteen wore a zarzuela-style polka dot dress; he was short, thin, white-skinned. Otto on the other hand was tall, well-proportioned, shirtless in black sweatpants. Together they lip-synched the Satanist version of a Kraftwerk song. After a while, Otto smashed his keytar across Pebeteen's helmet; Pebeteen, not the least bit intimidated, raised his own instrument and hammered Otto's thought-dome in turn. They went back and forth like this for some time.

The *choris cósmicos* were for sale at a stand in back, watched over by a friendly local fat guy and his brood. Little Kamtchowsky wolfed down her grilled sausage to the catchy rhythm of "La bomba" as sung by Carmen Miranda, who tapped her foot but was otherwise motionless. Then all the lights went out except for a few flickering yellow beams accompanied by a low frequency pedal effect, amorphous. The stage filled with mysterious figures dressed in black, wearing black helmets, brandishing machine guns that fired brilliant red beams of light.

ON THE FLOOR! EVERYBODY ON THE FLOOR! HANDS ON TOP OF YOUR HEAD!

Everyone obeyed, hiding their heads in their hands. The commandos walked amongst the prostrate bodies. They repeated the orders, shouted them over and over, swinging their weapons expressively left and right. Some of the people on the floor covered their plastic cups with their hands to keep from spilling. The noise grew deafening. ON THE FUCKING FLOOR! And now a police siren. Contagious laughter revealed that with this simulation of a simulation of a massacre, the show had come to its climax. The bodies of the dead crawled over one another, their arms and legs tangling, a mass of trembling tentacles. The shouted order changed to "Hands in the air!" just as the Pibes Chorros song of the same name started to play, and at the back wall a ritual took place—a poster was set on fire, some guy with a Leibnizian wig.

Llegamos los pibes chorros
queremos las manos de todos arriba
porque al primero que se haga el ortiba
por pancho y careta le vamos a dar.[xi]

After a while Kamtchowsky had had enough of being alternately astonished and bored, and went to look for a bathroom. Such trips were intimately connected to the core of her personality, linked as they were to general notions of female camaraderie and volubility. Between the ages of twelve and seventeen, whenever Kamtchowsky and her friends had announced that they were going to the bathroom, they were in fact about to "take a walk around," a tactical euphemism for getting a sense of the lay of the land, discovering who had come and where they could be found. Nothing memorable ever occurred, but the ritual kept them alert to possible interactions with the opposite sex.

In the course of this current expedition, she rubbed more or less lasciviously against twenty people or so; the spatial rhetoric of the hallway encouraged such flirting. The tightly packed bodies slowed her forward motion, and the low light turned everything red—not just her thoughts. At the end of the hallway she saw a half-open door and an old sink; once inside she noticed two boys smiling at her. One had curly red hair, was twenty-two or so, and quite cute; the other wore a checkered beanie and was extremely pale, infantile, disfigured, as if a very weak acid produced by some morbid form of maternal love had subtly corroded his features.

Kamtchowsky smiled back at them, and realized that she was mimicking Mara's seductive little gestures. The boys stood there, wordless. They look like imbeciles, she thought. She saw that on the toilet seat cover there was a swastika drawn in white powder; it made her feel dangerous. She gave a little hop, went to her knees, hunched forward and inhaled through her lucky dollar bill. Under the sweet gaze of her new friends, Kamtchowsky's bodily organism took in about two grams of ketamine, a general anesthetic often used on animals. The drug selectively diminishes the power of association in the cortex and thalamus, producing a dissociative phenomenon similar to an "out of body" experience. Kamtchowsky gasped for air—the chemical had gone in like a punch. The kid in the beanie drew near. He opened her left eye with his fingers and observed the behavior of her pupil. Kamtchowsky opened her mouth to speak; three seconds passed, and now she'd lost all control of her body. This discovery occurred just as she was formulating a desire: she wanted to make her way back to that packed hallway where acceptance came freely, but her legs would not respond.

Montaigne theorized that handicapped people make the best sexual partners, because the nutrients that would have served a given extremity are rerouted to the genitalia. Kamtchowsky had never heard of this, but mysteriously enough, she was in a position to provide corroboration of a sort. His name was Miguel; professionally speaking, he was the first differently-abled young man ever to be chosen Employee of the Month.

One afternoon back in April, at a McDonald's in the Belgrano district, she had ordered a McFiesta, and noticed that Miguel wanted to look her in the eyes as he handled her order, but couldn't quite manage it. Someone less romantic than Kamtchowsky would have admitted to herself that this was just because he was totally cross-eyed. Miguel, with all the aplomb that the scene required, invited her to join the McTour that was just beginning. Kamtchowsky, french fries and small soft drink in hand, couldn't bring herself to say no.

A dark-haired young man with a name tag reading "Germán" and a Mickey, two Minnies and a Ronald pinned to his tie—the equivalent of a *condestable* in the Napoleonic army—introduced himself as their guide, and led them down the line of cash registers. The other McTour guests were five eleven-year-olds in private school uniforms; they looked Kamtchowsky slowly up and down to make it clear that she didn't belong. Germán appeared not to have noticed the polarities that were destabilizing the group of humans under his command, concentrated as he was on more basic issues.

He spoke about the unique qualities of cheddar cheese and barbecue sauce, about maintaining the integrity of the cold chain, about the division of labor and the importance of creating value in order to build a better world: the very pillars of the McDonald's philosophy. Kamtchowsky listened carefully, calmly eating her French fries; from time to time she slipped in sarcastic questions of cryptic relevance, such as, Where *exactly* does Ronald McDonald live? and, What are the earliest symptoms of an *Escherichia coli* infection? Then out of nowhere, Miguel pressed his incandescent organ up against the Kamtchowskyan rearguard.

The indulgence often employed to mitigate the frenzy of such desire—the danger implicit in this type of lust—is downright legendary. Kamtchowsky turned to him in slow motion, but before she could raise a hand to slap him across the face, his bionic lips clamped on to her upper arm, and he began rubbing himself rhythmically against her near leg. The McTour had left them behind; even the slowest of the children had turned the far corner toward the refrigeration units that kept the chicken-based foodstuffs in optimum condition. Kamtchowsky brought her hands down, trying to protect herself, to parry his desperation. Miguel whipped out his private parts; seconds later he ejaculated onto Kamtchowsky's palms. Then, seeing that the McTour and its host of children were coming back, Miguel flew like a meteorite to the soft-serve ice cream machine, pushed the red button, and came back with a vanilla cone; realizing that he hadn't brought her any napkins with which to tidy up, he lowered his little pink mouth to her sticky hands and sucked them clean.

Kamtchowsky was reminded of Proposition IX, Part III of Spinoza's *Ethics*: Desire is "appetite accompanied by the consciousness thereof." Unable to exit the lane of pseudo-erudite mental associations down which she'd been swept, she also recalled an homage to Spinoza: the Borges sonnet about the Jewish hands. Miguel's gesture had been both ironic and protective, and she accepted the vanilla cone.

It amused her, the wisdom with which everything returned to normal. Thanks very much, she murmured, still shocked by what had happened. Then Miguel asked for her telephone number.

Kamtchowsky's hand was twisted brutally up behind her back, all the way to her shoulder blade; the rest of her body slipped off the toilet seat cover. She couldn't control her movements. She imagined that she was dead at the medullar level, that her body was being held hostage, captive to an optical nightmare, her eyes bisected by a plane that distorted her vision, as if she were watching the scene from two meters behind herself. She instinctively wanted to cover up, to protect her intimate parts; at the same time, something in the lower half of her body seemed to enjoy being exposed to the elements. Beanie, his pants down around his knees, worked his penis this way and that, trying to fit it into one or another of Kamtchowsky's holes. Curls, more pragmatically, took her by the hips and flipped her around, then drew her toward him. Suddenly Kamtchowsky's thoughts began to see themselves spatially: a burst of mental gunfire sprayed against a vortex where Curls had one eye open wide and was gasping, his teeth bared.

Hidden in the glowing fist of her very selfhood, she watched out of the corner of her eye. There was something sweet and triumphant in all this. She couldn't move. A strange peace came over her, a protothought in italics: *They are like bears, and I am the honey.* The door had been left half open, and *here come even more kids unbuckling their belts* (italics Kamtchowsky's). It was her body that attracted and distributed these vectors of manhood: this certainty lit her up inside. The fact that they were so desperate to intersect with the geometry of her flesh, that the vectors might crisscross in and toward her, that she might be the center of projection—all this made them in some way subordinate to *her*. One of those who'd just entered took out his cellphone and started recording; a few days later a video labeled *somegirl.avi* could be downloaded from any number of blogs and webpages.

Over at the bar, Mara and Pabst took their time eating their choripanes. It was the first time they'd ever found themselves alone together against the masses. Andy had wandered off to buy drugs or sell them, they weren't sure which; Kamtchowsky, they thought, was standing in line for the bathroom, which is why she was taking so long. Now there were shrieks, people running, others perking up their ears—a *performance* was about to start. The stage lights spun until they were shining directly into the audience's faces. Pabst instinctively closed his eyes; he found people expressing themselves enormously troubling.

On stage, the light came to rest on a young guy, his face decorated with glitter and brightly colored paint, his naked torso lined with lengths of Scotch tape. He began rubbing his chest with a piece of paper, muttering, "Text, text," louder and louder. Then five guys in yellow raincoats came to stand in a row facing the audience, unmoving. At the command "Gesture, gesture!" they opened their raincoats wide, showing bikini briefs hung with black ribbons. The Text guy shouted orders and the Gesture guys obeyed, throwing themselves to the floor, spitting on one another, biting each other, playing dead.

Pabst thought he recognized a certain Gallimardian odor coming off one of the texts, and said:

–At certain times of crisis, all myopic dwarves can be swapped out for priests who read Céline.

The kid in the bowler hat walked across the platform in his underwear, laughing. He tested the microphone that hung down over an array of soft drink bottles, fifteen of them or so. The stage lights made the bottles glow. A fat guy from Holland supervised the action; he wore a black T-shirt with a white skeleton on it, and a piano tie. Pabst took advantage of the pause to slide a few xenophobic notes into Mara's ear:

–These poorly educated Europeans emigrate in search of a culturally backward paradise where they can display whatever leadership qualities they possess against a background of urban third-worldness. They're just neighborhood demagogues pretending to be part of the vanguard here where it's easier to be such a thing, and then bragging about how cheap the rent is to their supermarket manager friends in Münster or Riga or Rouen. This is how they propagate the private mythology according to which the crest of their lives *still* hasn't completely passed them by.

Mara agreed delightedly.

The cap on every bottle had been tightened to a different degree, such that the gas escaping from each hissed out at a different frequency. The Dutch guy placed a little plastic chair in amongst the bottles; he took a seat, and very calmly removed his T-shirt. The kid dressed as a native stuck a number of sensors to the Dutch guy's belly, highly sensitive microphones that caught the sounds emanating from his intestinal domains.

The fat guy's stomach began to emit a series of subtle alien complaints; minor chords, meek at times, like someone doubting something, or asking a question. The thesis statement of his message to the human masses curled its way around to their delicate eardrums. On an electric signboard the little red lights spelled out:

> OH COME, BOARD THE TRAIN OF CONSCIOUSNESS OF THE INANIMATE. OH, CAN'T YOU SEE THAT PEOPLE AND PERSONALITIES ARE ONLY FALLACIES? COMPLETELY OVERVALUED FALLACIES! YOU ARE NOTHING MORE THAN AN ORGAN, AN ORGAN INSIDE A PURE SENTENCE, AN ORGANIZATIONAL CHART. FEEL THE ORGANICNESS OF THE ORGANIZATIONAL CHART, THE PUBLIC-PRIVATE HYMN THAT SPEAKS WITHIN YOU.

Andy returned to the environs of the bar accompanied by a pair of enthusiastic drug addicts ("I'm telling you, there isn't a single party, I promise you, not a single party in the world that is better than this one RIGHT NOW, nowhere in the world!") A guy who introduced himself as a "self-taught alchemist" offered them homemade absinthe, natural amphetamines, and cocaine made from animal placentas, all of which Mara politely declined. Andy glowed with sweat, which served only to highlight his firm, harmonious musculature. Mara covered his face with kisses, and they both laughed. I hope they don't start feeling each other up right in front of me, thought Pabst, who was starting to hate Kamtchowsky for leaving him alone so long.

His tongue still inside Mara's mouth, Andy handed Pabst a little plastic bag. Pabst took a disdainful look, and saw the pills inside.

–*This the very coinage of your brain*, quoted Andy, radiant. *This bodiless creation*, *ecstasy*, *is very cunning in*.

Pabst groaned something unintelligible; he enjoyed being difficult. A capsule slid into Mara's mouth while he was still whinging and trying to make up his mind.

–*Ecstasy! My pulse*, *as yours*, *doth temperately keep time*.

Andy closed the little bag, abandoned Hamlet and became more specific:

–I took a tab of ketamine, three pills, smoked two joints, did a little popper, two lines, a shot of grapita, a couple of—

–How can you even fit all that stuff inside?

There was no disdain in Pabst's words now; nor was their admiration, or even neutrality. Andy put a hand on his shoulder.

–Don't worry about it. The only neurons that die are the ones that got left behind, the stupidest ones. Drugs are natural selection's neuro-chemical means of determining the fastest and fittest members of the cerebral ecosystem.

Andy winked, and threw his head back for a drink of water; then he said hello to young Ludwig, who was likewise intoxicated. The kid now standing beside Pabst was panting hard. Everyone called him Woody Woodpecker—he didn't have red hair, but he did have a very wide forehead, and eyes that were perpetually on the verge of popping out. Pabst briefly imagined him pecking at a tree trunk; it wasn't pleasant. He was tempted to say *Rajá, turrito, rajá* but was afraid the kid would think he was quoting *Tango feroz* (1993) rather than the living-dead Roberto Arlt. He remembered the movie's plot with a fierce clarity: Tanguito smokes a joint, spends some time in jail, tangoes naked to "Malevaje" while pawing at the backside of his romantic interest, a *chica bien*, i.e. a rich, blond, treacherous snob. Basically he gets the shit beat out of him for being filthy, a drug addict, and a lover of Argentine rock and roll, all of which are more or less the same thing in this case. Near the end, a home movie shows him surrounded by his gang of filthy friends, and he secretes a posthumous rumination: "Not everything can be bought, and not everything's for sale." Cecilia Dopazo's high boots had caused quite a stir—she waved them around in the air each time they fucked. In addition to being a professional failure for the actors involved, the film was also a macabre premonition of the times to come. Pabst took Woody by the shoulder and let slip a reflection:

–Nothing is as disgusting as the theatrical capitalism developed by the left to sell their products. It's the kind of banality you often see in victorious sociological models: the practical syllogism according to which the truth is, by definition, on the side of the poor and afflicted for no reason other than that it flatters the reigning "democratic ideal" and a whole string of other euphemisms which must likewise never be interrogated. And the presence of a triumphant left in the cultural realm has consequences that are much worse than just bad movies. We watch bad movies because, as spectators, we've been condemned to the role of self-obsessed bourgeois ethnologists; *downwardly* self-obsessed. The victim's story is transformed into fable, and the poisonous air that envelops all notions of hierarchy and authority—notions that one so obviously must reject—now enfolds a fresh new operation: being victims protects us from any and all moral or ethical judgments regarding our actions. Police violence erases all previous acts, granting automatic sainthood to the unimpeachably virtuous victim. It's a good way to lose a war; in return one achieves a moral victory built on a philosophically flawed foundation.

Pabst fell quiet. The monologue had gotten him so worked up that his hands were trembling. Woody looked at him for half a second; Pabst noticed just as the kid was turning away, and kindly started talking again, in case anything hadn't been clear:

–Actually, it doesn't matter whether they've got their fist in the air (like in the '70s) or whether they've withdrawn all their threats (not that they could have made good on them regardless)—the left's lack of any real political strategies or texts served as nesting grounds for a *Zeitgeist* of settling for a stack of mediocrities, which is clearly all they were ever going to have to offer anyway.

And where had Kamtchowsky gone? He didn't like it

when she wandered off alone for so long. She wasn't with Mara, who was dancing cumbia up near the stage with B. and some girlfriends who taught in the French Department. Woody and Andy headed off to the bathroom for a snort of ketamine, and Pablo followed along behind.

2

Andy's shadow poured water over its head as it walked across the room—an obvious nod to Sigfrido Cutzarida's legendary Colbert Noir cologne ad. The lesbian modality of Andy's girlfriend was stretched out next to Pabst's girlfriend, their four long legs stretching up the wall, encaging the image of the 9 de Julio Expressway cut in two.

Pabst was curled up in a beanbag chair; he blinked as his dreams fell away, and pawed at his pants to make sure that his dong, flecked with dried semen, was safely out of the light. Outside it was sunny, probably; the Persian blinds were always closed, and the only light inside was electric. Andy widened his stance, stuck his hands in his pockets; his shadow now fell over the empty section of his desk where the CPU should have been. A few seconds passed.

Pabst opened one eye. There before him was Andy's crotch, its oblique geography elegantly arranged. *Zarpe Diem* was over and Kamtchowsky was asleep with Mara; Andy had fucked them both, Pabst hadn't, and there wasn't anything left to say. Spilled green tea had seeped into the flooring, and there were grains of rice stuck to the carpet. The television was on—the cheesy showgirl Moria Casán at the dawn of her mammiferous career. She was wearing a fuchsia wig, and had her fingernails buried in the wig of another showgirl, who looked a little like Luisa Albinoni. Without taking his eyes off the screen, Andy sat down on the floor.

–Our national sickness is definitely the hair weave.

Pabst looked at his friend, whose eyes were still boring into Moria; he remembered Sarmiento's bald pate, and let loose a spontaneous laugh.

Beside him was a stack of photocopies and a few effusively underlined books. Farther back, something shone in the dark, a piece of foil paper from a box of Sweet Mints, signaling the side entrance—far from the end—to the third chapter, the key to the evolution of the Theory of Egoic Transmissions.

3

I built the temple of Mars Ultor on private grounds and the forum of Augustus from war-spoils. Three times I gave shows of gladiators under my name and five times under the name of my sons and grandsons; in these shows about 10,000 men fought. I celebrated the Games under my name four times, and twenty-three times in place of other magistrates. Twenty-six times, under my name or that of my sons and grandsons, I gave the people hunts of African beasts in the circus, under the open sky, or in the amphitheater; in them about 3,500 beasts were killed.

The Deeds of the Divine Augustus abounds in passages where the words *bestia* and *venationes* are continuously intermixed to refer to Roman Games involving predators. In Suetonius we find *damnare aliquem ad bestias*, condemned to be torn apart by wild beasts. *Bestia* (in its first Latin declension, typically feminine) means *of obscure origin*, but its lexical importance to the Games led to the addition of human suffixes. *Bestius* and *bestiarius*, in Seneca and

Tertullian, are those condemned to be devoured by beasts; Cicero's usage refers to the gladiator who fights against them. Augustine of Hippo uses the adverb *bestialiter*—as would a beast, in a beastly manner—and keeps *bestiarius* separate to refer to the attributes of the beasts themselves; *bestius* is that which is ferocious, beast-like.

On the side of the beasts, one finds the lion of Biledulgerid, the leopard of Hindustan, the desert antelope, the British stag, and the Arctic reindeer; the albino bull of Northumberland, the unicorn of Tibet, the hippopotamus of the African coast and the elephant of Siam; ibex from Angora, the wild ass, dwarf giraffes, ostriches and zebras. "Their savage voices ascended in tumultuous uproar to the chambers of the capitol," (writes De Quincey) before the majesty of Jupiter Tonans—Caesar Augustus. On the side of the beasts, men crouched and ready for combat.

From a grammatical point of view, there is nothing keeping a man from converting himself into a beast; *bestius*, the ferocious beast-like creature who flaunts his beauty and deformity on the vast blood-fields of Rome, relies on his syntactic position to tell him which side he is killing for, which beast to strike. The name of the victim coincides with that of the aggressor—in the arena every beast is alike. It is thus only the beast's *place* within the sentence that determines its ontological nature, indicating *what* it is that one is. *Beast* can refer either to the one representing the State's power of Reason (in which case the spectacle consists of ripping apart some enemy of Rome—a Christian, a barbarian, et cetera), or to the one who is to be chased down by the sovereign human (in which case the human victor is celebrated by the multitudes, and what he annihilates is merely prey supplied to him by the Games).

The beauty of the beast—she of obscure origins—is displayed diachronically. In Latin, *bello*, *-avi*, *-atum* is the verbal form meaning *to wage and carry on war*, *to make war*. The dictionary follows these bellicose forms of *bello* with the adverbial forms of *belle*, used to indicate that something has been prepared deliciously well (*Attica belle se habet)*; exquisitely, with good taste and elegance, *praediola belle edificata*—small possessions built with taste (Cicero). We proceed past "Sweetly, softly, deliciously, delicately; in a kind, funny, friendly manner" to Bellerophon, grandson of Sisyphus, and from there to *bellicum*: in Cicero and Justinian, the word refers to a signal—a call to arms, to battle stations—which, in the field of rhetorical operations, is the moderately disdainful slap in the face that Cicero delivers with *bellicum:* "to strike a haughty tone." But *bellua* (of obscure origins) is the ferocious beast, the savage animal; *fera et immanis bellua*—cruel and ferocious beast. A monster, a monstrous thing; in Livy (a contemporary of Caesar Augustus), we find *Volo ego illi bellua ostendere*, meaning "I want to show this savage, this great beast, what goodness is" (note *bellua* at the center of the threat). *Bellipotens* (the God of War in Virgil) rests on *bellitudo*: loveliness, grace, beauty.

These are the roots that beauty and war have in common. This is the philological triangle of charm and brutality on the verge of blowing apart:

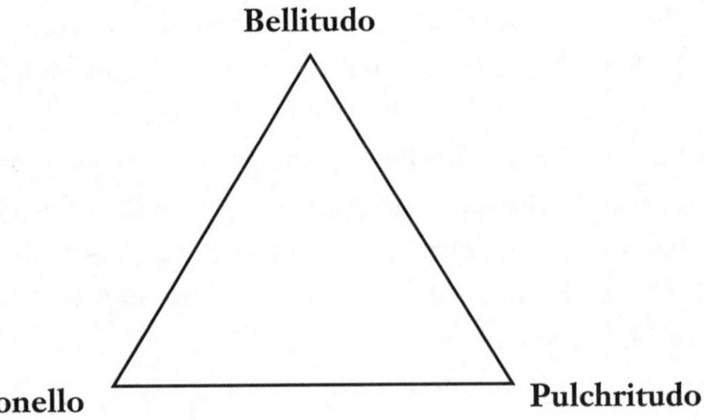

Each of the three vertices, the three synonyms for beauty, is a vector projected through time. *Bonello* mutates toward the idea of *bueno*, the good, conserving its roots in Spanish; it is the aspect of beauty that is carved out by the moral sense. *Pulchritudo* is the beauty that adorns the harmonic ratio of the precise, the ordered, the hygienic; the *pulchrum* posits the beautiful in opposition to the repugnant. *Pulchrum* and *bonello* are the facets of a Platonic diamond wherein what shines is Being itself. *Bellitudo* alone of the three synonyms has not been domesticated by Platonic ideals, by the imposition of pure being, the astral house of the just, the good. *Bellitudo* is beauty inhabited by war, much as beauty inhabits war. *Bellitudo* encloses a tumultuous seed: the beauty of the *bellum*, wherein roars the deadly, predatory nature of the *bestia*, the *bellua*, synthesis of sovereign Eros and Mars the Seducer.

The Deeds of the Divine Augustus contains several important illustrations, among them a reproduction of the central frieze of the temple of Mars the Avenger. As is all too well known—and there is nothing the least bit personal in this comment—in that frieze, Vulcan stands outside the temple calling desperately for Venus, unable to do anything about the fact that she has already left with Mars, her lover, at whom she smiles sweetly, enjoying her act of betrayal.

All of which reminds me of a certain accursed afternoon in the labyrinth that is the top floor of the Philosophy and Letters building. Augustus was walking hurriedly, poking around in one of his shirt pockets, the one where he always keeps his cigarettes and that pelican-blue Mont Blanc they gave him when he won the Ezequiel Martínez Estrada National Essay Prize. He was carrying folders, books, loose papers . . . and perhaps a manila envelope, one enclosing a dazzling message signed by Rosa Ostreech?[10]

Reacting quickly, I hid. It wasn't that I was afraid to see him or speak to him, but that I am wholly and terrifiedly conscious of the fact that words spoken aloud (the mysterious syntax nested within them) determine and actualize *transcendentally* the events in which they are embedded. My derailed heart beat wildly; when I saw that he was turning in my direction, I lost all control of my muscles and waved hello, the fat tome in my hand thrashing back and forth overhead. For an instant, it seemed that he'd noticed the eagle of my gaze alighting beside him, and was turning away. But I calmly watched as the scene played out—and in the end, the dove of peace devoured the raptor.

In his attempt to avoid a frontal encounter with an Ethics

10 This is the name behind which your faithful narrator hides.

adjunct who was dragging her existence through the vicinity, he failed to notice that the dark heavy object in my hand was nothing less than a volume of Byron. (In the previous class, Augustus had devoted a rather inopportune interlude to a number of "encrypted" sonnets that some dangerous madwoman had offered up to the poet, who wanted nothing to do with her, hated her and did everything possible to avoid her letters, propositions, and company. At one point it got so bad that he'd had to chase her away in public, in the middle of the town square.) I'd been looking for the passage Augustus had quoted, but still hadn't found it—in the annals of English philology, the title *Complete Works* is invariably either fraudulent or blasphemous. Of course, the Ethics adjunct couldn't infer anything from any of this; she deftly intercepted my dear theoretician, and poor ashen Augustus prolonged the lively encounter as if it were some Ciceronian *sententia*.

That would have been my final assessment of the episode, but then I detected the equine shadow of the odious one at the end of the hallway; her hair was tied up in a little bun, and her eyes were fixed on me. When he managed to free himself from the Ethics adjunct, Augustus headed directly for *that woman*, and she whispered something to him, whispered it almost directly into his ear. Both of them turned to look at me. Their lips continued to move.

I walked back to my house, kicking at piles of leaves and stepping in dog shit. Barely in through the door of my *pied-à-terre*, I realized that I'd forgotten to feed little Montaigne, who mewed resentfully as I crossed through the rarified darkness. As for Yorick, he'd managed to survive Montaigne's kittenish hunger, and was swimming peacefully in his bowl. I found the whole scene very moving. So many days without them. As if in slow motion, Yorick floated up to eat the food that drifted down through the rising bubbles. To please him, I brought a mirror up to the side of the bowl. He immediately went on high alert; he intended to fight this intruder, this other fish, this stranger swimming in front of him. I let him play like this for a time. When he began to tire, I covered the mirror, and instantly his feathery blood-red dorsal fin began to swell: the other had withdrawn, and Yorick had triumphed. The individual consciousness is a function of one's vanity, whose rank determines the body's spectra of possibilities. The truth of this axiom is verifiable even in populations most often ignored in psycho-political studies, including cold-blooded animals, whose miniature brains hearken back to pre-mammalian evolutionary phases. Oh the things I've never told you, Augustus, the things I've kept to myself.

Watching my pets at play, I get a sense of how the Voice who organizes the tale returns to float above her prey like some logical, succinct she-wolf. In short, Augustus, I just don't know. It's hard for me to keep going, following your signals. I let my thoughts travel through the dark until I can no longer hear them. When a state of amorous emergency is declared, the sovereign takes control of others' lives. He looks out over the long line of heads bowed in his honor, the long white strip that is the napes of the necks of those who revere him, and he rises, looks again at those necks: inside runs that which is surrendered in silence. He contemplates, he deciphers, he rises. But if he were up in the heavens, what would he see?

A canopy of black branches hanging over the pastures. Open spaces like stains; the black branches interlocked, a coven of spiders. Oily, dark green undergrowth. Black birds spiraling. Glittering fog, dragging itself along the grass. Totora reeds. A small boat at anchor, a barking dog.

Your hostage is down there. Motionless, somewhere.

4

Kamtchowsky made her way to 3960 Lt. General Domingo Perón Avenue: the Ronald McDonald House. She and Miguel had agreed to meet at six in the afternoon; just because he had Down syndrome, she reasoned, didn't mean he'd keep her waiting for an hour. Of course he did, but K had something to read to keep herself entertained, and her ass was perfectly comfortable—it was only the slightest bit wider than the stair on which she sat.

The text she had in hand had been a most fortuitous acquisition. On her way to this date with Miguel, Kamtchowsky had descried a hamster-colored mane next to the ticket machine in the Malabia station on the B line. They hadn't seen each other in months; her mother gave her a kiss, asked how she was doing, and informed her that she was on her way back from a meeting with the guys at the publisher. She had with her the proofs of Aunt Vivi's diary, and the book was almost ready. Do you want to have a look? Her mother's little claws, the hamstery hair on her forearms, the manuscript held out. Kamtchowsky took it with a smile. Vivi's notebooks had been her favorite thing to read as a child, not counting Emilio Salgari, the *Sissi* comic book series, the sagas of female inmates, and Che Guevara's diary, and also not counting the casuistic tomes of child psychiatry that infested the family library. Then when she was twelve or so, her mother had hidden the treasured notebooks and forbidden her to read them, without explaining why. And now the two women, who looked so unalike that no one would have taken them for mother and daughter, said their quick goodbyes.

Dear Moo:

On Monday I pulled on some jeans and an Oriental blouse, put on my new blue eyeshadow, and headed out. I'm tired, Moo, and it feels wrong to keep myself hidden safely indoors, cursing my country's fate. I feel like I have to do something, like the current situation is unsustainable, like something's got to give. I met up with Fernando, the dark-haired guy from the unit, remember? We sang beautiful songs about love and the battle for justice. He doesn't know that I'm a member of the Pro-China Insurgency Alliance—I'm pretty sure he thinks that any day now I'm going to sign up with his group. Anyway, I don't think we're going to be seeing each other much longer. Something pretty awful happened, Moo. I don't even know if I should tell you. We had sex. It was extremely pleasant. That wasn't the problem. But first he wanted me to give him, well, a fellatio, with my mouth, on his penis. I'd done it before with L., and before that just once with Juan Carlos. Fernando and I were kissing and he grabbed my head and pushed it downward, softly but firmly. I stopped right there in front of his thingy, so nervous that I started to laugh. It was if his dong was looking at me, saying hello like some merry caterpillar, coming happily up to see me as I went down. It was still half-covered by its little sleeve, and Fer (he always asked me to call him Fer) gave me a small, seductive smile. Then he started reciting a poem by Nicolás Guillén:

> I'm impure, what do you want me to say?
> That I love (women, naturally,
> my love dares to speak its name),
> and I love to eat pork with potatoes,
> and garbanzos and chorizo, and
> eggs, chicken, veal, turkey,
> fish and seafood,
> and I drink rum and beer and cane liquor and
> wine
> and I fornicate (even on a full stomach).

Fernando was still licking my ear at this point, and started kind of singing the poem, quietly (and with the accent of a Spaniard, though Guillén, as far as I know, is Cuban):

> I believe that there are many pure things in
> the world

that are nothing but pure shit.
The purity of clerics.
The purity of academics.
The purity of grammarians.
The purity of those who assure you
that you have to be pure, pure, pure.
The purity of those who've never had gonorrhea.
The purity of the woman who's never licked a glans.

Whoa, I thought! Nice way to make a "suggestion"! I gathered myself up to kiss him on the mouth, and I lifted my skirt to show him that I wanted it too, that I desired him, that we were still going to have sex and there wasn't any reason to make a big deal about it. What?! he said. You're not going to do it? (He was talking about the other thing.) He said that I was a prude with bourgeois values down to the marrow. That he'd thought I was different. That there is no sensation more beautiful than feeling the happiness spurting up out of someone else's body, and that he regretted having been so honest with me. But really, what was he thinking? That being honest and "winning" are synonyms? I told him that he was completely wrong. That I am a true revolutionary, and a member of the Pro-China Revolutionary Insurgency Alliance. He didn't believe me, so I showed him your official Party photographs and your Little Red Book. His face went deadly serious, and he started in with, Well, of course, of course you're one of those craven sepoy leftists. He said that any serious Marxist analysis of the Argentine situation would demonstrate the unrenounceable responsibility to unite with the Peronist masses. That I'm not on the side of the people and never will be. That I'd better get rid of all my Maoist books and photos or I'd end up in serious trouble. I felt awful. The argument kept getting louder and louder—he all but shouted that I was some prissy imperialist pro-Yankee proto-fascist bimbo.

Son of a bitch. I just don't get them, you know? I can't, I can't . . . Talking to you like this, having to talk to you like this, it seems like some macabre joke. Because you're a man too. I don't even want to think about this, don't want to, I want to act as if . . .

Later, looking for a little support, I met up with some people from the Party. Alcira and I drank some mate, *and she told me about L. She said that he's dating someone named Silvina. I got pissed off and told her everything. She said that I should go find this Silvina and settle things with her. That you can't trust men. That if Silvina was a full-fledged revolutionary and knew that L. was my man—well, if she was* truly *a revolutionary, she'd be in favor of abolishing private property, would say that if you're happy thinking of him as yours, then fuck you, go ahead and think it all you want, but nobody belongs to anyone else. Anyway, Alcira said, in the end your little speech might get out of hand, but Silvina's the one who would end up walking away. There are tons of guys out there, she said, especially in the Montoneros, tons of cute guys, much cuter than L. (I didn't get mad when she said this—she was just trying to make me feel better.) The thing is, I said, I'm all in favor of personal liberty, and as for abolishing private property, god, that goes without saying, but the problem is that I don't feel the need to be with any body except his; what I want is to be with him, and if I felt the need for someone else, well, I'd sign right up for open relationships and everything else, but I'd do it for real, I'd totally commit to it, not just say "fine" with a nod while my mind was somewhere else. The thing is, (this is still me talking to Alcira here,) L. would say that I'm contradicting myself, that I can't fight for the principles of social change out in the street and then forget them once I'm back home. Because the revolution is needed everywhere, Moo, and whoever doesn't like that can get as mad as they want, and then get lost. So I said, Fine, Alcira, why don't we heighten the contradictions? I'm going to find L. and say, If you don't want to be with me, tell me and we'll end things once and for all, goodbye to what we've shared, goodbye to our projects, and give me back all those Benedetti and Rimbaud books I lent you. Well, said Alcira, you don't have be so drastic. I thanked her for talking with me—she's the only one beside you, Moo, that I can talk to about these things. She told me to be careful about keeping a diary, that they can be extremely compromising evidence. Then she leaned back in her chair and gave me a serious look.*

Later I realized she told my superior everything, because the next day they called a meeting and said that as

Party militants we couldn't hold onto personal documents that might put anyone at risk—our comrades, ourselves, the Party itself; that as residents in a bourgeois society that has a century and a half of experience in total domination, we have to remain vigilant, able to foresee any and all reactionary violence on the part of the consorts of power, and so on and so forth for two hours.

They don't want me to write to you, Moo. The Party has forbidden the writing of texts documenting the past. They forbid the use of memory, Moo, and many of them don't understand that a revolution is built of both ideas and blood. The blood of thought, and the thought of blood. All the same, I know that Alcira had nothing but good intentions, that she did what she did because she felt it was her duty to protect me. I don't feel betrayed. She's a good comrade, and supports the revolution with all her might. The day that girl loses a little weight she's going to find a bunch of guys attracted to her kindness and intelligence.

I am so worried, Moo. I read and read all day long to get away from that feeling of anxiety. I just finished Eduardo Galeano's Vagamundo. *Alcira told me that a friend of hers had gotten together with him at work, a girl who writes for* Crisis. *(Guess who it was! Ha ha, yeah, Marisa, who always seems so prim and proper!) Galeano is a complete intellectual, totally committed to the cause. Just like Sabato, only cuter. Apparently Galeano likes to date several women at once. Still, it seems to me that Marisa is responsible for whatever happened. She gave herself to him too quickly. And look, he's a really great guy, maybe twenty years older than her, and Marisa, you whisper two words in her ear and boom, she's spreading her legs, giving up the treasure. I think her case is totally different from mine. L. and I had made our way together up a path of shared ideas, convictions and projects; it's not like one day we started merrily screwing our brains out and the next day I was complaining about him not respecting me. And also, L. and I are almost the same age, while Galeano is maybe twenty-five years older than Marisa. Boy, I don't know, Moo, all this talk about the miseries of others has me thinking about L., but from a place where there are no hard feelings, where peace is the only goal. Peace, that's what I need. I want to get away from everything that follows you around and fucks with your head, and dedicate myself to just being alive. I'm going to sign up for a Physical Theater course. That will help, will do me good.*

On top of all that, I have to get a root canal. While I was at the dentist's office, I was paging through a copy of Para Ti, *(believe me, Moo, the situation was dire—my only other options were* Great Chess Moves *and* Today's Textiles) *and I happened to open the magazine right to a personality test called, "What is hiding behind that mole?" There was a drawing of a face covered with numbers; each number stood for the location of a mole. I copied down the meanings of the ones that really caught my eye—actually, they're the moles L. has.*

05. Marriage to a celebrity, or at least to someone extremely important.

20. A sense of family.

29. Your sensuality needs to be expressed.

21. Be careful around water.

43. You love your independence.

30. You're vulnerable to flattery.

09. Predisposed to significant blows to the head.

36. A strong sense of order.

34. Erotic nature. If it's close to your nostril, that indicates a eventful fate.

35. Passionate, willful, irresistible.

40. Physical love predominates over sentimental love.

39. Happiness (of every kind).

It seems to me that #36 and #43 contradict one another a bit. Especially considering that L's biggest mole corresponds to #20. Unquestionably, though, #30, #43, and #29 all point at the same thing. Even if #29 is maybe a freckle, not a mole. Is #40 dominating his life just because he happens to be going through a particularly shitty period? Or is it the other way around? #9 is so weird. Is that what's going to happen to him? Will that mole disappear over time? #34 is totally true. L. has always been very passionate (#35) and his eyes glow with the promise of an amazing future. I hope he never reads #5.

Next I read my horoscope, and copied it down to see what you think of it:

Miss Sagitarius, and Her Relation to the Other Signs—Week of August 23.

With Mr. Taurus: You will find it difficult to control his love of independence. Mr. Taurus is extremely jealous, so your relationship with him will be tumultuous. He wants you to be an integral part of his life, to renounce your own independence and rights. You will become furious, and will tell him so. The two of you will wound one another. If your mutual regret is sincere, the relationship may be able to turn the page. But it would not be unusual if within a week you were once again starting from scratch. YOU MUST: leave your whims at the door, and make an effort to control your impulses. Remember this! Danger of the Week: making "intimate" confessions. Be very careful! Advice: date optimists.

It's true, Moo, that we have wounded one another. L. and I, and also Fernando and I—they're both Taurus. I got a little worried, not because of what the horoscope says, but just remembering what happened. I also think that we women have much more responsibility than it might seem at first glance. It's as if we have somehow been assigned two missions, one of peace and one of class struggle—we're never allowed to drop our feminine role as the one who provides love and security, yet we're responsible for destroying the bourgeois structures of alienation that limit us in so many ways (limit us as human beings, I mean). The dentist still hadn't called me in, and I kept reading. Next was the "Secrets from the Confessional" section.

Ema, from Barrio Norte: I'm twenty-four years old, married, two kids, a good job. But one day my husband and I had an argument about how much time I spend on the telephone, and since then he's started drinking too much, and hitting me. What can I do?

Para Ti: Under no circumstances should you let him hit you. That is a serious crime, and you never should have allowed it. But you also shouldn't have provoked such a violent attitude. Why do you spend so much time talking on the telephone, and with whom? I would also try to find out why he's drinking. Did he drink heavily before the marriage—is he an alcoholic? If so, the family doctor must step in, and you must summon all of your feminine prudence and love. Or did he start drinking because he'd stopped trusting you—to choke back his jealousy and disappointment? Accept your responsibility as a wife and a mother, and seek complete reconciliation with him, based on a deeper, more loyal, and fundamentally more serious mutual understanding.

Dear Moo,

I found out who Silvina is. Her nom de guerre *is Inés. Her comrades call her Inés, or la Flaca Inés. She's in the Evita Group of the Women's Branch of Precinct 13. In order to date her, L. has to execute counter-pursuit maneuvers. He met her at Ateneo 20 de Noviembre. She also works with the Union Coordinator. She's very committed to the hard line within her party. I'll bet it excites him to have to execute counter-pursuit maneuvers. She must be a very brave girl, no argument there. Each of us has our own form of bravery. She must have excellent contacts. Personally, I'm more, shall we say, discreet. But as for my plan, there's nothing cowardly about it. Quite the contrary. You won't find it written in any manual, and it hasn't been approved by any Party leader, or any horoscope for that matter.*

Ah, so, I went to sign up for Physical Theater but the class was already full, and they weren't taking any more names. I don't want you thinking I leave all my projects half-finished, as others might say, others who shall go nameless—perhaps, maybe, because I've already named him too often, because I can't think about anything else, because I'm suffering, and it hurts me, Moo, that I can't transcend all this, can't feel that my anguish might some day be transformed into something vibrant, something beautiful, something that will last.

I know that Inés is working as an activist in Avellaneda, near one of the slums. To get there I'll have to cross the bridge at La Boca, I don't know what it's called. I'll have to take the 152 and get off at the last stop. I'm going to track her down, and I'm going to say it, I'm going to tell her that L. is mine. Who does she think she is? You know what, Moo? If I go and find her and cuss her out, that's not violence, that's justice.

Kamtchowsky broke off reading; it surprised her to realize that just the mention of the bridge had created in her mind the image of Vivi hit by a burst of gunfire, collapsing *on* the bridge. (In Kamtchowsky's imagination it looked a lot like Puente Alsina, which had recently been repaired and repainted yellow. In fact she'd never seen the bridge at La Boca, and the image in her mind was from a music video, the punk band Dos Minutos, their album *Valentín Alsina*.) But that can't have been what happened.

Just then she saw Miguel arrive. Instead of his McDonald's uniform, he was wearing a loose Eminem T-shirt, and had a little Maradona-style earring. He came across the street and held out a bouquet of freesias. Kamtchowsky noticed that he'd put gel in his hair to get it to stand up straight. His leather pants were quite tight, and he looked very confident, very calm. The sight produced neither fondness nor disgust; Kamtchowsky's stunned mind was still caught in the imagined landscape of her aunt's death.

She smelled the flowers, and Miguel said something that she didn't quite catch. He mumbled on and on. And now she saw a long thin object emerging from under his belt.

It was a Luke Skywalker light saber, glowing, greenish. Miguel smiled with satisfaction. Then he let out a textbook Down syndrome laugh.

–You're Leia.

Kamtchowsky laughed too. Maybe having a little fling with a Down syndrome kid wasn't such a bad idea. She'd read that they tended to be much stronger than average guys. And, she wondered, were they also more in touch with their primal instincts? Less addled by their culture? Her young lover slashed at the air with his light saber. No one had ever compared her to Leia before; she made a mental note of his kind observation and decided not to look at his pants again.

They rang the doorbell. No one had been informed that they were coming, but Miguel's presence seemed to explain everything, and they were invited into the main dorm.

The volunteers who staff the Ronald McDonald House system offer lodging to the families of children from the provinces who have come to the city for medical treatment. People were playing cards and sipping *mate*, and there was a bulletin board covered with felt-tip drawings of suns, little houses, clouds, rainbows, and other icons of childhood optimism—fruit of the creativity of small organisms riddled with illness.

Kamtchowsky walked thoughtfully around the premises. She was wearing a black turtleneck that gave her a certain existentialist vibe, and also made her neck itch. Miguel was a bit fidgety, and did a brief rap of observations as they climbed the stairs. An only child, the word "retarded" was not to be found in his vocabulary; nonetheless, he'd always felt a bit *different*. Of course, like other kids his age he'd grown up believing he was surrounded by robots. He set little traps for them, leaving things where they didn't belong; later he'd return and see that once again the robots had put everything back in place. Thanks to his mother, an educational psychologist, he grew up healthy and strong: he played with dogs, drove the maids crazy, and destroyed his toys like any other kid his age. All the same, he recognized that just as his legs were growing too long for his pants, the gap distancing him from the rest of the world was growing wider; perhaps at the chromosomal level he understood what it was that separated him from others.

Being designated a *special* kid had allowed him to develop amidst a meticulous and profoundly generous affection which he knew was his by rights. Down syndrome or no, he seemed simply to assume that he was always in control of his situation. Defective synaptic connections notwithstanding, it was his indifference to Kamtchowsky's mental states that put her at a disadvantage. She decided to open a brief dialogue—maybe hearing his voice would get her back on track.

–Miguel, don't you sometimes have unbearable thoughts that follow you around?

Miguel shrugged.

–Yeah, sure. Sometimes I talk to my psychoanalyst about them.

–. . .

–But I don't worry about them. She just gives me the sweet pills, the ones that are like Prozac.

–. . .

–They help you grow. Look, right now for example, see how my wiener is growing?

–That's enough, Miguel, people are staring at us.

They were walking behind a woman in a blue apron; openings along the main hallway gave them glimpses of the belongings of families crowded comfortably into their little rooms. There were also rows of little beds that hadn't been slept in, their sheets in stridently bright colors, some of them hardly ever put to use by the sick kids in Ronald's care. Kamtchowsky walked confidently from one side of the dorm to the other. She felt just like she had the day she first heard the Roxette song "The Look," and started mimicking it in her gaze and gestures. It couldn't really be said that the combination of Kamtchowsky and "The Look" was creating a significant fan base or thickening anyone's warm penile mass; it couldn't even be said that it was getting her any particular attention from the young patients around her. Kamtchowsky exchanged skeptical glances with the most damaged of them. Would there come a time when they tired of calmly accepting their condition? When they would try to entertain themselves by hurting others, for lack of better options? She imagined that even their healthiest thoughts might occasionally take such a turn as they wove amongst malformed sensations.

Meanwhile, Miguel was slashing around with his light saber, and making gestures at the back of the woman in the blue apron. Yes, he was the coolest Down syndrome kid in all of Buenos Aires; he had it all, in his way, and not a care in the world. If Kamtchowsky were to accept the task of translating Miguel's facial expressions into propositional language, the idea of a quick fuck in the supply closet would definitely have gone through her mind. Miguel aroused her, but what was the best way to react? Then she heard an alarm of sorts—the melody of Michael Jackson's *Thriller.* It was Miguel's cell phone, and he set off into a moonwalk, grabbed his crotch, had a look at his phone to see who was calling, and decided not to answer. Kamtchowsky sighed. For some reason, she'd thought that with him things would be different.

Later on, she would have a very good idea.

5

Kamtchowsky's idea soon debuted on the mental stages of Andy, Mara and Pabst. They organized quickly: Mara would take charge of working up the digital backgrounds, with help from Kamtchowsky; Andy would ask Martin and Q to develop the necessary software; Pabst and Kamtchowsky would write the script. To the extent that their schedules and intellectual gifts permitted, they were all at liberty to pitch in on each other's tasks. A week later, their first test model was ready.

The Moral Games genre appeared on the heels of the commercial boom in Christian video games such as *Eternal War: Shadows of Light*, in which the mission is to travel into the depths of the suicidal mind of John Coronado to fight against the malignant spirits and the climate of destruction that afflict him. John is trapped in a vicious circle of drugs, pornography and self-mutilation. If God really existed, John wonders, would he allow these other things to exist as well? If the player wins, John goes to Heaven; if he loses, John goes to

Hell. (The game continues in both places.) John's lance emits lethal rays of Divine Light which swirl in the air like streamers made of razor wire. In another game called *Ominous Horizons: A Paladin's Calling*, we are in 16th century Germany; the Forces of Evil have destroyed Gutenberg's printing press and stolen his Bible. The mission here is to recover the Bible and thus ensure the spread of Christianity. Weaponry: a piece of wood inherited from Moses that can channel divine energy and destroy the henchmen of the Evil One. There is a high content of explicit violence; the New Age touch consists of a pagan warrior, the Grand Druid. At first, the main idea of these games was simply to provide a decisional context that would complexify the player's experience of the binary framework of the reciprocal interchange that is war. Before the first of the Moral Games appeared, there had been attempts to develop communities of followers through visually enriched variants wherein the tactical objective was camouflaged—much as in *Donkey Kong* and *Super Mario Bros.*, among other classics—by combining it with more specialized consumption dynamics.

The Argentine case in question was based on a modified version of the core content of a Christian war game. On the first screen of Stage 1, we see a long-haired young woman in a white nightgown standing on a terrace. The sun is rising over the conurban landscape, and a wind effect makes her nightgown flap around—it's too big for her thin body. The girl takes up a machine gun and starts shooting. Twenty police officers crowd together below and return fire. We hear the girl laugh.

(The provisional title of this adventure-style video game was *Dirty War 1975*; it would prove to be extremely popular.)

Next, a menu appears; as the girl in the nightgown continues to fire, the player is given the option of skipping the introduction and choosing a character from the following list:

Che I (black beret, Sierra Maestra uniform, no cigar).

Che II (cigar, bandana with red star, thin beard).

Hilda, 2nd in Command (skinny, valiant, her hair now cut short, white nightgown still flapping in the wind).

Susana, *nom de guerre* "La Gaby" (skin-and-bones, agile, black eyes, penetrating gaze, a woman of high prestige, Peronist).

"El Pelado" Flores (tall, green eyes, mustache, twenty-seven years old, dropped out of medical school to take part in the Struggle).

Father Manuel (angelic face, patrician family, thirty years old).

"Vladimiro" (could pass for a young Lenin, wears a beret and a red rosette).

The Revolutionary Author, *nom de guerre* "Pepe" (intelligent, thick-framed glasses, carries his typewriter everywhere, uses it as a weapon to crush his enemies' skulls).

To the left of the character menu is an image of the *Minimanual of the Urban Guerrilla*, a treatise written by Carlos Marighella, a Brazilian from Bahía.[11, xiv] Inside, there is

---

11 "O guerrilheiro urbano é um inimigo implacável do governo e infringe dano sistemático às autoridades e aos homens que dominam e exercem o poder. O guerrilheiro urbano é caracterizado por sua valentia e sua natureza decisiva. O guerrilheiro urbano não teme desmantelar ou destruir o presente sistema econômico, político e social brasileiro, já que sua meta é ajudar ao guerrilheiro rural e colaborar para a criação de um sistema totalmente novo e uma estrutura revolucionária social e política, com as massas armadas no

a diagram that explains the training process: all players start at the lowest rank, and must accumulate points in order to win promotion. Points are won by fulfilling the military objectives laid out at the beginning of each mission, and can be cashed in for additional recruits; when the mission is complete, the player sees how many new recruits have been gained as a result of his or her gameplay. (The total number of points available varies according to the mission assigned.)

Meanwhile, the right-hand side of the screen consists of a menu with character options pertaining to the enemy, along with a copy of *La guerre moderne*, by Roger Trinquier, the French officer who designed the methodology that would come to be known as "counterrevolutionary warfare," as practiced in Indochina and Algeria. (Andy had managed to get his hands on a copy of the actual manual.) The characters available here were:

"El Lobo" Bahndor (swarthy, hair slicked back, strongly built, lifelong Peronist, thirty-five years old).

"El Jaguar" Gómez (born in Paraguay, his motto is "No Retreat, No Surrender").

"El Tigre" Rosca (Argentine, career soldier, salt-and-pepper hair, blue eyes, thirty-eight years old, Chief of Operations).

---

poder. O guerrilheiro urbano tem que ter um mínimo de entendimento político. Para conseguir isto tem que ler certos trabalhos impressos ou mimeografados, como: *Guerra de Guerrilha* por Che Guevara, *Memórias de um Terrorista*, *Algumas Perguntas dos Guerrilheiros Brasileiros Sobre Problemas e Princípios estratégicos*, *Certos Princípios Táticos para Camaradas Levando em Conta Operações de Guerrilha*, *Perguntas Organizacionais O Guerrilheiro*, jornal dos grupos revolucionários Brasileiros." Marighella, Carlos, *MiniManual do Guerrilheiro Urbano*, from materials photocopied in June 1970.

Martín Romero Díaz (eighteen years old, conscripted into the Infantry, looks just like Palito Ortega, the singer from the 1970s).

Mónica "La Piba" Guzmán (fierce, buxom, bottle-blond hair, police officer).

Monsignor Faustino Orate de Echagüe (mysterious gaze, priestly robe).

Ranni I (the actor Rodolfo Ranni, thirty-five years old, black Ray-Bans, wearing a dress uniform and tie).

Ranni II (the same actor, no Ray-Bans, hair slicked back, olive green combat uniform).

The point of the game is to accumulate the greatest number of points, thus gaining the most new adepts, members, partisans and accomplices. Scores are tallied on displays to either side of the screen—the number of points earned next to the head of the character being played. The military objectives involved might include the destruction of enemy forces, the capture of weaponry, or the successful completion of tactical maneuvers. Each side also has a specific objective to accomplish, such as setting up an ambush in the streets, or taking over the ticket office at the train station. (At the beginning, the war was entirely urban; later on, the developers would add settings from all over the country, including tourist destinations up north and elsewhere.) Players are allowed to choose the musical accompaniment for their operation; there are songs by Palito Ortega ("Un muchacho como yo," "Se parece a mi mamá"), a deep house version of the Carlos Puebla hit "Hasta siempre, Comandante," courtesy of Etián, and a couple of Sandro songs. Once each player has made the necessary selections, the characters take their positions and the action begins. Each character chosen evolves in the course of the game, becoming ever more powerful.

Dirty War 1975 could be downloaded for free from both Pabst's blog and Kamtchowsky's; there was also a webpage they designed specifically to distribute the game. Pabst saw Kamtchowsky's idea as a massive sociological apparatus, one that was highly perfectible. Q, the project's chief engineer, had added a bit of malware that infected the players' computers and sent back information about their habits and preferences. (At university a few years later, Q would design a visual adventure game that consisted of killing students and professors from the Department of Natural and Applied Sciences in the hallways of Building 1.) Within a few weeks of launching the first prototype, the game's creators had a robust data base from which to elaborate new theories and extract statistical tendencies.

The data showed that forty percent of all players who played more than once suited up first for one side, then for the other; this produced fluctuations in the curve comparing performances and points scored. It was noted that of the growing number who started playing Pelado Flores and then alternated between Ranni II and Tigre Rosca, some twenty-three percent eventually settled on Vladimiro. Female players tended to begin playing Hilda on one side and Martín Romero Díaz on the other, but eventually switched to Lobo Bahndor or Che I. The Revolutionary Author lost out to the Rannis (especially Ranni II); however, it became clear that a majority of returning female players who'd begun with Jaguar Gómez also felt a special predilection for the Author. Eighty percent of all players chose either Ranni I or Ranni II at least once; some thirty percent were loyal to Che I or Vladimiro. A majority of the players who chose Susana and La Piba were men. A bit of code was rewritten to give Monsignor Faustino a large cross that shot death rays; Father Manuel, on the other hand, was given the power of coming back to life. Only a small percentage chose to play the Monsignor, but they tended to return to him faithfully. Most of those who played Father Manuel on one side alternated between Hilda and Che I on the other, with five percent switching over to Jaguar Gómez. La Piba was an extremely popular choice amongst the male players, and the development team received a number of emails requesting that they open the code so that players could give her more weapons and greater powers.

What explained all these fluctuations? Given the evenly distributed (that is, non-existent) moral load attached to each character, it wasn't easy to develop preference-based profiles; likewise, the motivational vectors showed no recognizable pattern. While it's true that many MMPG players tend to choose weaker characters who offer more of a challenge, the fact that *Dirty War 1975* was designed to confer equal chances of winning on all characters from both teams (a certain degree of poetic license allowed a molotov cocktail to have the same effect as a hand grenade) made short work of said guiding hypothesis. The Darwinian theory that each player chooses the character they think is capable of doing the most damage fell short as an explanation for the same reason. In general, the data gathered refused to allow for any definitive conclusions.

The best plays—or at any rate the most significant in terms of earning points—were always a function of the tactical distribution of weaponry. All operations took place concomitantly, so whichever player brought the greatest quantity of violence to bear was the player who took home the spoils. The game's creators counted on the fact that with the growth of the Internet, (both as a sort of public commons for entertainment and as an all-encompassing registry of, and space for, social and occupational interactions,) each player's character could enter the virtual worlds of the future with their characteristics and acquired powers intact. The development of technology would thus lead to common gaming platforms wherein points earned in new MMPGs could be used in games still laboring under more primitive paradigms, such as *World of Warcraft* and *Second Life*.

Little by little the game grew more sophisticated, thanks to the brilliant handiwork of Q and his friend Logical Backdoor, a skinny, diligently nerdy kid. As a child, Logical had seen the film *War Games* (1983) a million bazillion times. David, the film's protagonist, used the same tactics as Logical: both had modems fitted with acoustic couplings, and both had a gift for writing war dialing programs, which are designed to dial all possible numerical combinations within a given set of parameters in the hope of getting someone else's modem to respond. Once it did, Logical and David took control of the computers at the other end of the line, and used them as trampolines to vault themselves into other, still more powerful computers.

Then David runs into a mysterious mainframe. When he guesses its password, the computer takes him to be its creator, Professor Falken; it welcomes David, and invites him to play a game from a list that includes Falken's Maze, Chess, Poker, Guerrilla Engagement, Theaterwide Biotoxic and Chemical Warfare, and Global Thermonuclear War. The movie takes place in the 1980s, so naturally David chooses Global Thermonuclear War, and maps of the world's two superpowers appear on the screen:

United States.

Soviet Union.

The computer asks David which side he wants; he says, "I'll be the Russians," and chooses Option 2. The U.S. map then fills with potential targets, and he chooses to attack Las Vegas and Seattle. Of course, he isn't aware that he has just infiltrated NORAD, the United States nuclear defense program; his innocent game is in fact taking place on the cruel grounds of the "real" adult world. When the FBI captures him and accuses him of international espionage, one of the adults in charge says, "He does fit the profile perfectly. He's intelligent but an underachiever, alienated from his parents, has few friends. A classic case for recruitment by the Soviets." Logical possessed these same grim characteristics, and had spent years fantasizing about the moment the Russians arrived to take him home. By the time the Berlin Wall fell, Logical, then thirteen years old, had control of the network connecting all U.S. hospitals, and was capable of hijacking satellites.

The film contains three pearls of morality: 1. There are no human villains (the one omnipresent "character" is the impotence of humans faced with the futility of total war); 2.

It uses the terminology of logic to discuss the ethical problems of war (e.g. calculations of acceptable losses); 3. David knows from the very beginning that *the system is learning how to play*. "It's not just some machine," he explains to his friend Jennifer (daring, lively, athletic). "The system actually learned how to learn." In the film's final climax, after having examined all of the possible variations of a negative-sum game with no dominant strategy, the NORAD computer famously comments, "A strange game. The only winning move is not to play." David's logical intuition has saved the world from complete annihilation; congratulating him, one of the adults pointedly ruffles his hair. The film was criticized for the lack of sexual tension between David and Jennifer; shortly after, the groundbreaking film *The Goonies*, (its screenplay written by the same person who wrote *Gremlins*,) dealt decisively with the sexual awakening of young nerds through the French kiss that transpired (braces notwithstanding) between Mikey Walsh and the vivacious Andy, the cheerleader girlfriend of Mikey's big brother, Brand.

In *Dirty War 1975*, when a guerrilla characters dies, you hear an urgent, melodious off-screen voice say, "Compared to the melancholic Argentina of today, these bodies, these Montoneros who have ascended from their earthly city to the City of Heaven, represent the Argentina that was promised us, the Argentina that God intended to be born of their silence and their courage." This is an excerpt from the speech that Father Carlos Mugica gave at the Requiem mass for two guerrilla leaders. The recording was extremely well-known, and could (hypothetically) have provoked any number of kamikaze decisions amongst the game's players. Pabst criticized this feature, arguing that, given how compelling the little scene featuring Mugica's voice had turned out to be, one of the two teams now had more reason to die than the other, which affected the balance of team play, and thus the integrity of the statistics.

Another added feature widened the spectrum of what could be obtained with the points earned at the end of a successful mission: players could now buy uniforms and win medals. For example, a player who killed Martín Romero Díaz while keeping watch on a dark street corner would be rewarded with enough points to acquire either a set of new adepts or a replica of the uniform introduced by the Montoneros in the spring of 1975.

Fortunately, thanks to the aforementioned law of co-participation, many of Pabst's obsessions did not make it into the final version of the game. A scene showing the four Little Ponies of the Apocalypse, (their faces replaced with that of Elias Canetti, the audio consisting of excerpts from *Crowds and Power* read aloud) passed with the barest majority; the moment Pabst got distracted by something else, Q cut the scene without a word. Pabst muttered a bit in protest, but decided to let it go. He knew that at times it was best to take one's lumps and shut one's mouth.

In another way, these weren't actually defeats as such: they helped Pabst to feel controversial, to entertain himself with feelings of self-pity. As Marshall McLuhan once wrote, "The poet, the artist, the sleuth—whoever sharpens our perception tends to be antisocial; rarely 'well-adjusted,' he cannot go along with currents and trends." In fact Pabst felt terribly inspired; he couldn't stop posting on his blog.

Now he stood for a moment to scratch his nose; it was atrocious, the amount of bullshit he was capable of producing. He turned his head left and right, but couldn't quite get his neck joints to pop. He caressed his balls, flirting with the thought of rubbing one out. He closed his eyes to try out a few scenarios: girls from his primary school; humiliations suffered at the Club de Amigos, a camp at what used to be the Circuito KDT. He often found himself caught in a burst of metatheory as regarded the meaning of jerking himself off. Any given bit of mental content could self-activate and self-animate thanks to the introspective powers—the ability to manipulate the subtle substance of thought—of Pabst, Puppet-Master-in-Chief. Ultimately, all content was at the service of the ecstatic will of semen, the protein of pleasure. Detumescence at hand! he sighed happily. Then he noticed that he'd just said that out loud, and Andy was staring at him.

–Here you go, drink this, down in one.

Pabst's face was paralyzed with repressed fury. He hadn't moved a muscle to signal his thanks, and didn't plan to. He almost gagged when he felt Andy's big hand patting him on the shoulder, always more masculinely than was strictly necessary.

–Come on, drink up, it's good.

Pablo held the glass the way a little kid holds a bowl of chicken broth, drinking in sips. He was instantly drunk. Andy helped him to put on a wool sweater; the weather was still warm, but it was likely to cool down later on. Pabst glanced at his crotch on the way out—zipper closed, and no embarrassing stains. He asked aloud where his Kamtchowsky might be. Andy ignored this, and flagged down a taxi. It took them up Figueroa Alcorta to the gardens of the Planetarium.

Under a black sky shot through with lights, the Planetarium's sphere looked like an enormous tarantula. They had arrived at a massive open-air party; the human hordes writhed in all directions, powerful strobe lights spun, the bass notes made the ground shake, and the shadows of the surrounding trees were lost against the blind shapes of the sky. The event was sponsored by a beer company and a telephone company. The full measure of Andy's chemical artistry had gone into whatever Pabst had drunk; he couldn't do anything except stare in all directions, fascinated.

Andy exchanged handshakes with a number of young men and women, all of whom were extremely happy to see him—the customary delivery of pills. A guy in a Hare Krishna tunic walked mechanically toward them; he stood blinking in front of them for a few seconds, then walked away. Pabst pulled on Andy's sleeve, and Andy shrugged.

Pabst floated along beside his friend like a balloon filled with happiness and bewilderment as they left the Planetarium party behind and headed toward the lake. There weren't many ducks around. Pabst suggested throwing rocks at them, but Andy, the big brother, assured him that they would come back later.

–Are we going into the Rosedal now, at night? asked Pabst, his voice that of a kid on a field trip. Andy shook his head, walking slower and slower. The music from the party came to them as a murmur, mixed with the engine noise of passing cars. Andy winked, shot him a crooked grin. Pabst dreamily accepted that it didn't matter at all where they were headed, and pretended that the looks his friend got from everyone who drove by were meant for him as well.

A black car passed them, pulled to the side and parked. Andy examined the vehicle with a certain severity; he told Pabst to wait, and walked over to it. Calm and smiling, Pabst considered vomiting while Andy was away. He took a few stuttering old-woman steps toward the closest bushes, and laughed at himself.

Blurred in the shadows of the trees, Andy stepped to the car's open window and spoke with the driver, a sexually hybrid being—a sexual *homo faber*, Pabst laughed to himself, trying to calm down. Georgie got out of the car and started flirting with Andy. She had her boobs hanging out of her schoolgirl clothes, and her face, close-shaven, wasn't entirely unpleasant. Andy and Georgie talked as if they were old friends; Pabst assumed that he was selling her pills. Georgie didn't have a purse; her high heels were precisely those insisted upon by the Western canon as established by *Playboy* and *Penthouse*. It was common amongst *homo faber* (with *faber* here conserving its naughty connotation of "tool") to pick an English nickname with which to clad the socially acceptable modality of their glamorous gay selves. "The martyred saint of urban sodomites is the gemsmith Oscar Wilde, but the world's leading exporter of fairies, and of university-level fairy slang, is actually France," thought Pabst, on the verge of happiness as he fired back up. To entertain himself he cast about for additional conclusions based on his observations of Doña *Faber*, but none were forthcoming. Andy was taking his time, and Pabst started to feel uncomfortable, as if he were acting in one of those unjustifiable scenes that do nothing but add local color, the kind of scene that appeared in so many of the plays by contemporary poets he despised so much.

Andy opened the fly of his trousers and brought out his elegant member; Georgie promptly captured it in her mouth. As fellatio begun, Georgie had a look around, and her eyes met Pabst's. Pabst instantly let his gaze fall to the ground. His shoelaces were undone. He heard a voice ask, "Is that your little friend?" and looked back over. Georgie was staring at his crotch. He thought about waving to her from where he stood, as if it were daytime, hoping that his innocence would exculpate him, the way you'd let a good boy go just this once.

Andy, still standing in place, turned toward Pabst and shouted, "Pull it out! Georgie says to pull it out!"

Under other circumstances, Pabst would never have done what he did next. Under less stressful circumstances, he would have been able to ejaculate some relatively well-articulated argument into the ether. Generally speaking, such moments of personal splendor were what guaranteed his autonomy. But here and now, his usual burst of self-awareness petered out, and humiliation erased his memory.

His throat dry, Pabst spit on his penis and started tugging at it. The car's hazard lights blinked on and off, on and off, hypnotic. He could feel Georgie's eyes light up. He spit on his penis again and started tugging even harder. He thought of Celan's idea of poetic moments that consist of not knowing how to speak or what to say, because the world has fomented a revolt amongst its own contingencies. Then he imagined the face of Althusser. Andy continued to pump loads of organic material into an individual inside a car; Pabst contented himself with vomiting.

Now Andy came walking over, relaxed, almost triumphant. Pabst shivered. Andy wouldn't look him in the eye. Pabst considered issuing a clarification—that it had only been the sudden appearance of Althusser that had made him throw up.

–What just happened? he asked.

–Happened where?

–Just now.

–Nothing! Georgie's a friend.

– . . .

–Really. We used to play tennis together as kids.

–Enough! What happened? I mean, syntactically.

Andy scratched his head. As he thought, the light came to nest in his blond hair, making it glow exquisitely.

–Yeah, well, someone undertook an action that was followed by another action which was in turn followed by yet another.

–This is really unpleasant.

–Why?

–Please. I feel gross inside.

–There is no inside, Pabst.

–Of course there is, and don't call me Pabst, said Pabst, beginning to pout.

Andy slid a few bills into the hollow of Pabst's palm. Pabst, terrified and histrionic, threw himself down in the grass and sat there trembling. He wanted someone to rub his head while the time machine went into reverse and put the error back in its place, in the dimension of unconjugated verbs, in the one true Neverland.

–Of course there is an inside! he shouted, kicking at a pebble.

He got up, put his hands in his pockets and hunched his back in that scoliotic posture he had made his own–the cutest little outcast nerd. At least nobody had touched him. That would have been impossible to bear. And at least no one had made fun of him. He quickened his pace, then stopped as if suddenly sensing the meaning of the black trees that surrounded him.

He wished he had his notebook with him. He would have jotted down that the idea of Personhood is unquestionably linked to the idea of property, to the extent that the notion of that which is *mine*, understood as a *value*, interacts with the world at large. *Acts are one's own to the extent that subjectivity signs an ownership contract with a given situation or fact.* He started running, dodging the tree trunks of the woods of Palermo, headed toward Libertador. When he saw the cars, he was overcome by a strange certainty: the only possible property was ontologically interwoven with moral responsibility. He shuddered. The idea was neither particularly wise nor beautiful, and yet it shone inside him as if suddenly bathed in something peculiar, plausible, brightly gleaming.

6

Any passenger staring out the window of a bus heading from the Plaza de Mayo to La Noria bridge would have seen them gesturing as they walked along Rivadavia Avenue; that passenger would promptly have looked away. Pabst spoke nonstop, and from time to time he gave a little hop to keep from tripping on sidewalks under repair. Murmuring gravely, Kamtchowsky lurched alongside him, her gaze fixed on the ground, like a bird alert to Fate's key details. They were arguing, not for the first time, about a certain mode of poisoning.

They came to an alley leading off of Campichuelo Street, near the train tracks. An older woman opened the front door and said only that her son was in the basement. As they headed down the narrow staircase, Kamtchowsky almost stepped on a fat but sufficiently agile cat. The two guests stopped at the bottom of the stairs.

–Cartman, get down!

Q grabbed the cat with one hand, and gave a tight-lipped

smile. He had dark hair parted to the side, and big bright green eyes; the compressed facial features of adolescence would soon begin to space themselves out. He was wearing a duckling-yellow sweater and River Plate soccer shorts. The cat wore a little green hat like that of a certain *South Park* character, but not the one named Cartman.

–That's Kyle's hat, Pabst observed.

–Yes, but the cat is Cartman.

Kamtchowsky and Pabst made their way through the chaos of loose cables and dilapidated computers on the floor, and sat down on stools near their host's monitor. Despite the disorder, the room itself was clean and tidy, though some of the walls were starting to lose their paint, and bore craters ten to twenty centimeters wide, as well as several small holes that appeared to have been dug out. Kamtchowsky stood staring at the holes. Q assumed that her silence was a sign of powerful analytical capabilities.

–Impressive, right? I've had it like this for a couple of years. I told the girl who lives next door that I'm actually Superman. I told her a bunch of times, but she didn't believe me. So then I invited her over to see the holes in the walls that Superman makes when he masturbates. The proof is undeniable.

–Some of the holes are kind of high up, commented little Kamtchowsky.

–Precisely.

Standing beside his handiwork, Q crossed his arms.

–Superman's semen is capable of reaching supersonic speeds, and strikes with incredible force. The strength with which semen is ejaculated is entirely involuntary in the human male, and in all other earthly forms of life, but it would be illogical to expect Kryptonians to have the same limitations. With a body like Superman's, the spermatozoa blaze out like bullets from a machine gun. I'm still young, so my jizz has limited strength; when I get older, I'll probably be able to hit the ceiling. By that time it's extremely likely that I'll know more girls and be living somewhere else, but I can still show them pictures.

Q was delighted with the effect this had on Kamtchowsky, who at least looked girl-like. Ever knowledgable, Pabst calmly added:

–You ripped that off from Larry Niven's article about Kryptonian ejaculation. But I'll admit it's an excellent reference, and you've chosen an appropriate field of application.

–Just be careful where you aim, whispered Kamtchowsky, exchanging a meaningful look with Cartman, who mewed weakly.

Q was still staring at Pabst. Just then, his mother came down the stairs with a tray of cookies and chocolate milk. She spread the coasters out on top of the empty CPU case that Q used as a table, and left the room.

–Your mom is so cool! said Kamtchowsky.

–She knows she doesn't have any choice, answered Q.

He took a drink of chocolate milk; it left a little brown mustache on top of his own scant facial hair. He dropped the topic of ultra-powerful sperm and returned to his computer. He'd seen the online video of Kamtchowsky getting plowed, but had lost all memory of the impression, and wasn't capable of connecting it to anyone of flesh and blood. In fact, if anyone had asked for his opinion, Q would have affirmed that objectivity is merely a function of pixel resolution. He wiped his mustache away with his hand, and without looking away from the monitor, he said:

–The attack has to be orchestrated as a series of carefully coordinated steps. It's based on principles we've known for years; basically, they involve design flaws in the structural protocols of the Internet, flaws that can't be fixed unless you replace the entire architecture of the web with something more anarchical, more horizontal, and it's not at all clear when that's going to happen. The trick consists of infiltrating the Domain Name System, which translates all Internet names and addresses.[12] By poisoning the DNS with false information,

---

12 "Every computer connected to the Internet is assigned a unique IP address, an eight-bit set of four numbers, e.g. 192.168.0.1. For two computers to communicate with one another, they have to know each other's IP addresses. There is also a system of names used to refer to the computers connected to the Internet; the DNS (Domain Name System) translates easy-to-remember names (www.google.com) into IP addresses (64.233.161.99) and vice versa. It's a system of hierarchically organized domains: a site's position in the hierarchy is represented by the periods, and should be read from right to left. Thus, a generic root domain called "." includes a domain named ".com", which in turn includes a sub-domain called ".google.com", where a specific computer answering to the name "www.google.com" has a given IP address. The process of translation is conducted by a protocol (a series of ordered steps) consisting of successive questions and answers; each domain and sub-domain has a specific server with the authority to answer questions relevant to that server's place in the hierarchy. According to this protocol, each time a computer initiates a connection with another computer, the two computers must exchange several sets of questions and answers; in order to limit the number of such exchanges, and thus take advantage of all available bandwidth, there is also a system of temporary repositories holding pairs of names and addresses.

it's possible to make all of the Google Earth server connections that come out of Buenos Aires pass through a server we control.

Q closed the many chat windows that chimed out here and there on the screen, then opened Google Earth. Kamtchowsky looked at the back of his neck, at the tiny hairs standing straight out from his soft white skin. She thought of all the teen movies in which the oppressed class known as nerds rises up and triumphs over the dominant factions composed of young men far more gifted than the nerds at producing fluids and exchanging them with the opposite sex. The defiance of a single heroic nerd manages to jolt (cf. *shake*, *milkshake*, *shag*) the foundations of the stratified hierarchy: he affirms himself as an auto-regulating producer of pheromones and fluids by breaking the established class system apart. The ensuing assault on nerd heaven results in the nerds obtaining precisely that which is most desired by the most powerful class. The nerd's love for The Girl sets the male masturbator/female redeemer plot into motion; technology and know-how triumph over the privileges of birth and class. The vanguardist gesture of the rebel nerd is soon mimicked by other nerds who, seeing that they have nothing to break but their chains, are quickly infected with a desire for freedom and begin their march toward final conquest—"conquest" here maintaining the geopolitical connotation implicit in sexual appetite—as can clearly be seen in classics of the genre such as *High School U.S.A.* (1983), *Revenge of the Nerds* (1984), *Revenge of the Nerds*

These repositories are known as caches, and that's where the poisoning takes place." [Note from Q.]

II: Nerds in Paradise (1987), and *Can't Buy Me Love* (1987). All of these teen movies are organized around the essential narrative of the onano-emancipatory epic, wherein technical knowledge and initial oppression result necessarily in an advance on the warm core of sexual acceptance.

Q, his glass of chocolate milk in hand:

–That way, Google Earth's images of Buenos Aires will be replaced with whatever images we want; with a little reverse engineering, we can get our server to act exactly like the original, making the swap-out undetectable. When our server receives requests for information pertaining to specific coordinates in the city, it will respond with the materials we provide. To put it more technically, you could say that our DNS Cache Poisoning attack takes advantage of vulnerabilities in the authentication procedures of server responses to DNS protocols, by contaminating the temporary repositories with arbitrary information. This is possible because within the DNS question messages, there is a 16-bit number, allegedly chosen at random, which is used to identify the answer associated with a given question. An attacker capable of determining that number can cut in line, and get his own answer in before the authorized answer arrives from the domain in question, such that his answer will be cached instead. There are several vulnerabilities in the pseudo-random algorithms that computers use to simulate true randomness; these vulnerabilities allow the attacker to figure out the number that identifies the questions. Of course, that kind of crypto-analytical capability might not even be necessary: a 16-bit number represents only 65,536 distinct possibilities, and an attacker could design a program that tried them all in a matter of milliseconds.

Kamtchowsky had a stunned look on her face. Q's little speech had turned him into the cutest boy she'd seen since Michael J. Fox as Alex on *Family Ties* (1982-89). Eldest child of a pair of ex-hippies seeking to raise their children to value tolerance, freedom and progressiveness, Alex becomes a precocious admirer of Ronald Reagan, and a reader of the *Wall Street Journal;* he wears a shirt and tie in his own home, sticking his hands in his pockets from time to time. The pilot was particularly illuminating: Alex puts on airs as he prepares to accompany a girl named Kimberly (haughty, snobbish, perfect) to a dance at a restricted club; Alex's parents are afraid that he won't "fit in," and try to convince him—beg him to understand—that it's important to be honest and down-to-earth, that what truly matters is invisible to the human retina. In the end, Alex goes, conquers, has the entire gathering in the palm of his hand—the kid knows the worth of his assets. But the insidious father has nothing better to do and follows him to the party, horrifying everyone there, especially Alex.

Kamtchowsky imagined taking Q to the dentist to get his teeth fixed—that was the only defect she could see in him. He was such an infant that showing him a single nipple should be enough to make him jump her bones—mammarial and sexual hunger can so easily be confused. But how to go about getting him to love her a little, too? Kamtchowsky opened her mouth to speak, and nothing came out.

Pabst took Kamtchowsky's elbow, distracting her from her meditations:

–I've got it! We'll call it the Pornography of Space and Time.

–You've got the photographs?

–Yes, Mara's handling it, just a few more details to take care of, said Pabst, fascinated by all the possibilities he saw before him.

Q typed something into the computer and pushed back from the desk. He lifted Cartman up onto his River Plate lap, tightened one hand around the cat's neck, and looked his friends in the eyes, deadly serious:

–If you guys throw a party or whatever, with older girls, can I come?

Pabst nodded vigorously; Kamtchowsky looked down and smiled. Q laughed, the first time they'd heard the sound. His teeth really were a mess.

–Excellent, he said. Can I bring a friend?

7

–I love your photographs.

Kamtchowsky leaned in close over the laptop that Mara was holding on her knees. Mara gave her friend's little brown claw an affectionate squeeze.

–You mean it, you really like them?

Neither of them wanted to come right out and say it, but the rumors sparkled and glowed: Kamtchowsky had become quite the little diva of amateur porn. At first, her notoriety was limited to a few online chat groups and blog communities, but when the video showing her getting reamed in a bathroom by two pale guys with moronic expressions was uploaded by a certain *bigtool4U*, it went positively viral, and once *somegirl.avi* had infested all the big torrent sites, an additional novelty caught the eyes of thousands: the sequel, in which a kid with Down syndrome in a McDonald's uniform spilled semen brimming with flawed chromosomes into the hands of the very same tubby. The footage came from a McDonald's security camera; one of the keys to its popularity was that it had been filmed with a fisheye lens, and in the background stood Ronald McDonald himself, patron saint of hamburgers.

Every porn star creates his or her precursors. Kamtchowsky's sexual behavior had little in common with the canonical performances of Jenna Jameson, epitome of nymphomania; it had an uncontrolled, irresistible quality that was perhaps slightly closer in spirit to the *coitus more ferarum* (coitus in the manner of beasts) of Devon in *Island Fever 2*. Subtle, involuntary details gave the impression of a chubster who'd gone looking for trouble and was getting what she deserved. And as opposed to the case of Briana Banks, the talented and deserving German actress whose anal penetration scenes had brought her a number of awards, one factor that may have contributed to Kamtchowsky's popularity was a perceived difficulty in rolling her over. It wasn't that she was overly headstrong; if she didn't roll over, it was because she *couldn't*, though it seemed that she wanted to. She didn't shriek with pleasure or purposefully caterwaul, and it couldn't really be said that it looked like she was enjoying herself. She panted and puffed in deep concentration, trembling like flan with each thrust; her little cries seemed to be genuine expressions of fear, the sounds of a terrified little animal deep in the woods. The ketamine had caused her eyes to roll back as if she were on the verge of losing consciousness. K had participated in the creation of a film genre whose true precursors were the very things that made the world such a dangerous, hostile place, and which, precisely because of this, impelled the *I* to withdraw, to fold in on itself; in direct opposition to pornographic orthodoxy, both moral and aesthetic elements were brought into play.

–It's not that I *like* them, it's that I *love* them, Kamtchowsky was quick to clarify. Whenever I go by Retiro and see the Kavanagh Building standing there all spotless . . . I don't know, it actually kind of makes me sad.

Mara shot her a look that was both admonishing and seductive. It was hard for her to sort out her own opinion about this public obsession with Kamtchowsky's eroticism. She understood society's current taste for misogyny, and its morbid relationship to it, but not the stridency involved. She had just finished altering a set of digital photographs, coloring in the successive visual planes of devastation; in front of her now was Libertador Avenue, its sidewalk drenched in blood. The world must have changed in some absolute sense, must have escaped the reach of both rationality and instinct.

–For real? You're telling the truth? I love you so much I could crush your skull and eat your frontal lobes.

Kamtchowsky snuggled up against her, as if she could simply avert her eyes from all evil.

–And I'd eat your fingers and ribs, she answered.

A few months earlier, Kamtchowsky had decided to grow her market share by focusing on a specific sector of the population. She would release a new video, an autobiographical one, playing herself at the age of seven. The first showing had taken place at the second annual FU, Festival Urbano, which brought together cinema, video, theater, performance art, and multimedia—its interdisciplinary nature helped to stimulate dialogue. The theme was "*Otros y Otras*: Lives,

Flows and Voices," and Kamtchowsky's video was preceded by a panel discussion called "Daughter, from the Man to the Name." Her film was the only audiovisual element scheduled for discussion. The day of the premiere, she and Pabst wiped a few boogers on the "o" of the Welcome sign and took seats off to the side of the auditorium; they were very excited, but contented themselves with watching from a distance as the viewing public arrived. Kamtchowsky pinched Pabst's thigh, and he writhed with happiness.

The discount Parnassus before them consisted of a wooden dais, a formica-covered table, and a microphone. Two of the panelists had just arrived: a fat guy with long gray Susan Sontag hair, and a woman with sharply filed features, short mahogany-colored hair, and pointy eyeglasses, who was introduced as a member of AOL, the Asociación de Orientación Lacaniana. The long-haired dude set down a rumpled pack of cigarettes, and squared it to the table; when his status within the cultural bureaucracy was mentioned by the moderator, his eyes fell half-closed as if to acknowledge his own prestige and gravitas. Pabst swore he'd once come across an interview where the guy had declared, "Back then I was very Sartrean, and that was hardly a conga line, believe you me," but couldn't remember exactly where he'd read it.

The murmuring quickly died down. The flies kindly withdrew out into the hallway with the drinks and canapés. The Lacanian woman spoke first:

–When an interstice is filled, a sistance is chosen.

The sentence took its typical vestibular voyage, brushing up against the ear drums of the audience members, embedding itself in their earwax.

–K's film, the woman continued. She rested her elbows on the formica tabletop, confirmed that her machete was in place beneath her nails. She bent her avian, Lacan–o-maniacal neck forward and intoned:

–Let us say that K—'kay?—is likewise a Process, the name and protagonist of some other enclosing. What is it that occurs in the course of her unveiling, her demonstration—a word whose very etymology brings the monster into play? For *monster* comes from *demonstration*. The monster who menstruates, and here too the question of feminine desire in the postmodern age, the desire to make herself known to herself, face to face with herself, *desous* and *de soi*, her *I am*. How to think—and how to stop thinking—of a writing that comes into existence at the intersection of orality and genitality: in the *orar* of the daughter, in the *genito* of the father. An oral progenitor—and here is the paradox—it fills the mouth entirely. In effect it is the boundary itself that dissolves in one's mouth. In the mouth: the father finishes, and yet does not.

The horrendous old bird paused to take a sip of water; she had detected Kamtchowsky's presence.

–How to bind that sexuality—how to fix it to one's mouth—to that organ of speaking, and of saying? Your text, your documentary, it is likewise affected by the game present within the act of assisting oneself. *Assist:* the A-shaped cystitis, the beginning, the letter that opens one's mouth. Cystitis negates genitality: it forecloses upon it in that place where pleasure ungiven expires—it substitutes a place of pain for *squat down and just let it hurt.* It is the impossibility of allowing this organ trapped in a desire marked by the Urethra of the Other to function even as a means of escape. At the same time it is a cure, in the sense of care *(Sorge)*, for that which orders you around in your own name. Your father has given you a name, and with the same mouth that pronounces it he forces upon you the knowledge of the truth *in* (fitting into, beneath, against, of) the very prohibition of the father. Now I lift my gaze and move from my text to the audience: the Law of the Father enters and exits the speaking, the saying of the Daughter—daughter with her silent h, the exhalation, the hollow core—she is emptied out, and symbolically she encloses the h once again inside her through the affirmation-negation of genitality, through that mouth-filling-wholly of the Father's Daughter.

The necks of the audience members all craned distinguishedly toward Kamtchowsky. Pabst sunk down into his seat, repressing his vital impulse to run screaming from the auditorium.

Next, the Kamtchowskyan documentary was shown. She had shot it in digital: carpentry tools in a wood shop, and then a closet full of Papa's shoes. Blue bathtub, electric razor, an antique shaving brush; a few bottles of expensive cologne, perhaps empty. Papa in front of a refrigerator, the background consisting of a puzzle made of magnets—the human body, black and white, a few words scattered in. Papa pulling a stubborn cork from a bottle of wine; half drunk and telling the same joke twice; Papa stirring the ice cubes in his whisky with his finger, looking up at the fat white moon—but he isn't alone. A fixed camera filming the bed, the curtains ruffling in the violet light, Father taking his little girl in his arms before lowering her slowly, slowly to his hip, her little pink arms hugging him tightly, she breathes deeply, stretches out her neck, opens her mouth, et cetera. The digital image, given a faint sepia tone, had been transferred to Super 8 to strengthen its evocation of the past. Its main competitor in the Independent Film Festival's YouthEye-Cinema Level 0 category was thought to be the eclectic color-by-numbers piece *TransFormDimensional Gazes*; in the end they both lost to *Doc[u]mental: Unique Mental Documents.*

During the following debate, Kamtchowsky gritted her teeth and shook out her hair several times; there was talk of "the new sensibility," of art as social function and of social function as art. A while later those in attendance wandered out to the hallway to score a few mediocre tea sandwiches and inebriate themselves with Fernet Branca Menta, none of which would be likely to survive in the commercial market beyond art films and government-subsidized events. Pabst and Kamtchowsky gathered provisions at the bar that was sponsoring the event; then they wandered around for a bit, recalling for each other's pleasure every detail of the atavistic dress and behavior of the panel's participants. It was the high point of the day's entertainment.

8

In the villages of the !Kung people, being welcomed back into the human fold after committing a crime or series of crimes is a mystical event. Amongst the Maori tribes, returning warriors had to undergo the *whakahoa* ritual, designed to make them human once again: the hearts of their enemies were roasted and given in offering to the warrior gods, and what was left of the bodies was devoured by the priests, who howled out their spells in order to remove the "blood curse" and allow the warriors to recommence their lives. Among the Taulipang, triumphant warriors were seated on anthills, where they whipped one another, and threaded cords thick with poisonous ants in through their noses and out through their mouths.

I remember very little of what happened. I think I began to follow him, although in my memory it was the sun who was following me.

I walked for hours across the island. In the scrublands where the river alders grow dense, the ground is slippery, and the pampas grass tears at one's skin. The willows are enveloped in the insidious aroma of honeysuckle. The air is always still, windless. As I never reached the far coastline, it felt like I'd been walking in circles the whole time. I was thirsty, and wet my hands in a marshy puddle, but didn't drink. I kept an eye on the horizon, hoping to see the silhouette of a marsh deer, but only ever saw a coati and a few brightly colored birds. At times one's mind refuses to let go of its own inventions. It is the job of the intellect to guide the mind safely past each trap to the Great Hall, the accursed gulf where mankind dwells. Once another person has thought, acted, existed under our physical and mental control, that other person disappears. It is a beautiful moment, albeit sad; if they fail to cry out when we insert our arm, this means that their heart is dead, and the tiger within as well.

I still carry with me the incredible sensation of seeing him bent over in reverence, listening to me in spite of himself, vanquished, without even realizing it.

I let him go.

Then I walked for another few hours. The fog engulfed the motionless outlines of the trees and their yellowish leaves. And at some point I was no longer nowhere, could see a white sky broken in pieces.

Deep in the foliage I saw the sunlit profile of an enormous iron structure.

It was a man of colossal size, standing erect.

His head reached the treetops. His face was hidden in the dense upper reaches of the elms and eucalyptus; his body leaned slightly forward, a determined figure, at the ready, his hands down near his waist, a dagger tight to the hip. His facial features were hard to make out; the mouth seemed tense, the hair was on the longish side, the eyes stared out into the distance, fearless.

At his feet was a flagstone with an inscription: "He is a child, but he is also a giant." This enormous monument had been erected, hidden away on this island, to welcome Perón back, positioned such that he would be able see it from his airplane when he returned from exile. It could be seen from a thousand feet in the air if one was coming into Buenos Aires from the northeast and knew the exact coordinates in advance, but to an enemy patrol plane, it would have looked like nothing more than a black promontory, a shadow amongst the trees. They never saw it.

The Colossus had been the final dream of the Resistance while Perón was away, but they left the work half-done. Some parts, including the detailing on the shoes, the shirt and the arms, were barely even roughed out, the coarse stone still unshaped and formless. Weeds had grown tall all around, and lichen nestled in the clothing. Tension wires hung loose from broken limbs. The figure of the Colossus, though damaged and worn, was stunningly beautiful, and sad. Its silhouette was outlined by broken leaves of gray and brown, and beyond it, the sky, completely white. No birds could be seen; there was nothing but empty space above the treetops that swayed ever so slightly. The abandoned statue's color had changed with time but the incomplete face was still turned toward the same stretch of horizon, the tall thick jungle of the Tigre Delta. My fingers were wet, as if I had dipped them in darkness. I wiped my hands on my clothes, and it startled me to realize that I was no longer holding the gun. Turning, I saw it lying in the dead leaves.

On my way back, things no longer seemed to be *things*—it all looked so unreal.

9

The program was launched from Mara and Andy's downtown lair. Logical had hacked the delivery page of a supermarket website, sending twenty cases of beer and champagne to the ghost address next door. The party's curve had begun its climb toward apogee just as I arrived. There were colored lights—tiny little Christmas bulbs—and music that I'd never heard before. Ilona, Maurits, Raddy and a few others were dancing calmly. Aviv was doing a dance from the U.S., something called the Funky Chicken. Max was applying Martin's eye shadow, the same evil green I'd given to Ilona, and there was a group of girls over in the corner talking quietly with Logical. Wari, Beto, Gera, the Watas and a few others were having a look at the console, and Pabst was too excited to do any socializing. Etián was talking to someone, I couldn't see who; Dalia and Terleski were there too. Kamtchowsky was chatting with little Q, drawing closer and closer ever so carefully and slowly, and Mara was dancing with Jony, looking at him with deftly concealed fascination. I stayed off to the side for a while, sipping a Fanta; later I shared a friendly chat with Pola (people in the department sometimes get us confused, which is ridiculous—I'm much taller than she is, and she wears glasses). Then I hung out for a while with Martin, Andy and EK. Everyone seemed euphoric and calm at the same time; the bathtub, up high on its lion feet, brimmed with ice and bottles of bubbly.

The program worked perfectly. A delicate touch of a finger on the map of Buenos Aires brought up images of the red-drenched Liniers slaughterhouses, or of the Maldonado River flooding across the line that had once been Juan B. Justo Avenue, or of dotted boundaries indicating the smallpox and yellow fever quarantines of 1871. You could see Maciel Island, near La Boca, torched during Carnaval in 1905; the Plaza de Mayo destroyed by a hurricane, and the surrounding buildings ripped apart; the battle lines of the Guerras del Agua, the most powerful districts lifted to reroute the runoff of storms, leaving other districts helpless and drowned. On the hill crowned by the National Library you could see the house that Perón and his wife had shared, and the recently raised statue of John Paul II rearing up over that of Evita. The routes traveled in *Adán Buenosayres* as mapped by Marechal could be seen traced in blue; those of Arlt were a series of scribbled lines. There was a strange glow emanating from the house of Carlos Argentino Daneri. There were photos of the old Italpark, of children electrocuted inside the ghost train. Farther north, along the river, was the tree that bleeds red in the ESMA courtyard, and the remains of ships once buried beneath land since reclaimed from Río de la Plata. Toward the city center was a Chinese man weeping as his store was pillaged during a riot, and the Mercado Central where Tita Merello wove her seductions and Borges worked as a rabbit inspector; down below were the paths worn by Gombrowicz on the prowl for young fauns in the Constitución district, and the firefights that took place at the intersection of Juan B. Justo and Santa Fe during the Carapintada rebellion. In Schiaffino one could see the cover of Beatriz Guido's *El incendio y las vísperas* and a gif of Silvina making love to Alejandra while Adolfito was away. The scattered sites where the Disappeared were first ambushed; Mme. Ocampo locked up with the hookers in the Buen Pastor, and orgies thrown in Olivos by the Union of High School Students, and orgies in Palermo, and in the lost lovers' lanes of Villa Cariño; the body of a young girl found amongst the rental boats; Perón on his scooter, motoring up Centenario Avenue, trailing a rosary of blondes. The streets destroyed during the riots that marked the 23rd anniversary of Evita's death in 1975; the Jockey Club burned down; the Sheraton, converted into the Children's Hospital; the violent pile-up of buses near the Plaza de Mayo in March of 2006; the white and sky-blue ribbons crushed underfoot during the 1910 Catholic celebrations of the country's first centennial and the '86 World Cup championship; the official, military-march-style song of the '78 World Cup; the urban improv theater conducted by the military to make the bodies of the Disappeared reappear; the blueprints of the catacombs that lead to the Real Colegio de San Carlos, that connect the Casa Rosada to its swimming pool where a bleeding pig turns the waters red; Jorge Luis seated comfortably beside the river trying to pick up a girl; a collage of the many crowds that gathered in front of the Casa Rosada in the course of the 20th century—supporters of Yrigoyen, those willing him to fall, the mass demonstrations that filled the Plaza with Peronists, with anti-Peronists, with tanks, tents, fliers, blue-collar workers, grandmothers, transvestites, the anarchist martyrs in their coffins paraded along Avenida de Mayo, the military parades along that same route, the bright red, the black of other flags, the assault vehicles (always the same model) parked in the Plaza de Mayo, the façade of the Naval Hospital morphing into that of a building in Sarajevo. The geological strata of the region's speech patterns superimposed one on top of another, starting back in the days of the Organización Nacional; blood spilling over in the Matadero (*la ciudad circunvalada del Norte al Este por una cintura de agua y barro*[xiii]), the slumbering bodies sinking into the river, the umbrellas of the first crowds to gather before the Cabildo, and the limits between them and the pillaging mobs.

The city was an utter mess. And yet it was beautiful.

The juxtaposition of epochs gave definition to the map's specialized syntax. By abandoning the temporal determinations that assign facts to separate intervals, what emerged was the pure, syntactic relationship between the world on one hand and what took *place* in the world on the other; to a certain extent, the map sought to isolate the abstract form of the notion of consequence, separating it from the consolation of time understood as a series of stages. Facts, details, architecture, catastrophe, chaos, it all returned to write itself once more into the spatial history of repercussions. This history was neither an archive nor a memoir, but a set of graphic annals, witnesses to the phase of the chronicle that consists of the accumulation of tales void of linkage or hierarchy, and strictly speaking it isn't history at all; in one sense the program seemed to reclaim liberty from out of an anarchy of recountings, but at the same time it established the absence of history as a studiable phenomenon within which causes and effects could be identified in the name of change and improvement. This was the raw dough, the cyclical history of a country where events occurred and then revolved around one another, merely existing, unable to account for themselves. As an overarching phenomenon, this technological poisoning of the city map broke down a series of precepts all of which Pabst wrote about, at one moment or another, on his blog.

The program was all but untraceable. Q had designed its access point such that to enter it one had to track it back through a series of servers scattered all over the world. A cyberspy hired by Google or the Argentine government would have to follow the path taken by digital packets of information through Beirut, Santa Cruz de la Sierra, Denver, Budapest, Sebastopol, Marseille and Resistencia—it would be possible, but very difficult, and wasn't likely to occur.

The work that had begun in Buenos Aires would spread progressively to other parts of the country; this would create a series of non-trivial technical complications for the team, including the limited number of servers available for attack, and the different processes required for poisoning each one. Those who were interested in the project were welcome to participate by sending in digitally altered jpegs of their favorite street corners and neighborhoods. "Painting your village of course isn't painting the world," ran the slogan, "but at least you'll be painting your village." At first Pabst and Kamtchowsky received the images via their blogs, and Mara uploaded them into the poisoning program administered by Logical and Q. Later the team opened a public forum where anyone who wanted to could upload images and leave messages.

At times, the effects produced by the poisoning obey what seem to be strict formal laws: the cobbled streets now purified, melded, parallel lines appearing to unite. The trees look blurred, skeletal; several of the images are shot through with lightning. The team still hadn't composed its "Notes toward a Theory of Explosions," where they would compile the comments left by the map's users, and add notes on the digital effects used to alter the photographs. The text's main points described a sort of libertarian utopia based on non-visibility, laying out the importance of the establishment and role of anonymity. Its point of origin was undiscoverable. No one could see anyone else's golden rooftop or glowing marble floor. It becomes impossible to visualize the streets that we so calmly believe belong to us. And they do belong to us, which means, strictly speaking, that for us they are inaccessible.

Just then, Pabst and Kamtchowsky took each other's hand; something had told them that it would be a very romantic thing to do.

10

At long last, Augustus has agreed to meet me. We've set a date: this coming Tuesday. I'm extremely nervous, but I'm trying to keep myself under control. I've been working a great deal. At night I try to read as little as possible—when I read, ideas assault me constantly. But I must calm myself, must proofread, must think accurately and precisely. I cannot rule out the possibility of the existence of errors. (Perhaps I should recheck the page numbering?) I am tempted to print out everything in My Documents, the entire compendium of my thoughts on everything I've read as an adult, the totality of my anthropological intuitions, outlines of the new theories on which I'm working, my sociological history of perversity. But no. It would be better to summarize. To put things in order, to connect, to compose, to renumber. Augustus originally proposed that I stop by his office on Monday, but I suggested making it Tuesday, the day I clean the fish bowl, so that I can take Yorick with me, and show him the department.

Endnotes

i. *Knights of the Round Bed*, *Injection Experts*, *The King of Urges*, *A Slip of the Surgeon's Hand*, and *I'll Break Your Ratings Wide Open*: a series of Argentine sex comedies from the late 1970s and early 1980s, directed by Hugo Sofovich, most often starring Jorge Porcel and Alberto Olmedo.

ii. *Fun for the New Recruits*, *Big Rambo and Little Rambo: First Mission*, and *Recruits Attack!*

iii. Bosques de Palermo is a large urban park on the north side of Buenos Aires. It was built on land seized from Juan Manuel de Rosas, a 19th century governor, following his defeat at the Battle of Caseros.

iv. "I don't pretend to own you / I am nothing, I have no pride." From the song "Sabor a mí," a bolero written by the Mexican composer Álvaro Carrillo, and popularized by the Mexican group Trío Los Panchos.

v. "Who is worth more, a simple girl like me or you so proud, / or is your fragile beauty worth even more? / Think carefully, because deep down in the pit / we'll all be dressed the same." The song in question, "Ódiame," is based on a poem written around 1920 by the Peruvian poet Federico Barreto. The song itself, originally a Peruvian vals, was composed around 1950 by the Peruvian composer Rafael Otero López. It was popularized throughout South American some twenty years later by the Ecuadorian singer Julio Jaramillo. Many other versions exist, including a bolero composed by the Cuban singer Bienvenido Granda.

vi. The quote comes from the 2 April 1972 edition of *Potere Operaio del Lunedì*, a weekly pamplet produced by Potere Operaio, the radical left-wing Italian political group out of which the Red Brigades were born. The Spanish translation comes from *Montoneros, la soberbia armada* by Pablo Giussani, who found the original quote in Giampaolo Pansa's *Storie italiane di violenza e terrorismo* (Laterza, Bari, 1980, p. 33).

vii. Rosas's paramilitary security force was called the *Mazorca*, the name a pun uniting *mazorca* (an ear of corn—a common ruralist symbol) and *más horca* ("more gallows").

viii. The bolero in question is "Se te olvida," popularized by Trío Los Panchos. Lines 1–4 are identical to those of the song. The wording of lines 5–8 is correct, but the narrator has changed the punctuation, and with it the meaning. Small changes were made to the wording of lines 9–12.

ix. The cadence calls of the leftist urban guerrilla group known as the Montoneros were shot through with references to historical, political and military figures. They were also rife with sexual and military slang, and with insults directed at other political groups. Roughly:

We aren't rent-boys, we aren't druggies,
we are the soldiers of FAR and Montoneros.

x. Roughly:

Neither votes nor boots / but guns and balls.
Come here, El Brujo, come here El Brujo
come here / your ass is going to end up
looking like the Tango de París.
Traitor Rucci / give our best to Vandor.
We the people are asking you for it / we want
the head of Villar y Margaride.
Hard hard hard / those are the Montoneros /
who killed Aramburu.*
Five for one / you'll end up with none.
Loyal Mugica / we are going to avenge you.
What beautiful teeth you have / said Rucci to
Perón / Perón answered with a smile / Ha
ha! You'll die just like Vandor.
Voting urns are the path to government /
weapons are the path to power.
Smoking a cigar / I say fuck Aramburu / and if
that makes them mad / fuck Rojas too / and

if that makes them even madder / Fuck the Libertadora commandos.
Smoking a cigarette / I say fuck Santucho / and if that makes them mad / fuck Estrella Roja too / and if that makes them even madder / fuck the Left and all its commandos.
Look look look / what a beautiful thing / Peronists and Marxists / working for the socialist Fatherland.
We are going to build the Peronist Fatherland / we're going to make it Montonero and socialist.
We're going to make it a country of fighters / harmonious and custom-built.
If we aren't the people, who could the people be?
Abal, Medina, we want cocaine!
Quit busting my balls / there's only one Evita.
Fight fight fight / don't stop fighting / we're going to string up every gorilla.
With the bones of Aramburu (bis) / we will build a ladder (bis) / so that Evita our Montonera / can come down from Heaven.
What's going on, General? / The government is full of gorillas.
Yes sir, General, we agree / the gorillas agree too, and the people will fight.
What's going on, General? / We can't afford anything even with the raise.
I'll give you I'll give you / beautiful Fatherland /

something that starts with p . . .
The union bureaucracy / it's going to end, it's going to end.
This little piggy went to market / Now the people are leaving.
Youths: Present! / Perón, Perón or death.
It isn't time to vote / it's time to fight.
Spilled blood is non-negotiable.
If Evita were alive she'd be a Montonera.

*To which the unionist right wing responded, from the other side of the plaza, "Hard hard hard / the socialist Fatherland fucks them in the ass!

xi. Founded in 2001, Los Pibes Chorros are among the pioneers of a style of music called *cumbia villera*, which was born in the slums of Buenos Aires. Musically, it traces its roots to rock, rap, and reggae, and, somewhat less directly, to tango, punk, and narcocorrido. The lyrics often deal with poverty, drug abuse, and prostitution. They make ample use of Lunfardo, an argot that developed in the prisons of Buenos Aires in the late 19th and early 20th centuries. Lunfardo is shot through with various forms of wordplay including a form of syllable reversal called vesre (where, for example, "muchacho" becomes "chochamu,") and with slang terms derived from Italian, French, Portuguese, and Guaraní. It is thus something of a challenge to translate. The lyrics quoted here might be rendered, very roughly, as:

The kid thieves are here
we want to see all your hands in the air
because the first one to act like a snitch
is going to get the shit beat out of them.

xii. "Scram, idiot, scram."

xiii. "*(T)he city enclosed to the north and east by a belt of water and mud*": from "El Matadero," a short story by Esteban Echeverría, who was a central figure in the Romantic movement in Argentina.

On Translating Pola Oloixarac

by Roy Kesey

At last, at last: I finally get to speak to you directly about Pola Oloixarac and her magnificent debut novel, *Savage Theories*. Please know that I've been wanting to this whole time. Wanting to explain jokes of hers that have no English equivalent I could find. Wanting to explain the four layers of meaning she managed to fold into a given sentence where I was only able to fit two. Wanting.

That kind of explanation—of apology, really—has no place in the text, of course. Sometimes, though, I couldn't quite help myself. In those cases, there are endnotes, which I tried to keep to the barest minimum, and failed. Ah, the endnotes. Should you happen to be in the market for information on the punning titles of Argentine porn, or clues to the historical-geographic curiosities of modern-day Buenos Aires and environs, or long loose translations of Montonero cadence calls, you are very much in luck.

Fortunately, the sense of displacement that many readers feel moving from text to endnote and back again has its parallel in the work itself: the experience of reading Oloixarac in Spanish is an immensely rich one precisely in spite and because of the sense of displacement one feels on a regular basis. At times this is a function of the novel's jumps in time: the impossible but right meld of the ancient and the contemporary, with all manner of bridges built between. In other moments it is a function of jumps in space: we are whisked with little warning from New Guinea to Buenos Aires to the long-vanished African kingdom of Dahomey, with detours to, among other places, Paris and Zimbabwe and upstate New York, Crete and Athens and Rome in their respective A.C. heydays, and, in the end, back to Buenos Aires in our current era of MMOGs and DNS cache poisoning.

In fact, most of the action in *Savage Theories* takes place in the Argentine capital, and most of the main characters might best be described as children of the Years of Lead—the sons and daughters of those who survived the Dirty War, the twelve years (give or take) of state-sponsored terrorism in Argentina during which the military government and its right-wing death squad allies hunted down left-wing dissidents, guerrillas, students, journalists, and trade unionists, among others. This recent savagery darkens the novel's present, but it is hardly the book's only spilled blood. *Savage Theories* can be read as a history of a very specific sort of violence: the kind that is formative, for individuals, for cultures, and for our very species. One of its main through-lines theorizes as to how the relationship between predator and prey evolved across millennia, how it was transmitted across generations, and how it helps us to identify the very moment in which the human race began.

Savage Theories also creates a series of displacements through the arts and sciences. Marine biology gets a turn on stage, as do psychology, biochemistry, and linguistics; there is an obsession with film, with pop music, with painting and photography. Mostly, though, the novel sprouts from ground fertilized with anthropology and political philosophy, with nods to, among others, Sun Tzu, Hobbes and Montaigne, Marx and Freud, Spinoza and Leibniz, Wittgenstein, McLuhan and Althusser.

Occasionally, however, those nods are head-fakes, passages purposefully and pointedly misquoted, which brings us to the matters of voice and tone. The novel works primarily in a satiric key, and everyone comes in for their licks, but even the characters who live mainly for the pleasure of feeding their own bitterness and jealousy—which is to say, most of them—eventually find some measure of grace. Moreover, it is a satire shot through with a certain big-hearted love (and, let it be said, with sex that runs the gamut from pleasantly disturbing to delightedly transgressive.) And it resides in language that ranges fluidly from transparent to scientific to philosophical and back again, with occasional plunges into the darkest depths of poker-faced academic doublespeak.

If I were going to include a paragraph about "the greatest challenges I faced as the translator of this work," this is where it would go, but I suspect you're already getting the picture.

It is a great privilege to be writing this note, much as it was a privilege to spend so much time inside Oloixarac's work, and, even more so, to be the first translator to bring her into English at book-length. I hope I have carried the novel's displacements in successfully, because they are the heart of her project here. I hope her humor comes across, no matter how dark its contexts. I hope I have done right by her explorations of the many, many ways love can go wrong, and the few ways it can go right.

Oloixarac's second novel, *Las constelaciones oscuras*, has already been published. It is every bit as rich and enfoldingly complex as *Savage Theories*, and there is, I am certain, still more to come. We are witnessing the birth of something special, and I am proud and grateful to have played a role in widening the world of readers who can look forward to losing themselves in her work.

Acknowledgments

Other books and authors make cameos in this book. Pabst paraphrases René Girard's interpretation of Paolo and Francesca from his *To Double Business Bound: Essays on Literature, Mimesis and Anthropology*, as well as Malcom Gladwell's rendering of two behavioral experiments in *The Tipping Point*. *Blood Rites*, by Barbara Ehrenreich, is paraphrased on two occasions at the beginning of the book, as is the *Encyclopedia Britannica* entry for "Beast" in the third part of the book. Also in the third part, a paragraph of Caesar Augustus's diary (*The Deeds of the Divine Augustus*, in the English translation by Thomas Bushnell) is rendered with slight modifications of meaning. In Vivi's diaries, the Levi's jeans poem about the disappeared is reproduced almost verbatim from an ad run in *Siete Días* magazine in 1974; the horoscope and the woman's magazine advice are taken from 1970s original magazines that I found in the Hemeroteca (journals section) basement of the National Library of Argentina in Buenos Aires. The instructions and suggested readings for urban guerrillas come from a June, 1970 photocopy of Carlos Maringhella's *Minimanual of the Urban Guerrilla*. In the game *Dirty War 1975*, the description of a guerrilla girl in a flowing white dress belongs to Rodolfo Walsh's letter upon the killing of his daughter Vicki. I am indebted to many books and press articles about the 1970s in Argentina: Rodolfo Walsh's war writings, the *Lucha Armada en la Argentina* magazines, *La Voluntad* (Caparrós and Anguita), *Montoneros, final de cuentas* by Juan Gasparini, to name a few; the ultimate bibliography on the topic exists somewhere, but the juicy parts are probably still hidden among Henry Kissinger's love letters.

Many friends have helped and inspired me while working in this book. I would like to bid special thanks to the editors at editorial Entropía in Argentina, Gonzalo Castro and Juan Manuel Nadalini, who believed in the book from the start, and to Ana S. Pareja, editor of Alpha Decay in Spain. I'd like to thank Isabelle Gugnon, the French translator at Seuil, and to the immensely gifted, radically generous and laborious Roy Kesey, the translator of the present edition. Many artists and people working and thinking in Buenos Aires have inspired lines in the book: Maxine Swann, Jorge Eugenio Dotti, Dick el Demasiado, Pablo Messutti, Elsa Druccaroff, and Miguel Tomasín; my gratitude is with you all. Miguel is the Down syndrome drummer of one of my favorite cult bands in Buenos Aires, Burt Reynols Ensamble, and he is the inspiration for my Miguel—a true rock star. I went to say hello backstage once in the '90s; I don't think I was ever snubbed in a bigger way. The hack to Google Earth is based on an advisory for DNS cache poisoning written by Emiliano Kargieman and Ivan Arce in 1996; to this day, this continues to be an infrastructure problem for the Internet. My lovely aunt Martha, who was kidnapped and disappeared in 1975 by the Perón government, and later went into exile in Peru, was also a presence I'm indebted to, as well as my mother, who was a member of the Partido Comunista Revolucionário at the time and cemented, against her will, my fascination with the Dirty War years. Thank you Martin Caparrós and Juan Antin, who lent me their precious houses to write. Thank you nice librarians on the 5th and 6th floor of the National Library in Buenos Aires. For the present edition, I'd like to thank Hari Kunzru and Katie Kitamura, and very specially my editor Mark Doten and the team at Soho Press. Ultimately, I am grateful to my love and lionheart EK.